DARK SIDE OF THE MOON

NOVELS BY JERAMEY KRAATZ

Space Runners #1: The Moon Platoon
Space Runners #2: Dark Side of the Moon

The Cloak Society
Villains Rising
Fall of Heroes

SPACE RUNNERS

DARK SIDE OF THE MOON

JERAMEY KRAATZ

HARPER
An Imprint of HarperCollinsPublishers

Space Runners: Dark Side of the Moon
Copyright © 2018 by Full Fathom Five, LLC

All rights reserved. Printed in the United States of America.
No part of this book may be used or reproduced in any manner whatsoever
without written permission except in the case of brief quotations embodied
in critical articles and reviews. For information address HarperCollins
Children's Books, a division of HarperCollins Publishers, 195 Broadway,
New York, NY 10007.
www.harpercollinschildrens.com

Library of Congress Control Number: 2017942895
ISBN 978-0-06-244600-8

Typography by Michelle Gengaro-Kokmen
18 19 20 21 22   PC/LSCH   10 9 8 7 6 5 4 3 2 1
❖
First Edition

For the stargazers

Attention 2085 EW-SCAB Winners:

While the threat of the alien asteroid storm headed for Earth has been overcome thanks to the bravery of the newly minted Moon Platoon, the Pit Crew, and Elijah West, I know you are all still filled with questions and concerns. As such, I'd like to update you regarding our current situation and how it impacts your stay at the Lunar Taj.

All group activities are temporarily suspended until further notice. Due to the high level of alert we're under, it is requested that all guests at the Lunar Taj stay within the confines of the Grand Dome and the underground bunker. But that doesn't mean there's nothing to do! The "video game room," as many of you call it, is open and equipped with a catalog of immersive gaming experiences for you to enjoy at your leisure. And don't forget that your HoloTeks are also packed with custom programs that allow you to design your own Space Runners, holographic racetracks, and space suits. Also, please continue to meet in the common rooms on your floor! The best thing we can do in this time of stress is support one another. Remember, whether you flew out into space this morning or sought shelter underground, you are a united force—you are *all* part of the Moon Platoon.

Meals will continue to be served three times a day both

above and below ground, with selected snacks available in the kitchen at all times. Thanks to the Taj's state-of-the-art gardening and food-storage systems, I promise no one here is going to go hungry. If anyone is interested in seeing how my computerized kitchen functions and manages to feed countless guests, I'd be happy to give you a personal demonstration (bonus dessert!) at any time.

Your safety is my highest priority here at the Lunar Taj. Despite recent events, please rest assured that this resort remains perhaps the safest place in our solar system. With that in mind, please understand that your trip back to Earth will be delayed until we can ensure the voyage is 100 percent safe. I know many of you wish to be in contact with your loved ones at this time. Reestablishing communications with our home planet is a top priority.

For everyone who has asked about Elijah West, please let me clear a few things up. Yes, Elijah was taken aboard the alien mother ship that we encountered this morning. Yes, there was an explosion. But—and I say this as the person who perhaps knows Elijah West better than anyone in the universe—I have faith that he will be back at the Lunar Taj as soon as possible.

And, as always, I am available to address any questions or concerns you may have. Just say my name, and I'll be there.

On a personal note, I want to say how very proud I am of you—yes, *all* of you. The Elijah West Scholarship for Courage,

Ambition, and Brains has always attracted the best and brightest Earth has to offer, and the 2085 winners have proven to be exceptional in ways that Elijah could never have dreamed. You truly are the future of humanity.

Pinky Weyve
Lunar Taj intelligence and executive assistant to Mr. West

1.

Benny Love stared at Earth through a floor-to-ceiling
window inside the Lunar Taj. He'd seen plenty of pictures
of the planet taken from space, but he'd had no idea how
large it would loom above him from the surface of the
Moon until he'd gotten there. It took up so much of the
sky, a rotating ball of sand and water and rock and life that
seemed so close, like he could be back there in no time if
he just walked out onto the lunar landscape and jumped
hard enough. Somewhere—likely in the golden swath of the
Drylands in the western United States—his caravan was
on the move or setting up camp. His grandmother and two
younger brothers were probably in the ramshackle RV they
called home.

He didn't know exactly where they were at the moment,
but that didn't matter. The important thing—the reason
Benny couldn't take his eyes off the planet, could hardly

even blink as he looked at it—was that Earth was still there. Humanity still existed, still endured.

For now, at least.

He and his friends may have stopped the asteroid storm, but that didn't keep him from imagining what Earth would have looked like from the Moon if they hadn't flown into deep space that morning. Would there have been fire? A wall of water so huge that it destroyed cities and mountains? Would he have seen it all the way across the expanse of space?

A voice cut through the hallway Benny stood in, interrupting his thoughts. Drue.

"Uh, so, you haven't moved since I checked on you, like, five minutes ago," he said as he came up to Benny's side. He crossed his arms over the chest of his sleek gray space suit. All the other scholarship winners at the Taj wore the dark blue coveralls with gold stitching that had been waiting for them at the resort, but Drue had brought what seemed like a closet full of expensive clothes with him from Earth. It had been one of the first things Benny had noticed about him.

"It's kind of creepy," Drue continued when Benny didn't respond. Then he pursed his lips a bit and jabbed Benny in the shoulder with an index finger.

"*Ow*," Benny said, finally turning to him. "Why would you do that?"

"Oh, so you *are* real. I kinda thought you were using that bracelet Elijah gave you again and this was some glitched-out, frozen hologram." Drue put his hands on his hips and shook his head. "You've got to lighten up, man. We saved the world this morning. You should be exploding with excitement about that."

"*Exploding* is kind of the last word I want to hear," Benny said. He couldn't help but remember the image of Elijah's car being sucked inside the alien mother ship—how the creator of the Space Runners and the Lunar Taj had over-heated his hyperdrive and sacrificed himself to save them, or at least buy Earth some more time. To buy Benny's *family* more time.

He wondered what they were doing in the RV. Maybe still sleeping or waking up to sustenance squares for break-fast or trying to find some shade to park in to get a break from the dust and heat. Maybe they were even thinking of him, wondering what he was doing. Counting down the days until he was supposed to come home.

Drue rolled his eyes. "You *know* what I mean. We beat some alien butt!"

"Yeah," Benny said. "But it's not over. We don't know what they're going to do next."

Drue let out an exaggerated sigh. "You sound like Jazz. You two are really killing my Moon buzz." He turned away and started down the hall. "Pinky wrote a message like we talked about and sent it to all the HoloTeks. Jazz and everyone are waiting for you in the meeting room. Now's your chance to explain all the work we have to do next, which I can't wait to hear about." He looked back over his shoulder. "There'd better be more lasers involved is all I'm saying."

Benny's pulse thrummed as he considered all the things he'd learned in the past few days, trying to figure out which of the many problems they needed to address first. So much of it had seemed impossible. Just hours before he'd stood inside an Alpha Maraudi ship shaped like a giant asteroid. He'd actually *talked* to an alien, Commander Tull, who was still out there somewhere. Still after Earth.

They'd saved the planet, but they had no way of knowing when the aliens would be back—and they'd lost Elijah.

He took a few deep breaths as he tried to remind himself that the first part was what was really important. All he wanted was to stay in the hallway, staring at his home planet, reassuring himself that it was still there, but his friends were waiting for him. So he swallowed hard, trying to push all the concern out of his mind. Everyone at the Taj was worried, even if that was somewhat hidden by the morning's success right now. The least he could do to help was try to look like he wasn't scared.

He found his friends in the meeting room that Elijah West had locked them inside of just a few days before when they'd discovered that he had given up on Earth and planned to allow the aliens to destroy it, leaving the EW-SCABers as the last remnants of humanity. Hot Dog Wilkinson peered out a window overlooking the Sea of Tranquility, twirling a strand of curly blond hair between two fingers. Drue had plopped down in one of the floating chairs surrounding the holodesk in the center of the room. Trevone, the only member of Elijah's Pit Crew to help them out during their preparations over the last few days, sat a few seats over, swiping through holographic maps floating in the air in front of him. Jasmine Wu stood a few feet behind the older boy, mumbling to herself, her eyes scanning the charts as they passed by.

"Hey," Benny said as he walked in, coming to a stop at one end of the circular desk. "Sorry. I got a little distracted."

Hot Dog turned from the window and let out a breath. "*There* you are. I was starting to think our fearless leader was abandoning us."

Benny shoved his hands into his space suit pockets. "I'm not the leader here. We all helped—"

"I know, I know." Hot Dog walked over to the holodesk. "You keep telling us that, but you really should learn to take some credit." She frowned. "I hate to say this, but Drue might be right. Maybe you *do* need to chill out a little."

Benny looked at Drue and raised his arms out to his sides, but his friend just shrugged and spun in his chair.

Pinky, the artificial intelligence in charge of running the Taj, appeared as a hologram in one of the empty seats. Benny had gotten so used to her popping up out of nowhere that he barely gave the incredible nanotech projectors that brought her to life a second's thought anymore.

"Shall we begin?" Pinky asked, adjusting her black-rimmed glasses. "Or should I send for my favorite scholarship winner, Ramona? She's currently in one of the basement labs, staying far away from my programming, for once."

"Let's not interrupt her," Jasmine said. She looked to Benny. "Ramona's working on turning a few Space Runners into makeshift satellites so we can reestablish contact with Earth. Once we find a safe flight path, we can launch them. The problem is that there are still alien asteroids positioned between us and the planet. We've sent several unmanned Space Runners to run scans, looking for a way past them, but so far we haven't had any luck."

"And we can't just . . . go around those asteroids?" Benny asked.

"Obviously the entirety of space isn't blocked off. There has to be a way to avoid them, but it's a slow scanning process. We've already lost two SRs. These asteroids seem to be—for lack of a better word—*programmed* to hit anything that gets too close. They're basically space mines. The

Maraudi knew what they were doing when they set them up."

"Speaking of being blocked off," Drue said, "how am I *still* banned from the garage? I'm a space hero now!"

"Because as soon as you got back from the asteroid field you tried and failed to hot-wire one of Elijah's prototype muscle cars," Trevone said.

Hot Dog glanced at Benny. "He obviously didn't take notes whenever you stole that Chevelle."

"Borrowed," Benny said.

"Besides," Trevone continued, "the McGuyvers have enough on their plates trying to repair the SRs that were damaged in the attack. They're the best mechanics in the galaxy, but they're only two people. The last thing they need is you causing problems."

"I was trying to help!" Drue leaned over the holodesk. "We should know what we have to work with if we're going to war with some aliens." He shrugged. "Plus, it turns out that prototype didn't even have an engine in it, so it's totally not my fault I couldn't get it started."

"You're going to get banned from the entire Taj," Hot Dog said. "And we're not going to war with the Alpha Maraudi. We're . . ." She trailed off, biting her lower lip.

Drue looked back and forth between Hot Dog and Benny. "Really? Because I bet the aliens are pretty mad that we schooled them this morning. Maybe we should go on the offensive. Though we'd probably need more than lasers if we wanted to take down that big mother ship." His eyes lit up. "I bet Elijah has all kinds of prototypes for crazy stuff in his files that we could use. Pinky, what do you got for us? Show me the biggest, most ridiculous thing he was working on. Where are all the killer robots like the ones we fought in the video game room?"

The AI clasped her hands together on the holodesk. "Let's put a pin in that."

"We're not going to attack anyone," Benny said. "That would make us just as bad as they are. Besides, I told you guys, they're kind of not what we expected. They're . . . more like a space caravan."

Trying to wrap his head around the idea of extraterrestrial life coming for Earth was one thing, but the realization that the Alpha Maraudi weren't really some evil alien race was another, more difficult notion to process. They were just trying to find a new home. Doing everything they could to survive. In a way, Benny understood where they were coming from, and he didn't want to have to fight them.

That was the real problem, the thing sitting like a heavy lug nut in the pit of Benny's stomach: What were they supposed to do now? The day before, the stakes had been terrifying, sure, but their goals had been so simple: stop the asteroid storm, keep Earth safe, protect humanity. Now there were so many variables.

And despite his insistence that he wasn't the leader of the Moon Platoon, it felt like everyone kept looking to him for answers.

"Benny's right," Hot Dog said, taking a seat. "I just wish they'd find another place to set up camp."

"This is like game theory," Jasmine said, scrunching her eyebrows together. "Another species needs Earth to survive, but so do we. Normally I'd be into a logic problem like this, but it turns out this kind of thing isn't nearly as fun in real life."

"So . . ." Drue said, "we're taking 'blowing up the aliens who tried to kill all humanity' off the holodesk?"

"Pinky, if he gets within ten feet of a laser, let me know," Trevone said.

"What about this guy on the dark side of the Moon?" Benny asked, turning his attention to the Pit Crew member. "Could he help? Any idea how we find him?"

As if the shock of everything that had happened during their battle in space hadn't been enough, Trevone and Pinky had unexpected news when Benny had arrived back at the resort: the residents of the Taj weren't alone on the Moon.

"Dr. Austin Bale," Trevone said. He tapped on the desk in front of him and a hologram of a man appeared above it. He was maybe fifty years old in the image, with thick wire-rimmed glasses and a shock of black streaked across the front of his otherwise silver hair. "No clue. He's spent years avoiding all Elijah's sensors and expeditions. We have no idea what he's been up to."

"How do we know he's even alive out there, then?"

"Well, for one thing, he was probably the person who left supplies for Hot Dog when she crashed her Space Runner."

"I didn't crash," Hot Dog said. "I was *shot down*. Big difference." She leaned back in her seat and clicked her tongue. "I knew I wasn't crazy to think someone left me stuff. I can't believe Elijah tried to tell me I was confused."

"Remind me why we should care about this guy again?" Drue asked. "Let's imagine that I wasn't listening too carefully earlier. We had *just* gotten back from blowing up a bunch of asteroids."

"Dr. Bale was Elijah's right-hand man when he began the construction of the Lunar Taj and in-depth exploration of the Moon," Trevone said. "A renowned astrophysicist and engineer. He was with Elijah when he first discovered the base on the dark side of the Moon."

"Yeah, yeah, Elijah told us that part," Drue said. "He wanted to warn Earth about the aliens, but Elijah didn't want him to. So what's he doing on the Moon? Why stay up here?"

"Well, things are a bit more complicated than Elijah may have let on," Trevone continued. "Dr. Bale *did* go back to

Earth to warn people about everything he'd seen. He even took a bunch of artifacts from the Maraudi base with him."

"You mean, he *stole* them from the Taj," Pinky corrected. She drummed her holographic fingers on the desk silently.

"Right. But each time he tried to convince them that an extraterrestrial threat was out there some official would call Elijah, who assured them that nothing was out of the ordinary. He, uh . . ." Trevone paused for a moment. "He told everyone that being on the Moon had caused Dr. Bale to lose his mind."

"Yikes," Hot Dog said.

"The messages Dr. Bale sent to Elijah around this time were . . . *intense*," Pinky said. "So much so that at my recommendation we beefed up security around the Taj. And you wouldn't believe how much money Elijah spent keeping the man's comments out of the media." She shook her head. "I didn't exist as an AI back then. I was just a human, and I trusted Elijah. I mean, Dr. Bale *did* sound crazy, and he was definitely angry." She took a deep breath. "Neither of them acted like they should have. And while I don't love the idea of reaching out to someone potentially unstable, it's true: he could be helpful."

"Hopefully," Trevone continued. "In the end, he came back to the Moon along with a few research assistants who were convinced he was telling the truth. As far as we know, they've been living on the dark side ever since. He's masking his presence somehow, but we find evidence of old campsites every so often."

"Maybe he's using some of that alien tech to hide," Drue said. "Maybe he knows more about these ETs."

"Eesh," Hot Dog said. "A few days on the dark side is one thing, but how can someone live out there for years? It doesn't even seem possible."

Trevone shrugged. "The man's a genius. Or so I'm told. I've never met him."

"I have," Pinky said. "Or, at least, the real me has. And, yes, he *is* incredibly intelligent. Apart from Elijah, he's likely the only person on Earth capable of surviving out there for so long."

"But what's he been doing?" Benny asked, more to himself than the rest of the room.

"That's the trillion-dollar question," Trevone said.

"Whatever it is," Jasmine cut in, "he's in danger. Scouts from that alien mother ship broke rank in the middle of the asteroid fight. We lost track of them, but they were headed in the general direction of the Moon. If they wanted to hide out, the dark side would be the perfect place."

"Do we really need his help?" Hot Dog asked. "I mean, we've kind of been doing pretty good on our own."

Benny thought about this for a moment, memories of the last few days flashing through his head—the asteroids, the mother ship, Commander Tull. Finally, he nodded. "We need all the help we can get. We just have to figure out where he is."

"We could fly out to the dark side to try to spot him visually," Trevone said. "But I have the feeling he's the kind of person who finds you, not the other way around."

Benny nodded. The idea was maybe a little dangerous, sure, but at least it meant they would be doing *something*.

"Okay," he said. "Then let's head out."

"What, now?" Trevone asked.

"Yeah, now. We can't just sit around here talking all day or waiting to find a way to get in touch with Earth. We have to act, so why not start by finding this guy?"

"Because you're not in charge," a voice bellowed from the hallway.

Benny recognized it immediately. When the EW-SCAB winners had been split into four groups on the first day, Benny had ended up one of the Mustangs. The voice belonged to their leader, Ricardo Rocha, the "Beast from Brazil." Benny spun around to find him standing in the doorway. Behind him were the other remaining members of Elijah's Pit Crew—Sahar, and Kira and Kai Miyamura.

Ricardo held up a HoloTek as he glared at Benny. "I'm guessing this message came from you? How dare you think you have the right to give orders around here! You don't get to decide what happens now, or who can come and go as they please. As the oldest member of the Pit

Crew, the Taj is under my command."

"In the event of Elijah's absence, the chief operating officer would be Max Étoile, general manager and head of guest relations," Pinky said. "He left, though. And since we don't have any contact with Earth, the control of the Taj is actually sort of up in the air." She raised an eyebrow. "Technically, *I'm* the senior staff member."

Ricardo's boots were heavy on the floor as he took a few big steps into the room. "I was his number two, Pinky, and you know it." The fingers of his free hand curled into a tight fist at his side. "I'm the one in charge, and I say we're going to find Elijah. Every resource we have will be put to that task." He pointed at Benny. "That includes you, Pinky, and your friends here. No matter what it takes, we'll get him back."

2.

"Ricardo," Trevone said, standing, "you know things are more complicated than that."

"No," Ricardo said. "They aren't."

"We don't even know if Elijah's still alive."

"He may have survived the blast," Kai said. "No doubt he had a plan. Or five."

"If he did, he's probably waiting for us to come and save him," Kira added.

"Look, I'm just as concerned as the rest of you," Trevone said, "but—"

"Are you?" Ricardo interrupted, glaring at the other Pit Crew member. "Because, without your help, would they have taken the Space Runners out in the first place? No. Elijah would still be here."

"Don't you put that on me." Trevone's voice was softer now. Benny thought he saw one of his hands shake. "It was

Elijah's decision to join the fight in the end. That was his call. That's why we went up there."

"Also, we saved the world," Hot Dog said, raising her hand. "Let's not forget that part."

"What does that matter?" Ricardo asked, turning his furious gaze to her.

"So you were fine with Earth getting demolished and letting everyone die except us. Great. Good to know." She shook her head. "I wonder when all of you stopped thinking for yourselves and just started repeating whatever Elijah told you."

Trevone looked down at the holodesk. Sahar's piercing eyes narrowed as the Miyamura twins both scoffed, looking bored. Benny could see the muscles in Ricardo's jaw clench before he spoke again.

"Elijah had everything worked out. And you ruined it."

"*Hey*," Benny said, raising both palms into the air. "We're all in this together now. If we start fighting each other, we won't get anything done." He gestured to the holodesk. "We've been going over how to get back in touch with Earth and what to do next. There has to be a way to save the planet. You remember what Elijah said, right? When he was in that tractor beam? He told us to finish what we started. That was his last order."

Ricardo opened his mouth to say something but then grunted and stared down at the floor. "I don't care about what happens to Earth or these aliens. I only care about finding Elijah. I won't stop until we do." He looked back up at Benny. "It would be smart to stay out of my way."

"Ricardo," Pinky said, jumping to her feet, "there's something happening underground. A few EW-SCABers have gotten into a bit of an argument about resources on one of the floating greenhouse platforms." She sighed as she shrugged. "It would be best if you could address this before things get out of hand. Unfortunately, Elijah never got around to installing hologram projectors underground, so I'm little more than eyes and ears and a disembodied voice down there. Plus, the kids who sought refuge instead of flying out to try to stop the asteroids were following the Pit Crew, not me."

Ricardo gave the AI a long look before glancing at the others.

"This isn't over," he said. He looked at Trevone and then cocked his head toward the door. "I could use your help with this. Some of the kids underground have been looking for you. It's time for you to rejoin the Crew." He paused, and when he spoke again his voice was quieter, though no less intense. "You owe it to Elijah to help his plans succeed. To get him back."

Trevone nodded slowly and excused himself from the table. And then the Pit Crew was gone.

Silence settled on the room. Eventually, Benny spoke.

"So, the Pit Crew could be a problem. We may have convinced Elijah that Earth was worth saving, but I'm not sure Ricardo got the message."

"Saving the world and Elijah aren't mutually exclusive," Jasmine said. "But he seems to think they are."

"I can't believe I kind of liked that guy," Hot Dog said.

"Kind of?" Drue asked. "The jersey of his you stole is still in the trash can over there."

"It happens to the best of us," Pinky said. "But cut him some slack. These wounds are fresh, and Elijah meant everything to his Crew. This isn't easy on any of them."

"So is everything okay underground?" Benny asked. "The EW-SCABers who decided to hide down there . . . It's not getting bad or anything, is it?"

"Serves them right if it does," Drue said. "*We* saved Earth."

"How about you wait and hold that over their heads once we're sure the planet is gonna *stay* saved?" Hot Dog asked.

"What? It's true!"

"Maybe." Hot Dog leaned back in her seat. "But arrogance has never been a good look for you."

Drue gasped a little. Benny turned to Pinky. "So, like I was asking . . ."

"Don't worry." The AI smirked and inspected her holographic nails. "The Pit Crew will find things are in fairly calm order down there."

"You tricked them?" Jasmine asked.

"I was merely de-escalating the situation here." She shrugged. "No offense, but I don't think the four of you could take on the Pit Crew if they tried to stop you from leaving, and I happen to agree that Dr. Bale could be of some use—despite the horrible things he said about Elijah. If you want to hunt for him, I'd say now is the time to do it."

Benny scrunched his eyebrows together as he looked at Pinky. Ever since Ramona had fully unlocked her personality, she'd been a huge asset to him and the others. Without her help, there was no way they would have been able to stop the asteroid storm. Still, he hadn't had time to give much thought to the fact that with the AI's newfound freedom, she'd also have the ability to act on her own accord. Fortunately, she seemed to have agreed with him and his friends so far, but if the AI turned against them, there was little they could do at the Taj.

"Okay," he said. "If there's a dude living in some crater out there, we have to find him. Maybe he knows a way to help us get rid of those asteroids. Or how to communicate with the aliens or stop their ships—*anything* would be helpful." He grinned. "So, who's up for an exploration of the dark side?"

"Just the four of us?" Hot Dog asked.

"Yeah," Drue said. "The *original* Moon Platoon."

"Everyone's still really shaken up by everything that

happened earlier," Benny said. "It's probably not a good idea to send the whole fleet out when we're honestly not even sure what we're looking for yet."

"Ricardo seems to have actually *caused* an argument underground trying to figure out what was going on, so you likely don't have to worry about the Pit Crew for a little while. Get a plan together and go," Pinky said.

"You coming, Jazz?" Drue asked.

She nodded. "I guess now is as good a time as any to test out the things I learned in Hot Dog's crash course. We should gather some supplies first, though. Drue, can you grab some extra first aid kits and food and water just in case we run into any trouble? Or Dr. Bale needs help? Hot Dog, maybe see what kind of heat sensors the McGuyvers might have." She turned to Pinky. "Any records Elijah has about Dr. Bale and where you found those campsites would be useful in forming search parameters."

"Gladly," the AI said. "I'll transfer everything I have to your HoloTek and we can form a strategy together."

"Right," Benny said. "Let's take ten and meet down in the garage?"

"Aye, aye, Cap'n," Hot Dog said.

Benny started to respond, telling her for what felt like the hundredth time that day that he wasn't their leader. Instead, he nodded, and headed for the elevator.

He wasn't sure why he was going to his suite in the Lunar

Taj until he was there alone, and suddenly his breathing was heavier and his pulse was racing as questions rushed through his mind. How had he become such an integral part in the survival of his family, his planet, his *species* in just a few days? And, perhaps more frightening, what would have happened if he hadn't gone to the Taj? He took a seat on the edge of his bed and tried to get a hold of himself. They had a next move, which was good. But driving off to the far side of the Moon to search for some mysterious scientist who may or may not be able to help them didn't seem like it was enough. Especially when his family's safety was concerned. Whatever happened, he had to keep them safe. Somehow.

Benny looked at his nightstand where a silver hood ornament had been displayed for most of his stay on the Taj. It hadn't been all that long ago that his father had given it to him, before the man had trekked into the desert in search of water and never returned. But it was gone now, left behind in the alien ship and no doubt destroyed when Elijah West blew up his hyperdrive engine, and Benny suddenly wished more than anything that he could hold it again, as if doing so would make the homesickness that was growing in his chest go away.

Now a gold glove sat on the nightstand, the one thing Benny had taken from the alien spacecraft—the only way they'd managed to escape. He picked it up and slid it over his hand. It covered his palm, but his fingers stuck out. He made a fist, then spread his hand out again. Analysis in the Taj's research labs had confirmed that the glove was made up of unknown elements, which hadn't exactly been a surprise. On the alien ship, it had somehow controlled the rock walls of the craft, allowing its wearer to open up doorways. But he didn't know how it worked, and so far it had been useless on the Moon. He'd smashed it against the ground outside, but nothing had happened.

Still, if he was going out in a Space Runner, he felt like he should have it with him. Just in case.

There was a beeping in his room, and then Pinky's voice.

"May I have a word?"

"Uh, sure," Benny said.

The AI appeared in front of him.

"Benny . . ." She paused for a moment. "I don't disagree with the choices you're making right now. In fact, I think you're doing everything in your power to try to figure out the problem of the Alpha Maraudi. But that's the issue. I've been monitoring your heart rate, and I'm a bit concerned that you might be pushing yourself too hard. I don't want you to burn out. There's nothing wrong with taking a break and trying to relax."

"Relax?" Benny asked. "How am I supposed to relax? If anything, we're not moving fast enough. What if the aliens are already on their way back to Earth? What if they're *on the Moon*. What if at any moment—"

"You aren't making me feel any better." Pinky's expression softened as she put her hands on her hips. "I know a lot about you, Benny. All your background information and application materials are stored on my servers. I've watched you rally the kids here and lead them to victory. I can't imagine how tough that's been. I know . . ." She sat down on the bed beside him. "I know you're worried about your family. Alejandro. Justin. Your grandmother. The rest of your caravan. But you have to take care of yourself, too."

"There's just so much going on," Benny said, staring down at the shining metal on his palm. "How do I know if what we're doing is going to work or help us at all?"

"You don't. In the same way Elijah didn't know if his first Space Runner prototype would fly. And you didn't know if you could stop the asteroids. Sometimes you just have to believe in yourself and take a leap of faith."

"I'm pretty sure Elijah did a million tests on the Space Runner before he took it out. And it's not like we were flying blind up there earlier. We had all your charts and graphs and had tested some of the lasers ourselves."

"Benny, I'm trying to comfort you here, and as a holographic facsimile with no physical body, you're going to have to work with me a little on this."

He snorted, and then took a deep breath.

"Is there anything else I can do or say to make this easier?" Pinky asked.

Benny looked over at her. "Do you really think Elijah's alive? I know you said so in the thing you sent out, but . . ."

Pinky stood and took a few slow steps away from him. "I don't know," she said. She turned to the screen that made up the wall across from Benny's bed. Suddenly, videos of Elijah filled the space. He jetted across lunar mares in souped-up muscle cars. He winked at the camera while waving to Taj guests. In a smaller video in the background, he presented what must have been the real Pinky with a bouquet of shiny chrome roses. The AI smiled a sad smile. "But, despite all the mistakes he made, I really hope he is."

"Yeah," Benny said. "Me, too."

Pinky shook her head. The screen went black again. "Jasmine and Hot Dog are already down in the garage. You don't want to keep your friends waiting."

"Right," Benny said. "And, uh . . . thanks, Pinky."

"You were right in your application video, you know. You already *have* changed the world. I have the most advanced processing power of any computer known to man, and there's no scenario my programs can run in which your father wouldn't be beaming with pride at your accomplishments."

And then she was gone.

Benny took one last look at his hand before pulling off the golden glove and shoving it into the pocket of his space suit. Then, he took a deep breath and headed for the door.

3.

Everyone else was in the garage by the time Benny made his way down. The warehouse-like building hadn't changed much since the first time Benny had seen it a week before: a ceiling of bright white light reflected off the dark, polished floors, and the acrid scents of electronics and oil hung heavily in the air. Almost all the classic cars that had been retrofitted as Space Runners or Moon buggies had been hidden away underground by the McGuyvers—the solar system's best mechanics—just in case the asteroid storm had managed to break through the Taj's defenses, though. The only vehicles left were the ones they'd attached mining lasers to and flown into space earlier that day. Those Space Runners sat in neat lines on one side of the room, some blackened and scorched by enemy fire. On the other side, Jasmine chatted with Pinky and Ash McGuyver while Hot Dog cataloged the contents of a supply box in front of her. Off to the side, Drue sat in a chair with his arms crossed and lips pressed together in a sulk. Bo McGuyver, a huge, hulking man, stood over him, staring down at Drue over the bridge of his crooked nose while wiping his greasy hands on the front of his coveralls.

"I told you, I'm not going to touch anything I'm not supposed to!" Drue said. Bo remained silent. "Do you even know who I am? Who my dad is? I'm a *Lincoln*. We are *very important* on Earth." As Benny walked by, Drue perked up. "Hey, tell him it's okay for me to be here!"

Before Benny could respond, Jasmine's voice rang through the garage. "Yes! Here!"

Benny raised a finger to Drue. "One sec."

Drue huffed but stayed seated as Benny made his way to the huddle. "Tell me you've got some good news," he said.

"Jasmine thinks she's figured out where this Bale guy might be hiding out," Hot Dog said. "So much for Elijah being the smart one."

"Well, maybe," Jasmine said. "And I'm sure Elijah could have found him if he'd actually tried to. From everything Pinky and Trevone mentioned, it sounds like a reunion with Dr. Bale wasn't a big priority to him."

"True," Pinky said. "I think he'd rather have forgotten the man ever existed."

"Anyway, I looked at places where it seemed like he'd been camping based on evidence the Pit Crew or Elijah came across while exploring. Which, honestly, is mainly just a few footprints and Space Runner landing marks. Dr. Bale and his team did a great job of cleaning up after themselves."

She pulled on one chrome corner of her HoloTek to extend it and then held it up to Benny, showing him a map of the far side of the Moon with several yellow dots on it.

"I think he was hiding in the Daedalus crater for a while, but given when the footprints were discovered and factoring in the amount of time it would have taken to get to Hot Dog and leave her supplies after she went down, this might be his movement pattern." She tapped on the screen and blinking lines connected the dots. "Fortunately, he's heading closer to us."

"Yeah," Hot Dog said, pointing to the dot on the left side of the HoloTek. "Turns out there was some kind of energy ping around here right after I got shot down."

"It was just before our satellites were destroyed," Pinky said. "The energy signature was comparable to that of a hyperdrive engine."

"I'd suggest we search this group of mares," Jasmine continued, gesturing to a spot on the map. "It's actually not far from the alien base, relatively speaking, which means it's possible that's where he's headed. Maybe for shelter. He might have seen the storm coming."

"Uh." Hot Dog groaned. "Didn't we kind of leave a

big hole leading into the underground tunnels back there? Maybe we should get that fixed."

Ash McGuyver snapped her gum. "Bo and I will take care of it, no problem."

"Perfect!" Drue said, springing into the middle of their group. "So, what, we'll just head out and search the crater? Easy."

"It's not that simple." Jasmine waved two fingers across the map, zooming in. "These mares—if he's even there—can be almost a hundred kilometers in diameter."

"Uh, can you talk to me in miles, Jazz?" Benny asked. "Or, better yet, how many Tajs is that?"

"The search area is the size of two or three cities. Big ones." She shook her head. "Honestly, how has everyone not picked up the metric system yet?"

"Don't lump me into your science shaming," Drue said. "My tutors taught me both. This should still be pretty easy, though. It's a whole lot of nothing out there, right? Plus, don't we have sensors and stuff like that?"

"Heat sensors, energy sensors, you name it," Ash said. "But if Bale has a way of messing with those, you kids are on your own."

"So what are we waiting for?" Drue asked.

"One last thing," Pinky said, furrowing her eyebrows a bit. "Remember that Dr. Bale and Elijah don't have the greatest history together. And in a way . . . you *are* sort of intruding on his territory."

"Yeah," Benny said. He looked at Drue. "We'll be careful."

Even as Benny spoke, though, Drue was racing toward the Space Runners. "I call whatever goes fastest."

"You'll take the laser-armed SRs or you'll stay here," Ash yelled after him. She wiped her hands on her coveralls. "That boy'll be the death of me."

"Jazz, you'll navigate us, yeah?" Benny asked as they made their way to the vehicles.

"Sure," she said, but her cheeks flushed a little. "Just, uh, don't mind me if I get a little behind. I haven't had much actual experience flying these things."

Hot Dog winked at her. "Don't worry, we'll take care of you."

They slid into four of the Space Runners with Mustang-red stripes painted across them. A holographic map appeared on Benny's windshield, a blinking line cutting across the projected lunar surface.

"Here's our path," Jasmine's voice came through the comms, filling the cabin of Benny's vehicle. "I suggest a diamond flight pattern so we can keep an eye on the surface and each other."

"Agreed," Hot Dog said. "Benny, you take the front,

Drue and I will take the sides, and Jasmine can bring up the rear."

Benny waited for Drue to protest that he should take the lead, but he didn't say anything.

"All right," Benny said. "Pinky, open up the auxiliary pressurization tunnel. Uh, please."

And then they were off, shooting one by one out of the Grand Dome and into the stillness of the Moon's imperceptible atmosphere.

"Race you guys to the mare," Drue said over the comms. His Space Runner shot forward. "Last one there has to tell Ricardo we left."

"*Formation*, Drue," Hot Dog said. "We went over this."

"Oh. Yeah." He took his spot at Benny's right again.

"We're a good half hour away from this search zone," Jasmine said, "but we should keep an eye out for anything odd, just in case."

Benny laughed a little to himself, thinking what a strange thing this was to hear, considering the fact that they were setting out to hunt for a mysterious doctor hiding on the dark side of the Moon to possibly recruit him in their effort to save Earth from aliens. *All* of it was odd. Even the fact that Benny was sitting in a Space Runner. Despite the car having been in battle earlier that day, the inside was still sleek and clean, the surfaces all polished and the artificial-leather seats buffed. He caught his reflection in the rearview mirror and realized that he was pretty clean, too. At least compared to what he usually looked like in the Drylands, where it was impossible to scrub off all the dust even when they did have enough water to bathe, and his black hair was usually stiff with dried sweat, sprouting out in all directions. When he'd first gotten to the Taj, he'd felt so out of place. Even in the Space Runner on the way up to the Moon, he'd managed to get dirt everywhere because it had spilled out of his bag.

But now he'd changed. And for some reason that made him miss home even more.

Eventually, they were flying across the far side of the Moon. Benny pressed his face against the window, looking at the pocked landscape below him.

"I thought it'd be darker," he said. "I mean, it seemed darker when we were by that alien base."

"Probably because we were in a crater," Jasmine said. "The dark side of the Moon isn't really *dark*. It's just the side we can't see from Earth."

"Hey, remember when Iyabo was telling us that story about skeletons roaming the dark side?" Drue asked.

Benny did. How could he forget? The girl from Cameroon had painted such a clear picture of long-forgotten scientists pounding on the Grand Dome, desperate to get back inside the artificial environment. He'd tried to remember every detail to tell his brothers when he got back home—the perfect scary bedtime story.

"Well," Drue continued, "what if it wasn't an urban legend? What if that's what this doctor and his friends are? Moon zombies."

"Drue, are you getting enough oxygen in your Space Runner?" Benny asked.

"I'm just saying. They've got to get out of their space suits and wash them sometimes. Maybe all the radiation out here messed them up. Haven't you ever seen a horror movie? This is a classic zombie setup."

"That's actually kind of true," Hot Dog said.

"Not you, too," Benny said.

"What? After everything that's happened to us today, you want to draw the line of impossibility at Moon zombies? I head-butted a space medusa earlier."

"Okay. Good point."

Benny looked down at the craggy surface, imagining a dozen decomposing figures clawing their way out of the dust, mouths gaping as they reached toward the sky, toward *them*. He couldn't help but think of the skeletal faces of the flying robots they'd blasted in the video game room, which seemed like forever ago. Surely Elijah hadn't modeled them after Dr. Bale and his assistants . . . right?

"I'm not even going to begin to poke holes in this idea," Jasmine said. Then, after a pause, she continued. "But if I *were* going to, I'd start by—"

"Hey, guys," Hot Dog said, cutting into the comm feed. "I think I see something."

"Strange," Jasmine replied. "The scanners aren't picking anything up, and we're not very close to the mare."

"Not on the ground." Her voice was wavering now. "Above us."

It took Benny a moment to see what she was talking about, but then there it was. A dark spot, blotting out a few stars. A smudge of deep purple against the black sky.

And then there were more, four—no, *five* jagged shapes.

"Oh, crap," Benny muttered as the shard-like alien ships shot toward them.

4.

"Evasive maneuvers!" Hot Dog shouted as the ships sped closer.

Benny paused for only a second before twisting his flight yoke to the left, remembering some of the basic skills Hot Dog had taught him and the rest of the Moon Platoon in her piloting crash course. His Space Runner veered, dropping toward the dark crater below.

Moments later, the five alien ships were upon them, the same type that had come out of the mother ship during the asteroid storm. Their hulls were shaped like jagged arrowheads shooting through space, made out of some deep purple mineral. The backs of the crafts were capped with gleaming silver devices, as though some kind of metallic claw had latched on to the ships.

"They must have some sort of cloaks up," Jasmine said. "They're not on my radar. I can't get a target lock."

Benny glanced at his instrument panel, but only their four Space Runners showed as blips on the holographic screens.

"If they attack," Hot Dog said, "keep weaving. Just make sure we don't hit each—"

She stopped as ice-blue bolts of energy rained down around them.

Benny swerved, narrowly avoiding one of the blasts. He'd been hit by one of these before, and the result had been a total loss of control over his vehicle. All Space Runners were equipped with moderately strong antigravity shields, but from what he could tell they didn't offer all that much protection from whatever advanced weaponry the aliens had.

"I'm monitoring the situation!" Pinky's voice filled his car. "I'm calling more of the Moon Platoon to the garage for backup, but their ETA is twenty minutes at least."

"There's no time," Benny said. "Keep everyone else safe at the Taj. Be on high alert. We don't know how many of these things are out here."

"Benny . . ." She paused. "Please be careful."

He pushed his flight yoke forward and dove toward the Moon's surface, two ships in pursuit. "Yeah. Sure thing."

"All those foster families were right," Jasmine squeaked through the comms. "I should have played flight sims and video games instead of studying so much!"

Above Benny, his friends were fighting. Hot Dog and Drue were by far the most adept at maneuvering, their Space Runners spinning and darting around the alien vessels as they shot the lasers mounted to the fronts of their cars. But Jasmine was holding her own, too. She'd flown well away from the others and was sniping from a distance with precise shots. One of them hit the rear of a ship, causing the metal on the back to explode in an eruption of sparks.

"Oh my gosh," she said, her voice full of astonishment. "I hit one!"

"Woo-hoo!" Drue shouted. "Nice shot, Jazz!"

"Looks like the backs of their ships are their weak spots," Hot Dog added. "We know where to aim. Take 'em down!"

"I hope I didn't injure the thing inside," Jasmine said.

"Uhhh," Drue groaned into the comms. "Not exactly what I'd be worried about right now."

"Our goal *isn't* to hurt them," Benny said.

"Sure, but I don't think these dudes are trying to be very careful when it comes to my own safety."

Benny watched the damaged alien ship fly up into outer space—hopefully retreating. That was one down. At least they weren't technically outnumbered now—even if two ships were still gaining on him.

He clenched his jaw as his Space Runner jetted toward the ground, the dark surface of the Moon filling his windshield. Alarms began to go off throughout the cabin as he got closer. When he was within just a few yards of smashing into the lunar crust, he pulled back on the flight yoke and leveled out. He shot across the crater floor, pushing his car's hyperdrive as hard as he could as he twisted the flight yoke back and forth, avoiding enemy fire. For a split second he wished he were in something with wheels—he wasn't doing badly in the flying car, but he definitely would have felt more at home on the ground, in a buggy or something he was more familiar with. In the rearview and side mirrors, he watched the alien ships loop around each other, trading shots at him, before finally one of the crafts took position above the other, the two of them lining up directly behind him.

"Not good, not good, not good," he muttered to himself as sweat began to bead on his forehead. Suddenly, a barrage of red lights flashed on the windshield. He was about to hit the crater wall.

"Ahhh!" he shouted as he wrenched the yoke to the left just in time, until he was flying sideways, following the curve of the wall and dodging sharp outcroppings of rock. The two alien ships followed suit, firing their energy blasts. The cavern wall below him exploded with each missed attack, spraying debris and dust up all around Benny's Space Runner.

He tightened his grip on the flight yoke as he struggled to make out the terrain in front of him, and for a flash, he remembered a day he hadn't thought of in a long time. A few years before, his caravan had raced across the Drylands trying to outrun an approaching sandstorm. Benny's grandmother and brothers were in the RV, but his father was driving a truck full of gear at the time and had let Benny ride with him, buckling him into the passenger seat and covering his mouth with a bandana in an attempt to spare him from getting a mouth full of sand. It had seemed to Benny like they'd flown across the dunes at light speed, the two of them bringing up the rear of the group as they tried to reach an abandoned farm with a working well they'd planned on camping at for a while. They'd almost gotten there, too—Benny could see the huge, rusty barns just a few miles away—but in the last stretch the wind picked up, blowing sand across their path until Benny couldn't make out the other vehicles and trailers that had been in front of them. His father hit the brakes, and in seconds they were stopped.

"Standard procedure," his dad had said. "Nothing good'd come from driving in something like this."

The sound of the storm was so loud around them that Benny could hardly hear him.

"But we're *so close*," Benny had said.

His dad had just shaken his head and pulled off his own bandana now that he was sure the sand engulfing the truck wasn't going to get in too bad.

"What if we went over a cliff? What if we ran into someone from the caravan?" he'd asked as he slid his seat back and put his boots up on the dashboard. "Nah, we'll wait it out. There's no GPS or stars to help us through something like this, and it's too easy to get lost when you can't see where you're going. Only a fool would try."

Benny couldn't say that he'd always been able to see exactly where he was going the last few days, but the memory *did* give him an idea.

He aimed his Space Runner's laser as low as it could go and began blasting the crater wall beneath him, gouging a deep trench into the rock and sending clouds of debris floating into the paths of the ships behind him. He had just a few seconds of invisibility to work with and he tried to make the most of it. Pulling up on the flight yoke, he flew in a loop, hoping to take the ships by surprise.

And he did. Or one of them, at least. His laser hit its crystalline wing, causing it to ram into the crater wall and fall behind. The other ship, however, dodged him and corrected itself so quickly that Benny didn't have a chance of avoiding its counterattack. A bolt of energy slammed into the pilot's side of his Space Runner with such force that Benny was sure the whole car was going to break apart as he banged his head against the side window, straining against his seat belt. Lights all over the dashboard started blinking as he struggled to both catch his breath and regain control of the vehicle. But it was too late. He was too close to the ground, and before he could pull up on the yoke the car slammed into the bottom of the crater, spinning over the craggy ground, throwing Benny around until finally it skidded for twenty yards and came to a stop upside down.

Smoke began to fill the cabin of Benny's Space Runner. Coughing, he hurled himself against the door a few times. On the third try, it gave, and he rolled out onto the surface of the Moon, the force field helmet of his space suit automatically appearing around his head and filling with oxygen. He half crawled for a few seconds before managing to get to his feet just in time to see the alien ship returning, circling around and heading straight for him.

He tapped on his collar, trying to connect to his friends' comm systems. "Guys? Anyone? I'm kind of defenseless down here!"

Suddenly they were all shouting in his helmet, on their way to rescue him. But even as they raced toward the crater, he realized they'd never make it in time. The ship coming after him was too fast, and in the low gravity, there was no way he'd be able to avoid its blasts for long. It was homing in on him now, already within range to attack. Benny could see a surge of blue light on the back of the ship. This was it.

Suddenly, a bolt of gold light shot forth, briefly illuminating the dark corners of the crater and striking the side of the alien craft. The ship exploded in a flash of fire, quickly snuffed out by the lack of oxygen in the atmosphere. The few remaining pieces of the ship then fell toward the surface in a rain of smoking metal and minerals. Benny hit the ground and covered his head as the wreckage battered the rocky crater floor around him.

When he was sure that it was over he got to his knees, looking around, breathless. The alien ship had practically disintegrated, and the pilot inside . . .

The others were still shouting through the speakers in his collar, telling him that the two remaining ships were retreating after the explosion. He scanned the direction the gold bolt had come from.

And then he saw it. In the shadows near the crater wall there was some kind of vehicle that was too big to be a normal Space Runner. He watched as a long, cannon-like tube folded back into the hood of the craft as it lifted off the ground. It hovered in the air for a few seconds before jetting toward Benny.

Sweating and shaking, he held his breath and clenched his fists as the craft landed near him. The pilot-side door opened. A figure wearing a space suit that was patched in several places stepped out. Whoever it was also wore a force field helmet that was completely black, as though they had an inky egg for a head.

Benny had just enough time to breathe a sigh of relief that the figure looked human before the person was upon him, with one giant gloved hand around his neck, lifting him off the ground, fingers pressing against his collar.

"Stop!" Benny shouted, beating his fists against the figure's broad chest.

Then there was a beep inside his helmet and the hand let go. Benny drifted back down to the ground as a man's voice, low and gravelly, came out of his collar speaker.

"Who are you?" he asked.

"Benny Love," he replied in a wheeze as he scrambled to his feet. His hands immediately went up to his throat—the man had been manually connecting their radios, not attacking him. Or at least, he didn't *think* he'd attacked him. Behind him, his friends' three Space Runners landed.

The man tilted his head and pressed something on the back of his neck. His helmet slowly became transparent until Benny could see who was standing in front of him. The man's hair was matted and oily, gray but for a streak of jet-black across the front, contrasting the ghostly pallor of his skin. A thick, dark beard pushed up against the inside of his force field helmet. He stared at Benny through thick goggles.

Benny gaped at the man. "Um . . ." he started. "Dr. Austin Bale?"

The man raised one bushy eyebrow and nodded.

"Are you okay?" Hot Dog shouted as his friends rushed to his side.

Jasmine stopped in her tracks when she saw Dr. Bale. "It's you."

"Well, that was easier than I thought it would be," Drue said. Then he frowned. "Except for the aliens, I guess."

Dr. Bale looked them over one by one, stopping on Hot Dog. "You, I recognize. The girl in the crashed SR."

Hot Dog just nodded.

"It was a matter of good fortune for you," Dr. Bale continued. "I'd gone to see if the Taj was still standing after our radar picked up on that approaching storm." He looked to Benny. "You're welcome for saving your life just now."

"Yeah," Benny said. "I mean, you're right. Thanks! Sorry, I just . . . guess I didn't expect to find you so fast."

"You came looking for me?" he asked.

Benny nodded as his mind spun, hardly believing their luck. This man—the elusive scientist they'd been searching for—had utterly annihilated one of the alien ships with some sort of weapon unlike anything Benny had ever seen.

He had so many questions.

Dr. Bale's nose twitched, his overgrown beard and mustache scratching against the inside of his helmet.

"There's nothing for you here," he said, turning back to his big Space Runner. "Go back to your fancy hotel. Tell Elijah to keep a leash on his children. This is my side of the Moon."

"Wait," Benny said. "That's one of the reasons we're

here. Elijah's not at the Taj anymore."

Dr. Bale stopped, turning back to them slowly, staring at Benny. "What do you mean he's not there?"

"It's . . . kind of a long story," Benny said.

Dr. Bale narrowed his eyes before glancing at the sky. "It's not safe to be out here. You may have damaged the other four crafts, but they'll be back."

"How did you . . . ? I mean, that level of . . . *Where*? Up here?" Jasmine asked, the questions spilling out of her mouth.

Dr. Bale took a moment to look at each of them again, and then back at the three Space Runners parked a few yards away. Finally, he nodded toward his own vehicle. "Why don't I show you? My campsite isn't far." He glanced back at Benny. "I think we have a lot to talk about."

5.

There was something oddly familiar about the inside of Dr. Bale's vehicle. A coating of dust covered the consoles—touch surfaces that were scratched and practically obsolete compared to those inside the Space Runners Benny had been in. In fact, everything seemed dated, from the switches where there could have been holographic buttons right down to the strumming acoustic guitar that was pumping out of the speakers. The whole thing felt like a vehicle better suited for the caravan than the Moon, though it must have had a solid environmental system in it since Benny's helmet had disappeared after they'd taken off.

He glanced in the side mirror to make sure his friends were still following close behind, three chrome brushstrokes against the black sky. They'd been hesitant to let him ride alone with Dr. Bale when the man had suggested he do so, but Benny had figured if they were going to ask him for help, they should at least try to be friendly. And Dr. Bale *had* just saved his life.

Benny turned his attention to a stick shift between him and Dr. Bale. He'd seen them on Earth on the rare occasions that the caravan stumbled across ancient cars with primitive transmissions, but he couldn't imagine what one was doing here.

Dr. Bale must have noticed his staring, though he didn't look over at Benny when he spoke, his voice deep. "It controls the cannon. Not the most delicate instrument, but it gets the job done. As you saw."

Benny swallowed hard, thinking of the alien ship: there one moment, gone the next.

"So . . ." he began, unsure exactly what to say. "You have a . . . I don't know. It looks like a space truck?"

"We call this the Tank. It's my own design."

"That makes sense." Benny paused. "Powered by one of Elijah's hyperdrives?"

Dr. Bale grunted, which Benny took as a yes. He continued.

"And you built it to take down the Maraudi ships?"

At the mention of the alien species by name, Dr. Bale raised an eyebrow. "Let's not get ahead of ourselves," he said. "I saved you back there, so you owe me a little explanation as to why four kids are wandering around out here alone.

I assume you're some of Elijah's scholarship winners."

"You know about the EW-SCAB?"

"Just because I've been living on the dark side for a while doesn't mean that I'm not aware of what's going on in our solar system. I've been back and forth to Earth regularly over the years." He tried to smooth his beard down—finally free from the helmet, it was still curling up at the end. "Besides, Elijah's not the only one who can launch a satellite."

"So you're in contact with Earth?" Benny jerked forward. "Could you—"

"Don't get excited. That asteroid storm last week killed our communications. I take it the same can be said for the Taj's. From what I can tell it destroyed almost every usable satellite for hundreds of thousands of miles."

Benny hunched back in his seat. "Oh."

There was a brief silence between them before Dr. Bale spoke again. "Did he send you?"

"Did *who* send us?"

"Elijah," he said, his voice dropping even deeper at the last syllable. "Of course he did. Summoning me to that gaudy metal palace of his after the Maraudi finally made a move. I suppose he's seen reason at last and is ready to enact countermeasures. No doubt he's lobbying on Earth, trying to play the role of the white knight. I just can't believe he sent a bunch of *children* out to find me. He could have had the decency to come himself." He glanced at Benny. "Tell me he at least had military forces piloting the fleet that went out this morning."

"You don't know," Benny said. It hadn't occurred to him that he'd have to explain *everything* that had happened in the last few days to Dr. Bale. "Uh, where do I start? Okay, so you know about the aliens, but did you know that Elijah was using the EW-SCAB to recruit kids to basically sort of be the last of humanity once the Alpha Maraudi came for Earth?"

Benny went on, catching the man up to speed as best he could. By the time he was finished, Dr. Bale's face was contorted in disgust, his lips twisted and teeth half bared.

"The idiot, he . . ." Dr. Bale said, his eyes flashing wide for a second. Then he took a breath and adjusted his goggles as he shook his head. "Of all the preposterous ideas he had, I don't know why the plans behind the scholarship should surprise me. I always assumed the Taj would become a stronghold for the elite. I suppose I have to give him at least a sliver of credit."

"Yeah, well, things obviously didn't turn out like he planned," Benny continued. "We found out about the aliens and confronted him. I guess the important part is that a bunch of us weren't going to let Earth get destroyed, so we flew to the oncoming asteroid storm and tried to blow it up."

"How? I thought Elijah didn't have any weapons at the—Ah, wait. The lasers I saw you shooting. Let me guess, they were for excavating?"

"Yeah," Benny said.

Dr. Bale nodded. "Hmmm. Very clever."

"They worked pretty well until the aliens attacked. We did our best, but in the end it was Elijah who showed up and saved us. He got sucked into this big asteroid—a *mother ship*—by a tractor beam and overheated his Space Runner's hyperdrive."

"Causing it to explode." Dr. Bale pursed his lips for a moment. "Yes, I see. And the mother ship?"

"Retreated. I was inside it for a while. It was like the whole thing was made of rock. But I could *breathe* in there. My helmet didn't come on."

Dr. Bale twisted the end of his beard while staring out at the landscape in front of them. He nodded a few times but didn't say anything. The silence was just starting to get uncomfortable to Benny when the man finally spoke again. "Color me impressed. The lasers were a good idea, but they're primitive at best. You're lucky you didn't all get yourselves killed. You never should have had to go after the Alpha Maraudi yourself—for that, I must apologize on behalf of all the adults who failed you. Fortunately, I've been working on means of combating these invaders since we first encountered them all those years ago."

Benny glanced at the hood of the car where the cannon had disappeared. The word *invaders* lingered in his ear. "Yeah, I can see that. But, actually, the Alpha Maraudi aren't what you and Elijah—"

"Who's running the Taj now that he's gone?" Dr. Bale asked, cutting him off. "Not that simpering fool Max, I hope."

"Uh, that's kind of a good question. Pinky's sort of in charge."

"Pinky Weyve?" He let out a single grim laugh. "Elijah's personal-assistant-turned-girlfriend-turned-computer is in charge of the most sophisticated artificial environment humanity ever created?"

"Well, yeah," Benny said. "She and one of Elijah's Pit Crew thought you might be able to help us figure out what to do next."

Dr. Bale made a noise, but his lips never parted and Benny wasn't sure if it was a laugh or a groan. "So the Taj has lost contact with Earth and is being run by a bunch of kids and an AI."

"Basically," Benny said, and for some reason he got the feeling in his gut that maybe that wasn't the smartest thing to say to the man with a grudge against Elijah West. He tried to change the subject. "Plus, you know . . . We figured we should warn you. If there were aliens on this side of the

Moon. We'd tracked some headed this way at the battle this morning."

"As you saw, I'm more than capable of taking care of myself."

"Right." Benny looked at the stick shift again. "And, uh . . . where are we going?"

Dr. Bale nodded at the giant, shallow crater they were shooting toward. "Home sweet home."

Benny looked through the windshield, but there was nothing but empty space and rock ahead of them. "I don't see any—"

There was a slight shimmer as they passed through some sort of hologram field, and then suddenly everything outside the Tank changed.

"Holy whoa," Benny murmured as he tried to make sense of his surroundings, his eyes darting around.

"Holographic environmental mimicry equipped with sensor cloaks," Dr. Bale said. "The site's invisible from the outside, obviously."

Half a dozen boxy, dull metal sheds lined the right side of the camp, thick-looking canvas hanging over the doorways. Nearby, two older-model Space Runners were parked beside a row of trailers and what looked to Benny like some sort of missile launcher. The center of the site was filled with tables and benches, most of which were piled high with gadgets and tools that looked like they'd be at home in the Taj's research labs. To the left, three tents made of shining silver fabric had been pitched.

All around the perimeter, Benny could make out a sheen of distortion in the air that must have signaled the boundaries of the hologram.

"This is the reason I don't show up on radar," Dr. Bale continued. "We're not seen unless we want to be seen. Our vehicles have it, too." He pointed to a black box on the dashboard and touched a button in the center. The box glowed red as a glimmer of light spread over the outside of the car, and then suddenly all Benny saw when he looked out at the hood was the surface of the Moon.

Benny shook his head and blinked several times. "This is insane," he said. "This is *the coolest* use of holograms."

Dr. Bale grunted in approval and pulled the box off the dash. The Tank was visible again. He tapped the button on the box and its red glow disappeared. "Magnetically attached stealth drives. You should count yourself lucky that the aliens attacked. You never would have found me otherwise."

Dr. Bale parked near the tents and opened the door to his craft. Benny expected his helmet to power on, but it didn't. He took a few deep breaths—there seemed to be plenty of oxygen.

"That shield includes an environmental system," Dr. Bale said. "Not unlike the Grand Dome around the Taj, only this one has a permeable shell. Think of it as a bubble, not a force field."

"As long as it doesn't pop," Benny said to himself as he stepped out of the car, noting that the gravity felt like Earth's.

Behind them, three Space Runners landed, the pilots jumping out as soon as they touched the ground.

"What the what?" Drue asked. "It looked like you guys had disappeared and *then* I almost crashed out of surprise when I went through . . . *whatever* that was."

"Yeah, same," Hot Dog said, looking around with wide blue eyes. "Did we just, like, teleport somewhere?"

"Not at all," Jasmine said, her voice breathy. "This is a mobile research lab hidden by some sort of holographic field."

"Precisely," Dr. Bale said, crossing his arms. "Welcome to the most important location in the solar system as far as humanity's future is concerned."

Benny looked at his friends as Dr. Bale spread his arms wide, taking a few steps away from them. Hot Dog raised her eyebrows at him, while Jasmine squinted, trying to make out what was on the tables. Drue glanced around, curling up one side of his face like he'd just smelled something disgusting.

"He's been living in a place like *this* all these years?" he whispered.

The cloth draped over the door of one of the sheds was pulled aside, and two figures stepped out, both wearing patched space suits that looked like they were a size too big on each of them. They were both in their late twenties, Benny guessed. One was a pale man with perfectly square glasses and blond hair tied back in a small bun. The other was a woman with dark skin and her hair shaved short, almost to the scalp. They both paused just outside the shed entrance, staring silently at the new arrivals.

"We have . . . guests?" the man said.

"Children," the woman pointed out.

"Ah, and these are my research assistants, Todd and Mae," Dr. Bale said. "They've brought news from the Lunar Taj. Elijah West is gone." He glanced back at Benny and the others.

Mae and Todd looked at each other, obviously stunned by this news.

"Then he must have been involved in the attack on the asteroid field," Mae said.

"If he's gone," Todd started, "then who—"

"I know we all have questions," Dr. Bale interrupted him. "But our guests have been through quite an ordeal. Why don't you two dig up some refreshments."

The two researchers nodded to him, stared at Benny and his friends for a beat, and then disappeared back inside.

"What are you doing out here?" Jasmine asked. "What

is all this stuff? What was that explosion earlier?"

Dr. Bale started for one of the nearby sheds and Benny and the others followed. "Why don't I show you?" he asked. "If Pinky sent you, am I right in assuming she gave you some background on my history with Elijah?"

"A little," Benny said.

"Yeah," Drue agreed. "Sounded kind of . . . *rough*."

Hot Dog smacked his arm.

"'Rough' indeed," Dr. Bale said. "Elijah and I . . . We were very different men. At one point in my life I considered myself a mentor to him. It took a long time for me to realize that in order for that to have been true, Elijah would've had to have viewed himself as a student. That was never the case, despite the difference in ages. He was always a *visionary* or a *revolutionary*. Never a student." He stopped at the shed's entrance and turned to them. "Though, when it came down to it, he was more than willing to take on the role of a god, wasn't he? Allowing Earth to go out with a whimper while building his own civilization up here. Picking and choosing who would live and who would die. He gave up on humanity, but I didn't. Even when they laughed at me." His voice was turning into a soft growl now, and he was looking around the campsite, not at any of the kids in front of him. "Even when Elijah made me look like a fool, I found those who would listen, like Todd and Mae. I kept *preparing*."

He suddenly seemed lost in thought, like he'd forgotten what he was saying or that he had an audience of four in front of him.

"Um, preparing *what?*" Drue asked.

The man didn't say anything.

"Uh, Mr.—I mean *Dr.* Bale?" Hot Dog asked.

Dr. Bale took a deep breath and then looked at them, smiling.

"I'm sorry," he said. "My mind works so much faster than my mouth that I'm usually several thoughts ahead of whatever it is I'm talking about." He laughed a little. "And, let's be frank, it's been a while since we've had visitors. Let's get to the point, shall we. Benny, you asked me in the car what your next move should be."

He pulled back the canvas in the doorway, opening the shed to them. Inside, beneath harsh overhead lights, were rows and rows of overflowing shelves. Benny's eyes moved over the locked chests, canisters labeled with all sorts of warning signs he didn't recognize, HoloTeks, computer terminals covered in switches, blinking lights everywhere, and what looked to him like dozens of items that resembled the cannon that had taken down the alien ship, sitting alongside a stockpile of what Benny could only describe as futuristic guns.

"Dude," Drue muttered, and Benny couldn't tell if he was terrified or out of his mind with excitement.

"What is all of this?" Jasmine asked, stepping forward and peering into the shed.

"An armory," Dr. Bale said. "Your next move is simple. You must protect Earth."

6.

Jasmine blinked, looking back and forth between Dr. Bale and the weapons inside the shed. "You've been up here this entire time creating some sort of Moon arsenal?"

"That's merely a portion of what we've been doing," Dr. Bale said, letting the flap fall back down, hiding his armory once again.

"I can see why you and Elijah didn't get along," Jasmine continued. "He was completely against the further weaponization of the human race."

"And look how that worked out for him," Dr. Bale said quickly, his eyes wild for a flash.

"He could have survived," Hot Dog said.

Dr. Bale's features softened. "Well, I suppose we don't know what happened, exactly."

Benny shifted his weight. "What are you planning to do with those?" he asked, though he had a pretty good idea already after seeing what the Tank could do.

The man took a long breath, but before he could answer, Drue was talking again.

"Uh, also, where was all this earlier when we were gluing mining lasers to the fronts of our Space Runners and going to stop the aliens ourselves? Because I *bet* we could have used some of this."

"We did okay on our own," Hot Dog said.

"I got blasted by one of those ships!"

"Okay, sure, it didn't go perfectly." She thought for a second and then rolled her eyes at him. "Also, I was sucked into the mother ship and almost put in some kind of alien zoo, so, who should be complaining here?"

Dr. Bale grunted. "We didn't see this asteroid storm coming until you'd already deployed. We don't have scanners like those found in the Taj. For the most part, we've made do out here, but our equipment isn't exactly state-of-the-art. We didn't have a dozen spare satellites to launch after the first wave." He raised an eyebrow. "Now, if we had the resources of the Taj, that would be another story altogether."

Benny swallowed hard. He wasn't sure what he'd thought Dr. Bale would be like, but he definitely didn't expect him to be showing them a bunch of weapons within minutes of their finding his camp. And the way he talked about Elijah and the Taj was tinged with something that didn't sit well with Benny, despite Dr. Bale's calming, precise manner of speaking. The man may have been a genius, but the last time Benny had put his faith in someone on the Moon who supposedly knew better than him and his friends, Earth had almost been destroyed.

Still, they needed all the help they could get, and this man knew the Alpha Maraudi. Plus, he *had* saved Benny's life. He kind of owed him the benefit of the doubt.

"You said you were working on other projects," Jasmine said. "Is there anything *else* here that could help us?"

Dr. Bale nodded and began to walk to the next shed. Once he was in front of them, Jasmine turned to look at Benny. Her lips were pressed together tightly, and her eyes were wide as she shook her head.

"I know," Benny mouthed silently.

"The key to progress and success is to never rule out any possibility of advancement, no matter how remote," Dr. Bale said as they followed him. "That's one thing Elijah and I agreed on. The difference between us is that Elijah's thoughts were always stuck in his own solar system, whereas I have a much more open mind."

He held the flap covering the entrance of the shed back and let the four of them walk inside. When Benny saw the circuitry-filled stone terminals pulsing with a dim green light, he immediately recognized what they were looking at. This was Alpha Maraudi technology, the same kind he'd seen in the alien mother ship and . . .

"The abandoned Moon base," he murmured as he took in the dozens of asteroid chunks sitting on a table and a hologram of a three-sunned solar system in one corner. There were other things, too, that he didn't recognize: tools made out of some red metallic substance, glass cylinders housing various mineral samples floating in midair, and what looked to Benny like pieces of bone—long, narrow, and a dull bronze in color.

He swallowed hard.

"So you've seen it," Dr. Bale said.

"Yeah," Hot Dog said. "It's, uh . . . kind of a long story."

"You scavenged these things," Benny said. "That's why it looked so empty when we were there."

Dr. Bale stepped forward, picking up one of the asteroids as big as his fist. "*Scavenge* implies that these items were castoffs from the Maraudi we found. These items were . . . *inherited* after the extraterrestrials no longer existed. We brought what we could back to the resort with us. Well, the building site, at least. Everything was still under construction."

"Oh," Drue said. "I get it. This is the stuff you took from the Taj when you left."

"I didn't steal anything, if that's what you're implying."

Dr. Bale turned away from them slightly, surveying the items in the shed. "We found that base together, and contrary to what he may believe, Elijah does not own the Moon. I had as much a right to anything in that base as he did. *Earth* had a right to these things. Besides, what was he going to do with such important resources? Bury them away in his resort and pretend he was untouchable? Let them languish in some research lab? I couldn't let that happen."

There was a strange sensation against Benny's right leg as Dr. Bale spoke. Not quite strong enough to be called a buzzing, but some sort of dull energy, like the feeling he got when his HoloTek vibrated from across the RV and he could just barely, almost intuitively register it. He slid his hand into the pocket of his space suit, fingers grazing the golden glove.

It felt warm to the touch.

"And what *have* you learned?" Jasmine said, stepping farther into the room, looking at the collection of artifacts that had originated light-years away.

"Plenty," Bale said. He held up the asteroid rock. "You see, these beings are engineers beyond our wildest dreams. Imagine being able to create new elements. Stones that are partially organic, able to grow, veined with energies. Minerals you could control given the correct type of frequency. The way they've learned to use metals and rocks . . . They could reshape Earth if they wanted to."

"That must be why their ships look like pieces of quartz," Jasmine said.

"So, they can control rocks?" Benny asked. "How? With, like, their minds?"

"Of course not," Dr. Bale said. "With science. They have instruments of their own." He paused, smiling a bit as he walked over to a black case. He flipped it open, and, as he held up its contents, Benny's heart jumped.

It was a metallic glove, much like the one he had. Only this one had a gash through it, like something very hot had sliced through the palm.

Hot Dog glanced at Benny. He nodded slightly. The others kept their eyes forward, even though they both knew he had an alien glove of his own. It was still humming in his pocket, and he almost took it out. But he didn't. Something about the excited way that Dr. Bale talked made him think the scientist would want the glove if he knew Benny had it. And given the shed they'd just seen, Dr. Bale could probably force them to hand it over.

"When we found the aliens," Dr. Bale said, "I saw one of them control the door to their base with this, growing it into the huge slab it is now. Another—the Maraudi that got away . . . it looked like he was using it to *control* his ship."

Benny swallowed hard. Maybe this glove *was* going to come in handy.

"So, what about this one?" Jasmine said. "Can you show us how it works?"

Dr. Bale looked at the gash in the glove's palm. "Maybe I could if it were whole. But Elijah was careless with the architectural laser he was wielding when we made first contact."

That's when Benny remembered the details of the story Elijah had told them about when he and his top scientist had discovered the base—how there'd been a fight, and none of the aliens left on the Moon had survived. He shuddered as his eyes again fell on the bone-like items on the shelf.

It was almost difficult to imagine that all this had happened years and years ago, before the EW-SCAB had ever been created. And yet, here they were now, dealing with the ramifications.

Dr. Bale made his way to the hologram in the corner. "This is their solar system. You'll note that the middle of these three red dwarf stars is larger than the others. That's because it's expanding. Observe." He reached into the hologram and seemed to pull on it, until the whole image zoomed in on a blue and brown ball floating near one of the stars. "This is where they come from. And, as you can see . . ." He pressed on something at the base of the hologram, and slowly the star began to expand until it was overtaking the planet completely. "They're in trouble. I'm not sure what the timetable is on this—we haven't exactly been focusing on learning their language or communications techniques—but they're obviously looking to take Earth . . . Benny, you said you could breathe on their spaceship?"

"Yeah," he said. "I think they need our atmosphere?" It was more of a question than he meant it to be, considering Commander Tull—the alien in charge of the mother ship he'd been on that morning—had told him flat out that this was the reason. But Benny was preoccupied with something else. "So . . . you *know* they're not coming to take Earth just because they want to conquer it, then. They're coming for it because otherwise their species will die."

Dr. Bale nodded. "Let me guess. Elijah was still imagining they might turn Earth into a destination planet. Some sort of vacation resort for wealthy extraterrestrials." He let out a single, deep laugh. "Ever the entrepreneur."

"But, if you know that . . ." Benny started, shaking his head. "If you understand that they're just looking for a new home, why not use your skills to try to save their planet instead of making weapons to fight them. Maybe you could stop their star from expanding. Then they wouldn't need Earth."

"Who's to say that they wouldn't take it anyway?" Dr. Bale pulled on his beard. "In all honesty, their technology is far more advanced than ours. If they can't figure out a way to save themselves, there's no way I'm going to. Plus, my boy, when you're my age—when you've seen the things I've seen—you stop putting hope in the best possible solution and start to bet on the one most likely to come out in your favor. Or in this case, the favor of all mankind. We have to be able to defend ourselves if—*when* they return. That's why I've designed these weapons. I'll be waiting for them if they show their tentacled heads here again. The safety of our planet and our people is the highest priority. Everything else is negotiable."

Benny swallowed hard. His friends didn't say a word. The only thing that broke the silence was a rustling behind them. Benny turned to see Todd had pulled back the shed's canvas door flap. He and Mae both held trays with silver packages on them.

"It's probably not anything like Taj food," Todd said, "but we technically did break out the good stuff."

"It's better than nothing," Mae suggested. "After a while, you forget that most of your protein comes from soy powder."

Benny had eaten enough sustenance squares back on Earth to know that wasn't true, but he kept his mouth shut as they followed Dr. Bale and his assistants out into the center of the camp. Todd and Mae passed around the little silver pouches.

"Thanks," Drue said, taking his. "I think."

"So, you've come for help," Dr. Bale said, crossing his

arms. "I suppose you're hoping to take some of these weapons back with you now that you've seen them. But I must say, they were not meant for children to use, despite the bravery you showed this morning."

"No," Jasmine said, taking a step forward. "We didn't come here for weapons."

Dr. Bale looked at her, his eyebrows drawn together in puzzlement. "Oh?"

"We came for information," she continued. "Guidance. And to warn you."

"And to get in touch with Earth," Benny said, stepping up beside her. "That's one of our biggest priorities."

"I mean, we'll *take* some of those weapons," Drue said from behind them. "If you're offering."

Hot Dog sighed. "If you really want to save humanity, you won't give him anything remotely dangerous."

"Hey," Drue said. "I—"

"Can you help us with any of that?" Benny asked, talking over his friend.

Dr. Bale took off his thick goggles and began to wipe them with a cloth he pulled from his space suit pocket. "As you can see, we have a lot of very important work that we're doing here. But I'll confer with my colleagues and see what we can do. Contact with Earth would benefit everyone, after all." He nodded to Todd and Mae. "Between the three of us I'm sure we can come up with a few ideas."

Todd and Mae both nodded, still holding the trays.

Dr. Bale put his goggles back on and then pulled a thin HoloTek hardly bigger than a deck of cards from his pocket. "I'll be in touch. Call it nostalgia if you like, but I never deleted the resort's contact information from my datapad. I'll let Pinky know when we've come up with something."

"Oh," Benny said, kind of relieved at how well this was now going. "Well . . . Great."

"As humans, we're in this together," Dr. Bale said. "Whatever happens next, we must be united. Now, I really should be getting back to work. Your encounter with the Maraudi this morning has disrupted my schedule."

"Then I guess we'll be going?" Benny asked. "Hopefully we'll talk again soon."

"Ah," Dr. Bale said, smiling. "I've no doubt about that."

7.

"Okay, so that is not what I thought space camp on the dark side would be like," Hot Dog said through the comms as they flew back toward the Taj.

"I'm just saying," Drue said, glancing at Benny, who sat in his passenger seat, "those weapon things could come in useful in the future."

Hot Dog groaned. "I hate that I agree with you about that."

"How bad do you guys want to shoot that laser cannon he had?" Drue grinned. "I knew we needed space tanks. Remember? I told Elijah that he—"

"Drue," Jasmine came in, cutting him off. "I don't like even knowing that those weapons are up here. I always respected Elijah's stance about not using science to do harm. It's one thing I definitely think he was right about."

"I'm with Jazz on this," Benny said, looking out the

window and nodding toward her silver Space Runner flying at his right.

"Look, I know you don't want to hurt the aliens, but we should also think about protecting ourselves," Drue said. "Wouldn't it be nice to have one of those things mounted on top of the Grand Dome in case the Alpha Maraudi came and attacked?"

Benny didn't disagree, but everything was so complicated. Back in the caravan, they'd kept the amount of weapons floating around the trucks and RVs to a bare minimum, locked up as last resorts. They put their priorities on peace and being welcoming.

So he leaned back in his seat and avoided the question. "I'm just glad he didn't ask to come back to the Taj with us."

"Did you hear his voice when he was talking about Elijah and the Taj?" Hot Dog asked. "I was definitely getting some bitter vibes."

"Uh, he has to want to come back to the resort," Drue said. "Moon camping looked awful. Like, where were the bathrooms even?"

"Maybe he's waiting to have something to offer us so we invite him?" Jasmine asked. "Any person of science would want to have the Taj's resources."

"Imagine how excited he'd be if he got Benny's glove," Hot Dog said.

"Oh, *yeah*!" Drue said. "I almost forgot! Benny, you've got rock superpowers or something."

"If I could only figure out how to use them," Benny said. "When we were near all that alien tech in Dr. Bale's shed, the glove was doing something weird. I don't know. Like it was vibrating. Buzzy." He shrugged. "Maybe I should take some of the asteroid samples that we saw in that abandoned alien base and see if I can do something with them."

"You don't have to ask," Drue said, looking over at Benny and winking. "I'll be the brave one and test it out for you. Just don't be jealous when I've got a living rock statue as a bodyguard."

"In your dreams," Benny said.

Suddenly, there were gagging noises on the comms. It sounded like someone was choking.

"What's wrong?" Jasmine asked.

"Hot Dog!" Drue yelped.

"Gross." Hot Dog coughed. "What flavor are these protein bars they gave us supposed to be? Sunscreen? Dumpster fire? Oh, man, it's all stuck in my teeth."

"They're probably just Moon dust mixed with water," Drue said.

"This isn't funny!" Hot Dog shouted.

But the rest of them were already laughing. Eventually, even Hot Dog was, as they shot over the lunar landscape, heading back to the Taj as quickly as they could. When they were closer to the resort, Drue tapped on the dash, turning off the open comm line while Jasmine updated Pinky on everything they'd seen at Dr. Bale's camp.

"So I know you're all about not hurting these aliens and stuff, which I totally get," Drue said, not taking his eyes off their flight path. "But, in the end, if it has to be us or them . . ."

Benny shifted in his seat. All he could think of was the way Commander Tull had described the aliens when he and Hot Dog had been in the asteroid mother ship. How similar they were to his own caravan family back on Earth. People without a permanent home, just trying to survive.

How many others were on that alien world? How many lives were at stake? How many beings not unlike him and his family? Did they even have families?

His head started to pound. There was so much they didn't know, and the more he thought about it, the more questions plagued his mind, causing his palms to sweat.

"Hopefully it doesn't come to that," Benny said. "We'll figure something out."

"Sure," Drue said, though it didn't sound to Benny like he really believed it. "But if it *does* . . ."

He looked over at Benny, who just stared back at him. He didn't want to think about what he would do if he was forced to make that kind of decision. The obvious answer— the one that immediately came to mind when he thought about this dilemma—was that he would do everything in his power to protect his family. To make sure humanity was safe. But he didn't want to have to consider a future where doing that meant killing a bunch of aliens. Or, worse, an entire species.

The fact that so much of this felt like it was his responsibility terrified Benny, and a tiny part of him actually wished they had invited Dr. Bale back to the Taj to take over. At least then he wouldn't feel like this decision rested squarely on the Moon Platoon's shoulders.

Drue flashed his big white teeth. "Okay, you're right—we'll figure it out later." He laughed once. "You impressed? I'm getting better at knowing when to shut up." He paused. "You're welcome."

Pinky was waiting for them in the garage when they returned, pacing back and forth, her intangible body passing through a disassembled hyperdrive. Ramona sat in the pilot's seat of an oversize Space Runner on one side of the workshop area. As Benny got out of the car, he could hear Pinky talking to her.

"Ms. Robinson," she said, "should I be concerned that you've locked me out of your ancient piece of computing equipment? You'd better not be pirating my copyrighted program files again."

"Max paranoia, hologhost," Ramona said. The girl

smirked as she tapped on the custom HoloTek she'd brought from Earth and always had strapped to her left forearm. She tucked a coil of strawberry-blond hair behind her ear. "Don't get your processors worked up."

Pinky threw her hands out in exasperation and turned to Benny and the others as they gathered around her. "I'm glad to see the four of you back safe. Benny, how are you faring after the crash?"

"I'm fine," he said, though his body was starting to feel sore all over. "How have things been since we left? Anything we should know about?"

The AI bounced her head back and forth. "Bo and Ash are installing a force field barrier to fix the hole you left near the abandoned alien base. The Pit Crew decamped to Elijah's quarters. Trevone, too. They don't know you were gone as far as I'm aware. I think that's everything of note."

"Is your memory corrupted?" Ramona asked, leaning out of a Space Runner and pointing over her shoulder with a thumb. "One satellite installed. Ready to launch. Now I'm tinkering with a second. Plus upgrades."

"Great," Benny said. And then his shoulders slumped. "But that doesn't help if we can't get past the asteroids."

Ramona clicked her tongue. "Buzzkill."

"Sorry. Thank you, this is a huge help." He clenched his teeth and stared at the dark, shiny floor. "It's just that we're still no closer to getting back in touch with Earth unless Dr. Bale comes through. We're no closer to *anything*."

"Hmmm," Pinky said, taking a long look at Benny, "I am one hundred percent not your mothers, but I *am* trying to keep you all alive up here. What you all need now is food. Most of the EW-SCABers are in the restaurant for dinner. You're not going to come up with any good plans on empty stomachs, and I know for a fact that none of you have eaten since breakfast. Except for Ramona, who has consumed what I continuously point out is an alarming amount of energy bars and sodas."

Ramona glanced up from her HoloTek. "You want my skills, I need brain foods."

"Now that you mention it," Drue said, "I'm starving. And some of my tutors have said I get kind of moody when I haven't eaten."

"By all means, then, let's get you some food," Hot Dog said, making her way to one of the garage exits. "We can plan over whatever Pinky cooked."

They left the garage, walking across the dark gravel of the courtyard. Benny kept his eyes up on Earth, his hands shoved in his pockets, fingers grazing the gold alien glove. He was so focused on his home and trying to figure out what they should be doing next that he didn't notice the doors to the entrance of the Taj swing open until Drue stopped walking in front of him and muttered something.

Ricardo was making his way down the steps, followed by the Miyamura twins.

"Where have you been?" Ricardo's voice boomed as he approached.

None of them spoke. For a second, Benny thought about telling Ricardo everything they'd found on the dark side. But then he remembered how desperate Ricardo was to track down Elijah. If he told the Pit Crew about Dr. Bale, would they go after him themselves and try to use all those weapons against the Alpha Maraudi? Would they bring the cannons and the Tank back to the Taj?

And how mad was Ricardo going to be if he found out they'd disobeyed him and gone off to the dark side on their own?

Benny didn't know what to do or say, so he shoved his hands even deeper into his pockets and shrugged. "We've been around."

Jasmine turned to stare at him, but Benny didn't meet her gaze.

"They were obviously in the garage," Kai said, tossing his head back to get his dark bangs out of his face.

"Probably trying to steal another one of Elijah's classic cars," Kira said with a sneer.

Ricardo just glared at Benny. "What are you up to, Love?"

Drue stepped forward. "Oh, come on. You said yourself on our first tour of the Taj: the garage is the coolest place up here. Of course that's where we like to hang out."

Ricardo grunted. "I don't want you touching *anything* in there. Those SRs are *our* resources. We're putting together a plan to head into deep space to find Elijah just as soon as we figure out a way to track that mother ship."

"Yeah," Benny said. "Cool."

"I don't have time for this," Ricardo said as he walked away, the Miyamuras in tow. He pulled a HoloTek out of his space suit pocket and tapped on the device a few times. "Trevone," he said, once he'd connected the other Crew member. He glanced back at Benny. "We need to talk about locking down parts of the Taj to the EW-SCABers."

When the Pit Crew was inside the garage, Hot Dog let out a long sigh, like she'd been holding her breath the whole time.

"Well, that's just great," she said.

"He's really committed to this whole trying-to-find-Elijah-somewhere-in-literally-the-entire-universe-if-he's-even-still-alive plan," Drue said.

"I get that he's upset," Hot Dog continued. "But we almost got our butts kicked by just a few of those ships. Even if we sent out a whole fleet of Space Runners, we'd be outnumbered by . . . I don't know, a whole lot."

"Yeah. If the Pit Crew is going after Elijah, they'd at

least need some of the doc's weapons . . ."

"Right," Benny said. "And do we really want Ricardo and the rest of the Crew going after the aliens with all that tech Dr. Bale has? That's just begging for the aliens to declare war on us or something."

"Uh, Benny," Drue said, "I hate to break it to you but I kind of think we're already at war here."

"So that's why you lied to them?" Jasmine asked.

Benny turned to her. "I thought . . ." But he didn't know what to say. They were all quiet for a moment.

Jasmine shook her head. "We snuck out, yeah, but I figured we'd tell them whatever we'd found when we got back. They should know Dr. Bale is out there. What if they went out looking for him and got attacked? That would be on us."

"I don't know," Drue said. "I see Benny's point. If I were Ricardo, I'd totally go after that Tank of his and drive it into space, guns blazing." He paused. "I kind of want to do that already."

Jasmine looked over at Hot Dog, who raised her hands away from her sides and shrugged, her face scrunched up in confusion.

"We can't just start lying to the Pit Crew," Jasmine said. "To Trevone, who helped us destroy those asteroids. You're the one who said we were in this together, Benny."

"This is different," Benny said. "I'm just trying to do

the right thing. And we're not lying, we're just . . . not telling them everything."

"I know someone else who thought the same way," Jasmine said softly before turning away from them and heading up the stairs and into the Taj.

Benny wanted to call out to her, but he didn't know what to say. He knew what she meant. And she was right. Keeping this from the Pit Crew was sort of like Elijah keeping the truth about the aliens and the EW-SCAB from them. And even as he tried to tell himself this wasn't the same thing, that the Pit Crew wouldn't see the logic because they were too worried about saving Elijah, he could remember the world's most famous adventurer saying pretty much the same thing to him just days before.

It made him feel terrible.

8.

Jasmine wasn't in the lobby.

Benny looked for her in the restaurant, too, but he didn't see her anywhere. He assumed she'd gone up to her room. His body was beginning to feel heavy, but he wasn't sure if it was because of his hunger, the fact that he'd been thrown around in a Space Runner several times that day, or because he felt like he'd just disappointed one of his friends and didn't even know if it was for a good reason. Maybe it was a combination of all those things.

True to Pinky's message earlier in the day, dinner had indeed been served, and the air inside the restaurant was thick with the scent of spices Benny had no names for in his brain. On one side of the dimly lit room was a table piled high with tacos that sat beside what looked like a fountain of steaming, thick orange cheese.

"They usually have celebrity chefs up here in the busy

season," Drue said, inhaling deeply as he led the way. "I had my doubts about how good Pinky's computerized kitchen was going to be, but I gotta say she has yet to disappoint."

"I wonder what they're eating underground," Hot Dog said.

Drue shrugged. "Probably the same thing. I checked out some of the blueprints earlier, and there's a lot to that mined-out village we didn't see. Elijah was even building a spa down there."

"Of course he was." Hot Dog paused. "I don't guess it got completed, did it?"

Drue sighed deeply and shook his head. "No such luck."

They started for the food table, where various other kids were going back for seconds—maybe thirds or fourths as far as Benny knew. As they walked, the restaurant grew quieter, almost imperceptibly at first, and then so quickly that Benny was sure something had happened.

And it had. He and his friends—the ones who'd recruited, trained, and led the kids in the restaurant on the mission to stop the asteroid storm—had walked into the room, and everyone's attention had turned to them. Benny slowed until he came to a stop, suddenly feeling very exposed. All around him at the half-filled tables, kids were staring. These weren't just his fellow Mustangs or random EW-SCABers—they were the almost forty brave kids who had followed him into outer space that morning not knowing what their future held.

And then, all at once, they were talking and jumping out of their seats, rushing over to Benny and his friends. At first it was just a wall of sound that hit him so hard he almost had to take a few steps back.

"Hey, hey, hey," Iyabo, one of his fellow Mustangs, yelled. She jumped in front of the crowd and held up her hands as she faced them. "Let's *not* turn into a mob maybe? We can ask questions one at a time."

Benny felt a momentary wave of relief and said a silent thank you to Iyabo. She'd been a big help during their video game sims before everything went crazy, and had been a stellar pilot in the attack on the asteroid storm. She was obviously someone who knew how to take control of a situation and get stuff done.

But his relief faded as Iyabo turned to him, her braids flicking around her back. "I'll go first," she said. "Any word on Elijah?"

"No," Benny said.

"All right," she continued. "Are the aliens coming back?"

Benny was quiet for a few seconds. "I'm not sure."

The group behind Iyabo started whispering. She put her hands on her hips. "'Kay," she said. "So what are we supposed to do now?"

"I don't know."

And then they were all shouting again.

"How long will we be safe at the Taj?" Alexi, a dark-haired kid from Greece, wondered.

"Do we have to fight them again if they show up?"

"What if they go to Earth?"

"I don't know!" Benny said.

He'd been in the meeting room or out on the dark side most of the day since they'd returned from space, working alongside his friends without having to give answers to anyone. Now it seemed like all the fears and anxieties that had been building up inside the rest of the EW-SCABers were coming to a head there in the restaurant. Other questions filled the air around him as his pulse kicked into overdrive, even as Iyabo tried to calm everyone down.

"How much food is here?"

"Should we go underground just in case?"

"When can I call my parents?"

"I'm sorry!" Benny said, his voice growing louder and cracking. His cheeks felt hot. "I don't know!"

Hot Dog stepped up beside him.

"Drue," she said, "answer their questions."

"Huh?" Drue turned to her, eyes full of panic. "Why me?"

But Hot Dog didn't respond. Instead, she grabbed Benny's arm and dragged him through a swinging door that led back into the kitchen. His heart felt like it was a hammering piston, and all he could do was follow her, still muttering apologies.

"What are you doing?" he asked when she finally stopped pulling and he could start to think about catching his breath.

"You looked like you were about to faint out there," she said. There was a tray of fruit on a counter nearby. She tossed him an apple. "Here, eat something."

"I'm fine," he said. He didn't even feel hungry anymore. In fact, his stomach felt too full, like he might be sick.

"Eat," Hot Dog insisted, grabbing an orange for herself. "I don't wanna have to carry you to the elevators with Drue if you pass out. Can you imagine how nuts everyone would go if they saw you like that?"

He didn't answer.

She frowned. "I watched you stand head-to-head with an alien overlord this morning and you didn't look half as scared as you just did out there."

"I'm not scared," Benny said, despite knowing full well that he was. "It's just . . . a lot."

"I know. I mean, sorta. I was only the flight school teacher. You were . . ." She laughed a short, breathy laugh. "You were *a lot*."

Benny stared down at the red piece of fruit in his hands. "I haven't had a real apple in a long time. I'm not sure my brothers have ever had one that wasn't in an old can of fruit cocktail." He shook his head. "Why am I even thinking about that when there are so many other things to worry about? You heard them out there. Everyone's terrified. They think we—I—know what to do, but . . ."

He could still hear the muffled sounds of the other EW-SCABers shouting questions back in the restaurant. Standing there in the kitchen, he suddenly felt doomed to fail them.

Hot Dog bit her lip. "Pinky might be right. Maybe you are under too much pressure."

Benny looked up at her quickly, his forehead creasing. Hot Dog seemed to realize immediately that she'd said the wrong thing, her mouth forming words that didn't actually come out.

"You've been talking to Pinky about me?" he asked.

"No, no, she was just a little worried is all. And, you know, maybe she mentioned it to me earlier when I was getting supplies to go out and find Dr. Bale."

Benny's mind was racing, his head light as he once again realized there was so much out of his control, so many moving parts in their situation that he could never hope to get a handle on everything. And now he knew that others were talking about him behind his back. Plus, he'd upset Jasmine earlier, not to mention the fact that he was lying to the Pit Crew . . .

It all felt like too much. There was a pang in his chest. He looked at Hot Dog for a few more seconds before placing the apple on a nearby counter. "I'm not hungry."

"Benny . . ." Hot Dog said.

He glanced around the kitchen until his eyes landed on another door. He remembered from their tour on the first day at the Taj that it led out into the hallway.

"There's food in my room," he said, making a beeline for the exit. "Tell the others we'll meet in the morning. I just . . . I need some time alone to think."

"It's okay to be scared," Hot Dog said. "I'm scared. We all are. But we have to—"

The door closed behind him as he entered the hallway, darting for the nearest stairwell.

In no time he was back inside his suite, where he leaned against the door for several minutes until his pulse calmed down. Then he threw himself onto the bed. The glove in his pocket poked at his leg. He wondered if things would be better if he could just figure out how to use the alien tech to help them. Or, he thought, maybe he was just desperate, hoping that there was some simple solution that could solve all their problems. A magic glove. Another, habitable planet for the aliens. Some exiled genius living on the dark side who could tell him exactly what he was supposed to be doing.

He sat up, put the glove on the nightstand, and grabbed

the only bag he'd brought with him to the Taj. Inside he found the cracked old HoloTek that he'd been using for years. He'd said he wanted time away from Hot Dog and the others to think, but now that he was in his suite he didn't want to be alone with his thoughts and fears. He needed something to occupy his attention, to make him feel like everything was going to be okay. With a few taps, he was watching old videos of his family, of the caravan, of the endless dunes he never thought he'd miss so badly. The images were slightly fuzzy due to the Drylands dust embedded in the screen. He could have just played the clips on his new datapad or on the wall across from his bed, but this felt right. The weathered old piece of tech smelled like dirt. It reminded him of home.

He watched the hundred or so members of his caravan dance around a bonfire somewhere in what was once California, remembering how they all reeked of smoke for what seemed like weeks afterward. He watched his youngest brother, Alejandro, blow out a pillar of a candle that sat on a lopsided cake his grandmother had somehow put together using flour, an expired jar of applesauce, and the meat of a prickly pear cactus. He watched his family saying good-bye to him in the message they recorded the day before he left for the Moon, all so excited, so happy.

And finally, he pulled up videos of his father, who'd marched into the desert less than a year ago in search of water and never come back. Most of them were candid moments from everyday life—clips of him fixing cars, teaching his brother Justin how to filter water, or singing a song in Spanish that always delighted Benny's grandmother. In one, his father seemed upset. Benny could remember the night clearly, because it was so rare that his father was unhappy around them. Or, at least rare that he would let them see that he was worried or angry. But that night there had been some kind of caravan meeting about what their next destination would be, and his father had been outvoted.

"What's wrong, Dad?" Justin asked in the video.

His father's face—twisted with frustration—softened as he looked at his son.

"Nothing," he said. "Your dad's just being a worrywart."

"You should tell them they should do what you say," Benny said on the video, and his voice seemed so high-pitched and young that it took him a second to recognize it. "You're always right."

His dad looked at him and laughed the low, bellowing guffaw that always made Alejandro giggle. "No one is always right," he said. "Heck, half the time I'm playing life by ear. I just try to face the world head on and do what feels right. Sometimes things work out. Sometimes they don't, and I have to do better next time." He smiled. "If the rest of the caravan thinks this is what we should do, then we'll follow them."

"Are you scared?" Justin asked.

"Of course not," his dad said. He grinned a little. "But even if I was, you can't let fear get the best of you. Then you'd never get anything done."

"We could just go off on our own instead," Benny suggested.

His dad looked puzzled for a moment. "Benicio," he said, the full name his father reserved for when he was being serious. "We might not always agree, but the caravan makes us stronger. We have to work together. It's how we survive. Sometimes you just have to trust others." He grinned, raising both his dark eyebrows. "Or trust that they'll realize their mistakes on their own. Don't you know we're nothing without each other?"

The clip ended with his father lunging forward, scooping both Benny and Justin up in his arms, the camera shaking back and forth and unable to focus as the boys squealed. In his suite, Benny stared at the frozen image of his father the video ended on before starting it over again. He watched it several more times, his body heavy with a strange mixture of feelings—the comfort of seeing this moment again and the intense longing to be with his family. Eventually, his eyes got heavy, and he let himself fall into the memories of the videos he'd just watched, until it was almost like he was living them again.

Benny woke up with his old HoloTek on his stomach.
It was early—had he been in the Drylands, the sun wouldn't have risen for several more hours—and there was a knot of hunger in his stomach. He'd never eaten the night before, which, combined with everything that had happened yesterday, was probably why he'd passed out so hard on his bed, lying on top of the covers with no memory of falling asleep. As he sat up and stretched, sharp pains shot through his body. Every inch of him was sore and tender. In the bathroom mirror, he saw bruises forming on his chest and shoulders, maybe from when he'd crashed against the asteroid mother ship. Or when he'd tackled the alien. Or when he'd been shot out of the sky on the dark side of the Moon.

He was kind of surprised he was able to get up and move around at all.

After cleaning himself up and throwing on a fresh space suit, he tore through a bunch of the snacks in his suite. And then he sat on his bed, unsure what to do. Eventually, the quiet stillness of the room became claustrophobic, and he started to feel the same anxieties he'd had the night before tingling in his chest. He looked at the old HoloTek. His father's words rang in his head.

You can't let fear get the best of you.

He knew he couldn't stay in his room, waiting for the rest of the Taj to wake up. He had to do something to make himself feel like he was making strides toward solving at least one of the many problems he and his friends had been burdened with. And so he pocketed the alien glove and headed down to the meeting room, trying to stretch out his tight muscles along the way. He kept thinking of words from the video, and he repeated them in a silent whisper as he walked through the halls of the Taj.

Do what feels right.

The mantra—plus a solid night's sleep dreaming of the old days in the caravan—gave him some comfort. A renewed sense of purpose. The only problem, though, was that Benny was completely unsure what felt right anymore.

The lights of the meeting room powered on as he stepped inside. Pinky appeared in one of the floating chairs.

"You're up very early," she said.

"But you already know I was asleep very early, too," he responded.

Pinky just smiled a little and nodded.

"Update me, please," he said, coming to a stop in front of the holodesk.

"On what?" Pinky asked.

Face the world head on.

Technically, Benny was facing *several* worlds, but he figured that didn't change the spirit of his dad's words.

"Everything," he said. "If the rest of the Taj has questions for me, then I want all the information I can get."

They went over reports, scans, and calculations Pinky had put together throughout the night, but nothing had really changed much since the day before. There was still no sign of alien activity—though, now that they knew their radars didn't register the purple-colored ships, that wasn't very comforting—or a clear way to reestablish communications with Earth. The Pit Crew was all still asleep. Ricardo had passed out at Elijah's desk, plotting possible ways to find Elijah deep into the night.

"He's probably driving himself insane," Benny said. "I'm guessing it's only a matter of time before he gets tired of feeling like he's not doing anything and does something crazy."

Pinky raised an eyebrow and murmured in agreement. "And you're sure you aren't going to end up doing something crazy yourself?"

He thought about this for a second and then shook his head. "I had a better mentor than him. And I've got friends watching my back and keeping me focused. Speaking of which, can you wake up Hot Dog and Jazz and Drue for me? And Ramona, too. We have work to do."

"Actually, Jasmine has been baking for the last half hour in my kitchen, Hot Dog just started up a flight sim in her suite, and I'm not actually sure that Ramona ever sleeps. Drue's the only one I'll have to drag out of bed."

Benny laughed a little. "Never mind. Let them keep doing what they're doing. Give them an hour."

Pinky smiled. "A little time to blow off steam. It's not a bad idea."

"Right." Benny started for the exit. "And I need to talk to Jazz, anyway. Oh, and Pinky . . ." He paused at the door for a moment before turning to face her. "It would be cool if you didn't talk to Hot Dog about me behind my back. Or anyone, I guess. Please."

The AI looked surprised, only for a moment.

"Of course." She tilted her head back, looking at him over the bridge of her nose. "You know, there's something about you this morning. You sound kind of like he did once upon a time."

"You mean Elijah?" Benny asked. "That doesn't really make me feel great."

She looked off to the side at something Benny couldn't see. Something that wasn't there. "It should. Elijah was many things, but you can't argue that he wasn't a strong leader."

She turned back to him and smiled.

"Thanks," Benny said, and then he headed out the door.

He found Jasmine in the Taj's kitchen. Despite all the high-tech lasers and kitchen gadgets lining the walls, she was standing alone with a big mixing bowl and a few bags of ingredients at a clean work space in the center of the room.

"Hey," he said.

She jumped, clearly not expecting anyone. A little cloud of flour plumed around her hands. Then she stood very still.

"Hi," she said.

We're stronger together.

"I don't mean to interrupt or anything," Benny said as he walked farther into the room. "But . . . I wanted to say that I'm sorry about yesterday. I shouldn't have lied to Ricardo and the others. We should have all talked about what we were going to do first. It *was* the kind of thing Elijah would do."

She seemed to relax a little. "I didn't mean it like that. Well, I did, but I was so surprised and confused and . . ." She trailed off.

"No, you were right," Benny said. "I'll talk to them later, when they're up, and take the heat for it."

"Ricardo's going to be so mad." She sighed. "I *guess* I could go with you and make sure you don't get murdered. Plus, I bet Trevone will want to know all about the tech we saw."

"That would be cool," Benny said. He walked to the other side of the table she was working at. "What are you making?" he asked.

"Cookies. They're my favorite things to bake."

"I've never made cookies before."

"It's super simple," she said. "You can help me."

He looked at the measuring cups, the big bag of sugar, the little vials that could have held anything as far as he was concerned. He was way out of his element, their tiny kitchen RV not up to the task of cooking much, even if they'd had the ingredients.

"Maybe I'll just watch this time."

She nodded as she poured some amber-colored liquid into a spoon. "I know you're frustrated," she said. "I am, too. So I've been thinking about things we can do. Baking actually helps me do that sometimes." She began to stir the mixture. "I agree that we need to find a way to fix all this without hurting anyone. We're still trying to figure out how to get past the asteroids so we can put Ramona's satellites up, but . . . what if we tried to get in contact with the Alpha

Maraudi instead? Communication could be the key to all this, and Dr. Bale obviously hasn't tried that. Not that we have any idea how to connect with them right now. But I asked Ramona to think about it."

"Yeah," Benny said, and the more he thought about it, the better it sounded. "*Yeah*. That's a great idea."

"I'm glad you think so," Jasmine said. "This is all so crazy that sometimes I'm not sure if I'm having a really smart moment or going nuts."

"I can kind of relate." Benny smiled. "I'm glad we've got you on our side to help us. We couldn't have done any of this without you."

Her cheeks flushed and she looked at the floor. "Thanks."

Someone snickered behind them. Benny turned to see Ramona in the doorway.

"Heart holograms all around," she said, turning her attention to the HoloTek on her arm. "Don't mind me, though. I'm just the real brains behind everything."

"I'm glad we have you, too, Ramona," Benny said.

"Agreed," Jasmine added.

Ramona opened up one of the giant refrigerators that lined the walls. "Some hacker's been stealing my soda stock in the garage. Not cool."

Benny and Jasmine looked at each other.

"Um," Jasmine said. "Not to be rude, but I'm pretty sure you're the one drinking all of them."

Ramona just burped as she headed toward the door with half a dozen cans in her arms. "Whatever, newbz."

Dozens of cookies sat on a counter in the meeting room an hour later.

"In retrospect, something more breakfasty would probably have been a better idea," Jasmine said, a dusting of flour still coating strands of her shiny black hair.

"What's not breakfasty about cookies?" Drue asked, biting into one of the six he'd grabbed and tossed on the holodesk. "Whoa . . . This is . . . this is like the best thing I've ever tasted, Jazz. Seriously."

She smiled wide, and then tried to hide it. "There's lavender in the caramel drizzle."

"Super health power-up," Ramona chirped as she tore a small piece off one of the cookies and shoved it into her mouth. "Max impressed, J."

"Do you have any idea how expensive that piece of tech is that you're getting crumbs all over?" Pinky asked, glaring at Drue.

He shrugged. "Bill me."

Hot Dog pointed at his black space suit with silver rivets on the shoulders. "You're kidding me with these, right? Just how many space suits did you bring from home?"

"What?" he said through a mouthful. "The blue ones you guys have are so plain. They look itchy, to be honest."

He shrugged. "Besides, my dad always says a Lincoln should *look* like a Lincoln."

"Your dad sounds like a ton of fun."

"He . . ." Drue paused for a second. "He has his moments. Besides, the Lincoln family does have an image to maintain."

"An image? If I'm not mistaken, Drue Bob Lincoln the First argued in Congress that climate change wasn't real and so we shouldn't waste time or money trying to stop it," Jasmine said. "Maybe you should ask Benny how that worked out for the Drylands."

Drue just laughed nervously and picked at his cookie. Benny shook his head—the Lincoln family was the least of his concerns.

Hot Dog turned her attention to him, barely meeting his gaze. They hadn't spoken since the night before. "What's first?" she asked.

"Something Drue suggested to me yesterday," he said.

"Sweet!" the other boy said. "Uh, what was it?"

Benny looked to Pinky. "Let's go through Elijah's files. Prototypes, research, special projects, anything even remotely connected to the aliens. Especially in terms of communication. Also, anything that could help us get rid of the asteroids between here and Earth."

"Of course," Pinky said. "Though, I warn you that for someone who was always on the cutting edge of technology, he was a bit old-fashioned when it came to the creative process. His brainstorming was almost always done with pen and paper. Unfortunately, those journals are all in his office, which—"

"Has been taken over by the Pit Crew," Benny said.

"I'm uploading everything I can find to your HoloTeks," Pinky said.

"There's so much here," Jasmine said, swiping through files on her screen. "There must be hundreds of Space Runner prototypes alone, not to mention reports from researchers he hired, engineers, astrophysicists. It could take us forever to get through these, much less come up with any way they might be useful."

"Many of these projects are purely hypothetical, never meant to be executed," Pinky said.

"Uh, I think I'm looking at a model of the Taj being shot into space," Hot Dog said.

"Exactly. Elijah often spent a fortune—and an absurd amount of time—just to see if he could come up with a way to do something, with no intention of ever *actually* doing it." She smiled a little. "Also, it turns out you *can* shoot the Taj into space. It would just require a lot of time and planning combined with a ridiculous amount of money."

"Okay," Benny said. "So, where do we begin?"

Pinky snapped her fingers. Benny's HoloTek screen flashed, and a series of folders appeared.

"I've taken the liberty of compiling the projects that might be most helpful to you," she said. "Possible Taj defense systems. Experimental hyperdrives. Plans for large-scale Space Runners primed for deep-space travel."

Benny tapped on his screen, opening up blueprints for what looked like a giant Space Runner bus, big enough for several people to live in reasonably comfortably.

"It's like an SR RV," he murmured to himself.

"Awesome," Drue said. "But isn't there like—I don't know—a giant asteroid-shredding missile launcher in here somewhere?"

"From what I've heard, you'll have to talk to Dr. Bale about something like that," Pinky said. "Elijah was always adamant that his innovations not be applied to any sort of weapons. You wouldn't believe the government contracts and licensing deals he turned down."

"Ugh," Drue groaned, reaching for more cookies. "All I'm finding is stuff about how the gravity can be controlled on a room by room basis at the Taj, which I'm sure will be super helpful if I ever want to hang a portrait of myself in the lobby, but not right now. Talk to me about some of these prototype SRs, Pinky. Where are the dual-engine hyper-drives? Or a Moon motorcycle?"

"I hesitate to point out that something like that *has* been produced," Pinky said. "But it was far less practical than a normal Space Runner."

Drue's eyes practically sparkled. "Where is it?" he whispered.

Within a few minutes, Pinky had led them down into the basement and through a series of corridors. Eventually, they came to a long spot in the hallway where there appeared to be no doors. Pinky stopped.

"I advise you not to touch anything down here," the AI said, keeping her gaze planted firmly on Drue.

"Scout's honor," Drue said.

Pinky sighed. "I know for a fact that you were never a scout, Drue Bob Lincoln the Third."

"Uh, in *where*, though?" Hot Dog asked.

Pinky waved her hand, and a section of the wall slid away, revealing the entrance to a pitch-black room.

"Secret level," Ramona chirped. "Woot."

"I don't know why I'm surprised by this," Hot Dog said, shaking her head.

"What is this place?" Benny asked, staring into the darkness.

Lights flickered on overhead as Pinky walked in, revealing a huge room filled with row after row of shelving racks holding all sorts of devices, tools, and hulking shapes draped in white dust covers. On one side of the room, five Space Runner—or Space Runner-*inspired*—models lined the wall.

"It was originally designed as a sort of vault area, but

in practice it's become a storeroom for Elijah's failed or discarded toys," Pinky said. "Many of the projects he abandoned or that never lived up to his expectations ended up here. All these should be in the plans I sent to your HoloTeks."

Drue darted straight for the prototypes. "*This* is what I'm talking about. You've been holding out on us, Pinks."

"How did this stuff even get down here?" Jasmine asked, wandering farther into the room.

Pinky pointed to a square on the cement ceiling. "This opens up. We're underneath the courtyard. The fountain out front is directly above us and moves aside to allow easy access to and from the garage."

Hot Dog had wandered down one of the rows of shelves, and was now holding up what looked to Benny like a metal skull with wires dangling from the neck. "Elijah was building robots?" she asked.

"No way," Benny said.

"Before settling on a holographic interface for me, he did toy with the idea of giving me a more palpable form," Pinky said.

"Analog realness," Ramona said.

Hot Dog looked back down at the skull in her hands. "This is terrifying."

Benny picked up one of many sets of gloves sitting on a shelf, a thick band across the knuckles.

"These look like the gravity gloves we used in the video game sim," he said.

"Close," the AI replied. "Those actually emit high-voltage, supertargeted magnetic fields. Elijah used them to move around dead Space Runners back in his early testing phases."

From across the room, Drue gasped. "What. Is. This?!"

Benny found him beside a red Space Runner that stood on four short, shining metal disks.

"Ah," Pinky said. "For a while Elijah was entertaining the idea of landing on an approaching comet and riding it for a few days." She motioned to the disks. "These are designed to shoot off of the vehicle and latch on a passing celestial body. Then, the powerful electromagnets hidden inside could theoretically pull the Space Runner to, say, a comet, holding it stable on the celestial body. Eventually he lost interest in the idea."

"He really went through a whole magnet phase, huh?" Hot Dog asked.

"Brilliant," Jasmine said, coming up beside Benny. "To design something like this and keep it in storage. Most people would kill to even have a working concept."

"Why land on a comet when he could just race beside it and—" Drue stopped mid-sentence, his mouth hanging open. "There it is."

He darted away from them, making a beeline to a yellow

bike-shaped craft in the corner.

"A Moon motorcycle!" he shouted.

"That would be the Galaxicle, yes," Pinky said.

"How does it work? No, let me guess—mini hyperdrives in each wheel? Pinky, I'm taking this for a spin."

"Absolutely not," Pinky said. "That prototype hasn't been tested in years, and it proved to be far too impractical for use in space. It was little more than a novelty."

"I just want to go for a ride around the Taj!"

"It's far too fast for—"

"*Too fast?*" Drue asked. "I think I'm in love."

"You'd probably break every bone in your body," Hot Dog said.

Ramona smirked. "Let him do it."

"Put one finger on that and—" Pinky started, but she abruptly turned back to the others. "There's a call."

"A what?" Benny asked.

"It's Dr. Bale."

Benny looked around, unsure of whether he should be excited or concerned. From what he could tell, they felt the same way.

"Okay," he said. "So what do we do?"

"Well?" Drue asked. "Answer it, dummy."

"Yeah," Hot Dog agreed. "Maybe he's got news about the aliens or something. He could've seen them headed our way."

"I can route it to your HoloTek," Pinky said.

Benny nodded and pulled out his datapad. He took a deep breath before tapping on the screen. The scientist's face appeared. He was back in his strange space truck—the Tank.

"Benny," he said, peering into his HoloTek camera. "Very good. I was hoping you'd be the one who answered. I suppose I have Pinky to thank for that."

"Yeah, you—" Benny started.

"I'll cut to the chase, my boy. I have something I think you'll be very interested in."

Benny blinked. "What?" he asked.

Dr. Bale's lips spread over his teeth, revealing a toothy grin. "Contact with Earth."

"What?" Benny asked. "How? When?"

"I'll show you." Bale paused, adjusting his thick goggles. "We'll be at the garage's auxiliary port in ten minutes. See you then."

Before Benny could react, the screen went black.

10.

Hot Dog's eyes went wide. "Ten minutes?" she half shouted. "He's almost here!"

"Could he really have a way to contact Earth?" Benny asked.

"Of course," Jasmine said. "I mean, anything is possible."

"If he wants to carve a message into the Moon with lasers," Drue said, "you can tell him I already had that idea and it got shot down."

"I'm much more concerned that he might have brought a bunch of those weapons with him." Jasmine shook her head. "He could have called us before he left his camp. He didn't want us to have much notice."

"They've disengaged whatever cloaking technology they were using," Pinky said. "I've got five vehicles approaching the Taj perimeter. There appear to be three drivers.

The two unmanned crafts are quite large, likely floating containers."

"Right." Benny raised a hand to his temple, rubbing the side of his head as he turned away from the Space Runner prototypes. "Let's get up there." He started for the door, and then paused, looking to Pinky. "Call the Pit Crew," he said. "Tell them what's happening. Tell them everything we know about Dr. Bale. This could be big, and we should be figuring this out together." He groaned. "I'm sorry about how much Ricardo is about to yell at you."

"I appreciate that," Pinky said. "But save the concern for yourself."

"Wait," Hot Dog said, catching up with him as he headed into the hallway. "So we're just going to let Dr. Bale in?"

"I don't know," Benny said. "We've got, what, eight or nine minutes to decide?"

"I'm not thrilled by the idea," Jasmine said. "But not letting him inside the Taj *could* provoke him. We don't want to do that."

"Maybe he's not as nutso as we thought he was," Drue said as they piled into an elevator that would take them up to the lobby. "Maybe he just wants some tacos instead of Moon dust bars."

"Plus, if he has figured out a way to get in contact with Earth . . ."

Benny's thoughts turned to what this could mean for

them, just how important it was that they be able to warn humanity of the alien threat. It had been almost a week since they'd had any sort of contact with the planet. And it wasn't just Taj satellites that were destroyed in the first asteroid assault; who knew how many telescopes, communications hubs, and unmanned space stations had been obliterated? Had people sent up Space Runners to check on the Taj? Were they aware of the threats floating between Earth and the Moon? Or was the planet still blissfully unaware that anything major was happening? If Dr. Bale could get them in touch with Earth, they could *finally* have answers to at least some of their questions.

He thought, too, of what else contact with Earth would mean for him: a chance to call home. To see and talk to his family. He wasn't sure how he'd break the news of everything that had happened—was *happening*—to them, but he knew that just seeing their faces and hearing their voices again would make everything better somehow.

They tore through the lobby and out into the courtyard, none of them speaking. When they made it to the garage, they found Bo McGuyver reassembling a hyperdrive engine while Ash tinkered with a laser mounting. Benny and his friends must have looked worried when they entered, because Ash immediately hurried over to them, her eyebrows raised in concern.

"What's wrong?" she asked.

"Dr. Bale is coming," Benny said. "He's on his way now."

Pinky appeared beside them. "I'm estimating his time of arrival at five minutes and forty-seven seconds."

"He's coming *here*?" Ash asked. "When that man left the Taj the last time, he made off with a bunch of prototype SRs." She turned to her brother. "Yo, Bo. Help me hide anything valuable we haven't already stashed underground."

She whipped out a HoloTek and tapped on it, causing the floor to shift on the far side of the garage. Several rows of Space Runners sank below the concrete. With a nod of satisfaction, Ash motioned her brother toward their gadget-filled toolboxes against the far wall. Ramona sat in one of the two oversize satellite Space Runners next to them, face buried in her HoloTek, seemingly oblivious to everyone else.

"The auxiliary tunnel is still sealed," Pinky said, a hesitancy in her voice. "Would you like me to open it?"

There was a stomping of boots behind them as Ricardo and Trevone burst into the garage, Ricardo leading.

"Where is he?" he shouted. He glared at Benny as he practically snarled each word.

"Four minutes and twenty-four seconds away," Pinky said.

"Pinky told us he has an *arsenal*," Trevone said. "What if this whole thing is just a trick to—"

Ricardo raised a hand in the air so quickly that Trevone

jumped and stopped speaking midsentence.

"I can't believe you," he said, pointing at Benny, then gesturing to the rest of them. "*All* of you. Going out there. Finding him and then not telling us."

"I know," Benny said. "I'm sorry, but we—"

"You need to leave." Ricardo took a few steps toward him.

"Uh." Drue came up to Benny's side. "Dr. Bale is kind of expecting *us*."

"Also," Jasmine said. "About those weapons."

"Yeah." Hot Dog pulled on a blond curl. "Are we letting this guy in here for sure?"

"He obviously has resources that we need," Ricardo said. "We can't ignore whatever he's offering if he really can get us back in contact with Earth. That would mean reinforcements. We could get together a whole search party for Elijah. And as far as his weapons go . . ." He turned his attention to Trevone. "We could use them."

Trevone clenched his jaw.

"So, you think we should let him in?" Benny asked.

"We *are* letting him in. It's not your decision to make."

"Gentlemen," Pinky said carefully. "You are putting me in a very awkward situation. I'm going to need the two of you to find some common ground very quickly."

Benny looked up at Ricardo, thinking again of his

father's words. About trusting others. About the impor-
tance of the caravan sticking together. If he said no now,
he'd just be making the Pit Crew *and* Dr. Bale mad. Plus,
they *did* need all the help they could get.

Finally, he nodded. "Ricardo's right."

Drue took a few steps away from the group, looking
around the garage floor, before finally picking up a long,
thick torque wrench.

"What are you doing?" Jasmine asked.

Drue shrugged. "I dunno. If he pulls anything funny
or tries to hold up the Taj, I kind of want to be prepared.
This may shock you, but I've never actually been in a fight
before, so I don't know how to throw a punch."

"Put that down," Hot Dog said. "Not that I think he's
going to look at you and be scared, but it's probably not
going to help things at all."

"ETA fifty-two seconds," Pinky said.

"The brat has a point," Ricardo said. "We should have
some sort of plan if this goes bad."

The AI waved to a row of SR trainers in one corner of
the garage. "Perhaps you're forgetting that I have control of
most everything in here. If he so much as implies a threat,
I'll have him pinned against the wall."

Benny turned to her. "Good. Be on your guard, just in
case."

"You're *not* in charge, Love," Ricardo said, taking a step toward Benny and puffing out his chest. Then he glanced at Pinky. "Be ready."

They stood there, staring at the corridor that led outside the Grand Dome. Apart from Pinky's updates and the sounds of the McGuyvers tucking sensitive equipment and plans into locked cabinets, the garage was silent. And then the vehicles were shooting in from the tunnel, their hyperdrives rattling, louder than any Space Runner Benny had heard.

They parked at the far end of the garage and took their time getting out of their vehicles. Benny and the others stood back, unmoving.

"Here goes nothing," Hot Dog murmured as Dr. Bale stepped out of his car. He said something to his assistants, and Todd and Mae hurried to one of the giant rectangular boxes that had floated in behind them.

"Hello again," Dr. Bale said as he walked toward Benny's group. He nodded to Pinky. "Ms. Weyve. It's been many years." He smiled a little. "He chose a good time to upload your image."

Pinky let out a short, breathy laugh as she crossed her arms. "Dr. Austin Bale. You certainly look as though you've spent the last few years on the dark side. The Taj's spa, fortunately, can do wonders for a tired face."

"*Pinky,*" Ricardo muttered.

But Dr. Bale didn't seem to be concerned by the AI's comments. Instead he grinned and smoothed down his oily hair. "I haven't been living in luxury up here on the Moon, no. Too much work to be done to worry about keeping up appearances."

Mae and Todd pulled a big metal trunk from one of the containers and carried it between the two of them. Benny couldn't tell if it was exceptionally heavy, or if the two thin assistants were just weak from spending so much time on the dark side, surviving on sustenance packets.

"I can't tell what's inside." Pinky's voice came through the speaker in Benny's collar, so quiet he could barely hear her. "But I'm sensing dozens of small power sources."

"You said you had a way for us to contact Earth," Benny said, taking a few steps forward.

In a flash, Ricardo was standing beside him. When he spoke, his voice was deeper than usual. "My name is Ricardo Rocha. As the senior member of Elijah West's Pit Crew, I'd like to welcome you to the Lunar Taj on his behalf, and hope—"

"Yes, it's a pleasure," Dr. Bale interrupted. "I know who you are and you know who I am, so I think we can go ahead and dispense with the formalities in the essence of time."

He pulled off a glove and reached down, touching the side of the trunk. It sprang open, and Benny instinctively held his breath. Inside he could see what looked like a pile of small black objects. Bale picked one up, holding it in his open palm so they could see its twelve equal, flat sides, which gleamed in the light.

"That's what's reestablishing our comms?" Benny asked.

"Close," Dr. Bale said. He nodded to Mae, who pulled out a HoloTek. After a few taps, the device flew from Bale's hands and hovered in the air twenty feet above them. He continued. "The remaining asteroids between here and Earth are your problem. As long as they're around, there's no safe place to park a satellite. And SRs aren't primed for automated tactical response when threatened—one of Elijah's grosser oversights."

He pulled something out of the pocket of his patched space suit, holding it up to them between his thumb and index finger: a piece of alien asteroid rock no bigger than a lug nut.

"What you need is protection," he said. "That's what I've come to offer you."

Dr. Bale tossed the asteroid bit high into the room above them. It came within five feet of the floating black device before a golden blip of energy shot out. The asteroid piece went up in a small explosion of dust and fire, tiny specks of debris raining down around them.

"Whoa," Benny murmured.

"Hey!" Ash shouted, charging a few steps toward him.

"Don't you dare shoot anything off in my garage."

"Defensive drones." Dr. Bale grinned, ignoring her. He waved to the trunk beside him. "These are all primed to fire when a mineral of alien composition is within range."

"We could have used those here last week," Pinky muttered. "Or yesterday morning."

"That's . . ." Jasmine said, pausing as a smile spread across her face, "*perfect*. I assume we could program them to orbit a few Space Runners with satellite links inside, allowing us to create a makeshift communications line with Earth."

"I want one floating around *me*," Drue said, "programmed to zap any aliens that show up."

"This tech could also be utilized to fortify the Taj defenses," Trevone said. "Imagine if we could simply shoot hundreds of them into future asteroid fields."

Dr. Bale smiled wryly as he listened to them. "Very clever, indeed. I can see why Elijah chose all of you."

"You brought these for us to use?" Benny asked. His mind was already trying to put together a plan. "How fast can we get them in the air?"

"Immediately, to answer your second question." Dr. Bale paused, letting his eyes roam over the group.

That's when Benny realized that Dr. Bale wasn't just handing over this technology without getting something in return.

"What is it that you want?" Ricardo asked, obviously having come to the same conclusion.

Dr. Bale smiled. Beside him, his two assistants stood with their hands clasped behind their backs.

"As Pinky mentioned, I've been gone a long time," he said, smoothing down his beard. "I wouldn't mind a hot shower. Supplies. We, too, have people on Earth we are in dire need of contacting." He shrugged. "And, of course, access to some of the state-of-the-art tools and instruments you no doubt have lying around the Taj would be indispensable in furthering my work."

"Which is what, exactly?" Pinky asked.

Bale's face grew solemn. "Saving the human race, of course."

Benny wondered how, specifically, he planned on doing that. After all Elijah's assurances that everything would be okay in the end if they just trusted him, Benny wasn't exactly keen on putting his faith in someone who promised to save the human race without giving any actual details. He looked at Bale's vehicles parked on the other end of the garage.

"What's in the other containers back there?" Benny asked.

"The future. Many of the innovations you saw in my camp. I couldn't just leave them out there."

"You brought all those weapons into the Taj?" Jasmine asked.

"Uh, and you're sure they're all safe?" Hot Dog asked.

"I do *not* want a bunch of bombs and laser guns hot-wired together on the dark side of the Moon sitting in my garage," Ash said.

But Ricardo raised a hand, motioning for everyone else to be quiet. His eyes were narrowed—Benny could see him trying to work out a plan of his own.

"I think you and I should have a long talk, Dr. Bale." He glanced at Benny and his friends. "Alone."

11.

Ricardo and Trevone whisked Dr. Bale out into the Taj's courtyard, leaving his assistants behind to stand watch over the cargo. Jasmine and Drue crouched beside the trunk filled with black devices, both speaking at once.

"So, are these gold things laser beams or plasma blasts or what?" Drue asked.

"Why the dodecahedron shape?" Jasmine asked.

"And, like, how powerful are we talking about here? How much can they destroy? We could test them out on Pluto or something! That's where they found that first abandoned alien base! It's perfect!"

"More important, what's the internal energy source?"

"They're run on modified fission cores," Todd said. "Like a hyperdrive."

"They're Dr. Bale's design," Mae added. "The man is a genius."

"Completely," Todd agreed. "History will no doubt view him as such."

Jasmine and Drue looked at each other before they both started talking again. Benny stood near the exit to the courtyard. His focus was less on what was going on in the garage and more on what Ricardo was discussing with Dr. Bale.

"Any idea what they're saying out there?" Benny asked Pinky. He'd thought about trying to sneak around outside and eavesdrop, but in the open space of the Grand Dome there was nowhere for him to hide.

Pinky frowned. "Trevone has temporarily shut me out of the courtyard. I'm trying to work around him, but there's a reason he's on the Pit Crew."

"Can Ramona maybe hack the system?" Hot Dog asked. "No offense, Pinky."

The AI waved a hand back and forth. "None taken."

"Ramona should focus on the satellites," Benny said, nodding to the girl in a nearby Space Runner. "That takes priority, I think."

Hot Dog sighed. "I thought Trevone was on our side."

"We're all supposed to be on the *same* side." Benny shook his head. "I realize how dumb that sounds when *I'm* the one who didn't tell them about Dr. Bale."

"No use worrying about that now."

"I wonder what Elijah would say if he knew the Taj's

garage was housing a load of weapons," Pinky said. "Actually, strike that. I know exactly what he'd say, and I don't care to speak those words while children are present."

"I just have a bad feeling about this for some reason," Hot Dog said.

Benny looked at the Space Runner that Ramona was still tinkering with, and then over to the research assistants. Jasmine turned one of the drones in her hands slowly, while Drue continued asking Todd and Mae questions. Behind all of them, the two big storage trailers loomed. He could only guess what all was inside.

With every move they'd made since first finding out about the Alpha Maraudi, it seemed like their problems had just gotten more complicated. Nothing had been what it had seemed. An asteroid turned out to be some kind of mother ship. A conquering alien race was really just trying to survive. Something told him, too, that there was more to Dr. Bale than they realized, but he had no way of knowing what.

"If we're getting back in touch with Earth," Benny said, "then it's worth it. Right?"

Hot Dog nodded a bit, a hesitant agreement that mirrored his own feelings.

Ramona leaned out of the Space Runner. "Upstream, downstream connections are maxed. Both satellite SRs ready for launch. My work here is done." She crumpled a soda can in her hand and tossed it over to a trash can yards away, a perfect shot. "Level complete."

Benny watched Mae and Todd smile at each other as they heard this news, and then they were carrying several of the black devices over to the Space Runners, chattering back and forth.

"I'm assigning two drones to each vehicle," Mae said.

"Brilliant." Todd tapped on his HoloTek. "That should be plenty. I've already plotted the most efficient course for them to take."

"Dr. Bale will be pleased."

Hot Dog leaned in close to Benny. "I think they're the only two members of his fan club," she whispered as Drue and Jasmine rejoined them.

Jasmine still held one of the drones. "It really *is* a genius design," she said.

"Guys, these things shoot out particle beams," Drue said, his eyes wide and glittering under the lights. "*Particle beams*. This is crazy-go-nuts tech."

"It's strange, though," Jasmine said, turning the drone over in her hands. "I can't imagine this sort of technology being honed in a camp like the one we saw. Especially so quickly. They would need so much manufacturing equipment and time. The logistics of creating these weapons must have been extremely complicated. He obviously had these lying around already." She looked at the trailers. "I wonder what else he has in there."

Drue's eyes lit up. "Maybe we should find out."

He started toward the trailer at a fast clip. Benny and the others looked at one another for a second before following him. They were a few feet from the containers when a voice sounded behind them.

"New Apollo Lockdown, Code Armstrong," Mae said.

In front of them, the open door to one of the trailers slammed shut.

"There's sensitive equipment inside," Todd said. "It's not for children."

Drue turned to him, eyes narrowed. "We're not just children, we're . . ." He paused. "We're Moon heroes!"

Todd smirked, but before he could respond the door to the courtyard opened and Dr. Bale walked back inside, Ricardo and Trevone following him.

"What's our progress?" Dr. Bale called to his assistants.

"We're ready to launch," Mae said, looking up from a HoloTek. "The drones are programmed to protect these two SRs."

"On your order," Todd said, straightening his posture.

"Wait," Benny murmured, taking a few steps forward.

Dr. Bale paused in the center of the room, surveying the satellite Space Runners before nodding. "Good work.

Let's not waste any time. We'll launch immediately."

"You're welcome," Ramona said, from her seat in the corner of the room, not looking up from her HoloTek.

"What's going on?" Benny asked, feeling as though some big decision had been made without him.

"Just as I said," Dr. Bale said. "I'm reestablishing communications with Earth."

"I meant what did you guys talk about out there?"

Dr. Bale looked at Ricardo, who raised his head a little higher.

"Dr. Bale knows people on Earth who will be able to help us find Elijah," he said. "We need manpower. We need an *army* to get him back. Dr. Bale is giving us that."

"An *army*?" Hot Dog asked.

Dr. Bale nodded. "I have a wide range of contacts on Earth. They'll no doubt be wondering what the status of the Moon is. Once they understand what's happened, they'll send reinforcements."

"I thought everyone on Earth thought he was nuts," Drue whispered.

"What's your plan?" Benny asked.

"Simple," Dr. Bale said. "We're going to protect humanity."

"And in doing so, we'll get Elijah back," Ricardo said.

"Yes. Of course." The man pulled a HoloTek from his

space suit pocket. "Now, first things first. Let's get these satellites in the air."

"That's not a plan, though," Benny said. "*How* are you going to protect the planet?"

But Dr. Bale didn't answer. He tapped his device, and the two Space Runners rose a few feet off the ground.

"Something's wrong," Pinky said, before Benny could think of what to do next. "I don't have access to the mainframes of these Space Runners and the auxiliary tunnel is open."

"Oh, that," Dr. Bale said. "In order to ensure that my drones work perfectly, I need complete control over the vehicles. Trevone let me tap into your operating systems. I'm sure you understand."

"What?" is all Benny could say as the Space Runners shot forward out of the garage.

"Trevone?" Pinky asked, her voice breaking slightly.

The Pit Crew member kept his eyes on the dark concrete floor of the garage.

"If it's a problem, we can try to work something else out," Dr. Bale said, pocketing his HoloTek again. "But for the sake of time I figured no one would take issue with it. I'm here to help. Soon we'll be back in touch with Earth again, and we'll get everything sorted out." He turned to Ricardo. "Speaking of which, we have several hours before the satellites will be in position, and I wouldn't mind seeing that suite you mentioned."

"We'll put you up in one of the wings that isn't being used by the scholarship winners," Ricardo said. "You should find everything you need in your room. If not, please let Pinky know and she'll do her best to accommodate you." He looked at the AI. "Right, Pinky?"

"Of course," she said, adjusting her glasses, a slight edge to her voice. "It's my duty to serve."

Dr. Bale looked at Benny and his friends. "Don't worry. This will all be taken care of now. You've done admirable jobs. You saved the planet. You are true champions of humanity. So relax. Everything will be handled, you'll see." Then he turned on his heel and started toward the exit, Ricardo beside him.

"Trevone," Jasmine whispered, raising her hands in confusion.

He glanced at her and opened his mouth, about to speak. But then he turned away and followed the other Pit Crew member out.

A few seconds passed in silence before Pinky spoke.

"Um, I hate to be the bearer of bad news," she said. "But Ricardo has requested that the garage remain off-limits to all unauthorized personnel." She grimaced. "That includes all of you."

"What gives him the right?" Drue asked. "I'm not going anywhere!"

"Wait, we're *all* getting banned?" Hot Dog asked. She crossed her arms. "He can come and drag us out if he wants us to leave."

Benny bit the inside of his cheeks. The morning before, he and his friends had been leading the charge against the dangers that faced Earth, and now it seemed like they'd been cut out completely. Frustration welled up in him, but there was something else, too: deep down, he felt almost relieved to have lost control. To know that someone else was in charge of making the decisions and keeping Earth safe.

"No," he finally said. He shook his head and looked at her. "We've got to try to work together, which means we should probably pick our battles. Besides, we don't want to do anything to rock the Taj until comms are reestablished. Let's just see how this plays out over the next few hours and hope for the best."

Hot Dog bit her lip. "I don't like this."

"Me neither," Jasmine said. "But I think Benny's right."

He smiled at her a little. Still, he couldn't help shake the feeling that something was wrong—that there was a puzzle piece he was missing from the overall picture. He'd felt this sort of relief before, when Elijah had guaranteed that everything was fine at the Taj. And that, obviously, hadn't turned out well. He swallowed hard, and looked at the others—the Moon Platoon. No matter what happened next, he told himself, they'd get through this together.

They'd figure out a way.

But even as he repeated these thoughts, the sheer immensity of the situation threatened to crush all hope inside him.

12.

"Wait, so, some other dude is taking charge of the
Taj now?" Iyabo asked, whipping her long braids back and
forth as she looked from Benny to Jasmine, the silver ribbons threaded in them glinting. "And you actually went out
there and found him?" She let out a long sigh. "I don't get
you guys. We had this place to ourselves and you went and
ruined it with more adults to tell us what to do."

She plopped down into one of the plush chairs in the
Mustangs' common room, where Benny, Drue, Hot Dog,
and Jasmine had retreated following their exile from the
garage. Iyabo had been talking with another group of kids
in the room when they'd first arrived, but the others had
filtered out. She'd stuck behind, though, insisting that if
something were going on, she deserved to know what it was.
Apparently, the fact that they'd been sitting around hardly

saying a word to each other was an obvious sign that something was wrong.

"It's not exactly how we planned it to go," Drue said as he put his feet up on the coffee table in front of the cluster of chairs where they all sat.

Iyabo picked at a bag of dried fruit she'd brought from her room. "Yeah, well, I'd planned on having a fun-filled two weeks on the Moon, and we all know how that turned out."

Pinky walked out of one of the walls where an animated red Mustang was rearing back and neighing silently. "Good news. Any minute now we should have a usable connection to Earth."

Benny felt the hair on the back of his neck stand up. Jasmine let out a loud sigh of relief. Finally, at least one of their big problems was about to be solved. Communications were being reestablished.

"Great," Hot Dog said, jumping to her feet. "So who are we calling first?"

"That's . . . the bad news." Pinky took off a pair of black-rimmed glasses and rubbed the bridge of her nose. "I've been blocked from controlling the satellite transmissions. Trevone is continuing to limit my abilities at Dr. Bale's request. I am, apparently, too much of a *variable* as someone who can think for herself."

"What?" Jasmine asked, her voice louder than usual. She pressed her lips together hard for a moment. "What is he thinking? This is so disappointing."

"Currently, Dr. Bale and a few others are gathered around the holodesk in the meeting room downstairs preparing for satellite uplink." Pinky's expression twisted. "I . . . don't seem to have control of that door anymore."

"Okay, this is ridiculous," Hot Dog said, beginning to pace. "You're, like, the brain of the Taj. They can't just cut you off from doing your job."

"Why is the Spit Crew going along with this?" Drue asked.

Hot Dog came to a stop. "Spit Crew? Really? That's the best you've got?"

"You don't want to hear the names I've come up with for Ricardo," Drue said.

She sighed. "I take *one* jersey from his room and I never hear the end of it."

"Please think about what you just said."

"Guys," Iyabo said, cutting in. "Maybe you two should stop flirting with each other and focus on the actual issues?"

Drue and Hot Dog stared back at her, mouths slightly ajar, before both of them gagged like they'd just bitten into something spoiled.

"The Pit Crew is scared," Jasmine said. "They're just trying to get Elijah back. He's like a father to them."

"Yeah, one who almost got the world blown up," Iyabo said.

Pinky perked up, taking in a sharp breath. "They're trying to make a connection now."

"You still have eyes and ears in there, right?" Benny asked, getting to his feet. Even if they weren't calling the shots, he didn't want to be left in the dark. "Can you show us what's happening?"

She nodded. In a flash two of the intersecting walls of the common room changed. One was a side view of those gathered in the meeting room. Dr. Bale looked different from before. His beard was trimmed much shorter and his hair was clean and slicked back. He wore a pristine new space suit and had traded out his thick goggles for a pair of wire-rimmed glasses. Ricardo and Trevone stood on one side of him, his assistants on the other. The second wall in the Mustang common room gave them a frontal view of the holodesk. A squiggly blue hologram pulsed in the air above it as Dr. Bale attempted to make contact with Earth. Benny and his friends all walked closer to the video-feed walls, staring at the scene playing out before them.

"Where are Sahar and the Miyamuras?" Jasmine asked.

"Ricardo sent them on patrol outside the Taj," Pinky said.

"That's crazy," Benny said. "Did you tell them we were attacked out there earlier?"

"They all seem to agree that the Pit Crew can handle themselves."

Hot Dog took a step closer to the video walls. "How long do you think it'll take before—"

The line above the desk in the meeting room flashed and was replaced by a hologram of an office where serious-looking men and women in dark suits sat around a circular table, all staring into the camera.

"Yes!" Benny shouted. "It worked. We've got contact."

His attention was immediately focused on the one man who didn't look like he belonged there. His minty-green hair was like a dollop of foam on the top of his head, complementing his similarly dyed mustache and short, pointy beard. Max Étoile, the tall, thin man who had run the Taj under Elijah's command and had fled when the major asteroid storm approached.

On the video feed, Max squinted. "You?" he asked. "Where's Elijah?"

"Wait . . ." Drue said. "That Max guy actually made it back to Earth?"

"And he knows who Dr. Bale is," Jasmine whispered.

A woman with red hair pulled back into a severe bun sat at the center of the hologram. She turned to someone offscreen. "Get the chairman."

"He's in a meeting with—" a voice started.

"Get the chairman," the woman repeated, her tone

unchanged. Then she turned her attention to the camera. "Doctor. It's good to see you're alive. When we lost contact with the Moon, we'd feared the worst. Asteroids took out NASA's orbiting telescopes and our satellites, giving us limited visibility. We're working off older, Earthbound models now." She pursed her lips. "Is the Taj secure?"

"It is," Dr. Bale said. "Despite our insufficient preparedness." His voice took a harsh tone. "Elijah's children here on the Moon managed to stop an Alpha Maraudi assault that would have wiped out Earth."

"I'm sure you could have handled the aliens yourself if you had to, with all the weaponry at your disposal," the woman on camera said.

"True." Dr. Bale shrugged. "But I suppose we'll never know."

"Guys, you did not say anything about weapons," Iyabo said.

"Wait . . ." Benny said. "They *know* about the Alpha Maraudi?" He shook his head, trying to make sense of what he was hearing.

"And from the way they're talking about the weaponry," Jasmine said, "I wonder if it was made on Earth."

Drue stepped closer to the screen. "I feel like I've seen this lady before."

The woman paused a few beats before tilting her head to one side. None of the other people in suits had moved since the call started. "And Elijah West?" she asked.

"Elijah was captured during the alien attack," Ricardo said, stepping forward. "Our number one priority is to find him and—"

"His current status is unknown," Dr. Bale said, raising a hand to silence the leader of the Pit Crew.

Ricardo looked like he was going to say more, but closed his mouth instead.

"Who are . . ." the woman started, looking at him. She stopped, though, either because she recognized him or because it didn't matter, Benny wasn't sure. "Well, at least we won't have to worry about Elijah getting in the way of—"

"This had better be good," a man boomed offscreen.

Beside Benny, Drue flinched.

The woman with the red bun looked at the man in the chair to her left and cleared her throat. The man stood and hurried out of the way as another figure came on-screen. He sat down, his brown hair slicked over in a severe part. He stared into the camera with piercing gray eyes as the woman leaned over and whispered into his ear. Something about him looked familiar, but Benny couldn't quite figure out why until Drue stepped even closer to the wall, his eyes wide.

"Dad?" he asked, his voice cracking through the single syllable.

"Whaaaaaat?" Hot Dog said, drawing out the word. "No way."

"Hello, Senator Lincoln," Dr. Bale said with a smile.

"Dr. Bale." Drue's father nodded.

"I should let him know I'm okay," Drue said. He took a few steps toward the door but then stopped, likely remembering that he couldn't get into the meeting room. In a flash he was back at the wall, practically bouncing on his feet. Benny had never seen him look so on edge, and after all they'd been through together in the past week, that was saying a lot.

But Drue's father didn't ask about his son or *any* of the EW-SCABers. Instead, he put his hands together on the desk in front of him and spoke to Dr. Bale. "What is going on? I've got a fleet of top secret, weaponized Space Runners ready for takeoff here, and you can't even keep a single line of communication open?"

"Weaponized Space Runners?" Jasmine asked.

"There were complications," Dr. Bale said. "The asteroid storm—"

"I don't want excuses," Drue's father said.

"Your dad is super intense," Hot Dog said.

"Yeah, he's great," Drue said flatly, in barely more than a whisper, his eyes glued to the screen.

"Update us on the alien threat," Senator Lincoln continued.

"They've retreated," Dr. Bale said. "Likely gearing up for another, more vicious assault on Earth. There were five scouts on the dark side earlier, but I have no further evidence of them on radar. That being said, we have a very limited understanding of how fast their ships can travel, and our current satellite capabilities on the Moon are less than ideal. I'll be launching deep space probes as soon as I can get them put together, but we need to move quickly and strike hard." He crossed his arms. "The resort is ready to become our base of operations. Project New Apollo can begin."

Ricardo and Trevone both turned to look at each other, before Ricardo took a few steps forward. In one swift movement, Trevone's hand was on Ricardo's shoulder, holding him still.

"What is he talking about?" Benny asked.

Max leaned into the camera. "If Elijah could hear you now, don't you know he'd just *die* if he found out what was going on."

Ricardo opened his mouth to say something, but either thought better of it or couldn't figure out the right words. Watching him, Benny could relate.

"I'm glad to see you made it back to Earth, Max," Dr. Bale said. "I trust the drones I supplied you with enabled a safe journey."

"I don't know if I'd call it safe," Max said, sneering. "It was certainly the most anxiety-filled flight I've ever been on, what with the asteroids exploding around me near constantly." He raised a hand to his chest and gave an exaggerated sigh.

"Mr. Étoile, the information you've given us about the Taj has been useful over the years, and you'll be handsomely rewarded for your work," Senator Lincoln said. "But with Elijah West out of the picture and your documented support of our plans moving forward, I see no roadblocks to the government taking control of the Taj. You're excused."

Max stared at him for a beat before stammering, "B-but I can still help—"

"That will be *all*, Mr. Étoile," Drue's father said, never even looking at Max.

"Max and Dr. Bale and the government were all working together this whole time?" Hot Dog asked as Max huffed and stomped out of the meeting room.

"This is some conspiracy-theory kinda stuff," Iyabo said. "Right?"

"It's not a theory if it's *real*," Jasmine said.

Benny kept his eyes focused on Dr. Bale, trying to piece everything together. There was a brick of dread in the pit of his stomach making his guts churn.

"The war is here, ladies and gentlemen," Dr. Bale continued, clasping his hands behind his back. "Just as I warned you it would be. When all this is over and Earth is safe, we'll be seen as heroes. Saviors. And you, the ones who trusted in me when all the others thought I was mad—who saw through Elijah West's deceptions—will be lauded as visionaries."

"I'm not totally sure what's happening," Hot Dog said, "but I don't like it."

"All those trips back and forth to Earth he mentioned," Jasmine said. "He was gathering allies. There *were* people on Earth who believed him."

"Well," Drue's father said with a grim edge to his voice, "at least we weren't sinking money into preparation for nothing. You're sure your superweapon is ready?"

Benny took in a quick breath.

"What is he talking about?" Jasmine asked, wringing her hands.

"We haven't been able to field-test it, given the circumstances, but I stand by its design," Dr. Bale said. "You have my guarantee it will fulfill its purpose."

"It had better," Senator Lincoln said.

"I can clear out the rest of the asteroids between here and Earth with my drones. That won't be a problem," Dr. Bale continued. He motioned to Todd and Mae. "I'll have my assistants launch them now. It will take a while, but I'll get you a viable path to the Moon. Then we'll send the children here home, and the Taj will be opened up to the forces you've put together."

"Oh, heck no," Hot Dog said. "I'm not going anywhere."

"I know, I'm getting used to resort life," Iyabo said. She

scoffed. "I told you we were better off here alone."

"Once we've secured the Taj," Senator Lincoln said, "I want us striking as soon as possible."

"Of course," Dr. Bale said. "We'll take this fight to them and stop the enemy before they have a chance to hit us again."

"They're going to try to destroy the aliens with something horrible," Benny said.

"But wait," Hot Dog said. "He can't just give the Taj over to the government or whoever."

"Who's going to stop them?" Jasmine asked.

"Um, us," Hot Dog said.

On the screen, Senator Drue Bob Lincoln, Jr. nodded to Dr. Bale. "We have much to do on our end. The president won't be thrilled when she hears about what we've been doing, but I'm sure she'll be on board once she understands the full extent of the alien problem. For the time being, this entire incident will remain top secret. With any luck, we can handle it covertly, before the American people have to know anything about it."

Dr. Bale tapped on his HoloTek. "I'm sending you all the information gathered by my team and the artificial intelligence here at the Taj."

"Is she going to be a problem? Max tells me she's quite . . . *spirited*."

"Spirited?" Pinky asked. "What is *that* supposed to

mean? I'm contacting the real me and getting her to track him down and slap him."

"Pinky won't be a problem," Dr. Bale said, motioning to Trevone. "We have a leash on her."

In the common room, Pinky gasped, then clenched her fists.

Trevone's eyebrows were knitted together. "Yes," he said. And then something in his expression changed. He glanced to one side. It looked to Benny like he was staring right at them for a few seconds. Then he turned his attention back to the hologram. "Pinky is under our control now. It would take a programmer far smarter than anyone in this room to get past my firewalls."

"Good," Senator Lincoln said. "We'll be in touch in a few hours, Doctor. The Congressional Committee on Lunar Affairs thanks you for your work."

And then the hologram floating above the table disappeared.

"What was that?" Ricardo asked, covering the few feet between him and Dr. Bale in a single bound, until the tall boy was glaring down at the man. "You told me we were going to find Elijah. You said—"

"My boy," Bale said, digging into the second word. "This *is* your best chance of finding him. With an army at your back." He narrowed his eyes. "We *need* these reinforcements. Trust me. You've seen how strong these aliens are. As passionate as you and your Crew may be, you can't take them on alone."

Ricardo took a long look at him before taking a step back.

Dr. Bale turned away from the Pit Crew and marched toward the door. "Come on, then. I'd like to take a look at the research labs. We have a war to prepare for."

13.

For a moment, everyone in the Mustangs' common room stood silent, unsure of what to say. Finally, Benny spoke up.

"We can't let them do this," he said. "I know the Alpha Maraudi are a threat to humanity, but they're *people*. I mean, sort of. You know what I mean. There's got to be something we can do. Another way."

"He's using the Pit Crew's desperation to get them to go along with this," Jasmine said. "To bring an army here."

"To *exterminate* the aliens."

"Is that even possible?" Hot Dog asked. "I mean, I know they said they had armed Space Runners, and Dr. Bale definitely has some crazy weapons, but . . ."

"I don't know." Jasmine shook her head. "Elijah was right when he said that humans are pretty good at destroying things. And we have no idea what this super-weapon might be."

"Yeah," Iyabo said. "That does *not* sound good."

"Is it here?" Benny asked. "On the Moon? Could we find it?"

"If it's here," Pinky said, "it's cloaked with the same sort of device that kept us from tracking Dr. Bale and his team over the years."

Hot Dog scoffed. "How could Elijah have let this happen?"

Benny looked over at Drue, figuring he'd at least want to weigh in on this and talk about blowing up planets or how powerful particle beams could be. But he just stood there staring at the wall, which had returned to its previous animated state, red mustangs running in place, galloping without ever moving forward. His eyebrows were scrunched together, a deep crease between them.

"He didn't ask about me," Drue said quietly.

In the shock of everything, Benny had almost forgotten that Senator Lincoln—Drue's *father*—had been the chairman of the group that seemed to be behind all this on Earth.

Hot Dog turned to him, her mouth twisting as she inhaled a breath through her teeth. "Well," she said eventually, "I mean, maybe Dr. Bale already sent him stuff saying everyone was okay?"

Drue didn't respond.

Benny couldn't stop shaking his head as he thought of how everything was rocketing out of control. Drue had asked him what he would do if it came down to the fate of Earth versus the fate of the Alpha Maraudi, if only one could survive. He'd avoided answering this, even *thinking* about it too much. And that was because deep inside, he knew he'd always choose Earth. Part of him even wondered if maybe Dr. Bale's solution was for the best after all. And that made him feel even worse.

But in his heart, he knew this wasn't right. That there had to be a better way—he just had to figure out what that was. And this wasn't just because he'd seen his own caravan reflected in the Alpha Maraudi. It was something else. He didn't want to be the kind of person who was okay with a bunch of aliens being killed.

"Whatever we do now, it has to be quick," Jasmine said. "Before Dr. Bale can clear a path back to Earth."

"And before a bunch of army dudes show up," Iyabo added.

"Todd and Mae are in the garage now," Pinky said, "activating most of the remaining drones."

Hot Dog twisted a blond curl. "So what's our next move?"

Benny was lost in his head. He didn't realize everyone was staring at him until the room was silent. Even Pinky seemed to be looking to him for guidance. And realizing that, his chest suddenly felt tight.

"I don't know," he said. "Maybe we could try to warn the Alpha Maraudi? Crap, does that make us traitors to the human race?"

"Uh, maybe," Iyabo said.

"Ramona's looking into setting up another satellite for us," Jasmine said. "But we'll have to figure out a way to actually contact them."

"Drue," Hot Dog said, "what if you called your dad and tried to explain things to him?"

Drue looked like he'd been woken up out of a daze, and stared back at Hot Dog in confusion for a few beats. "Are you kidding me? You heard him. He's made up his mind."

"Yeah, but you're his son," Jasmine said. "Maybe . . ."

"That's not how this works," he said. "Trust me. He's not going to listen to anything I have to say."

"Okay," Hot Dog said. She spoke slowly, taking great care to choose each word. "You said that sometimes you peeked at your dad's files, right? Is there anything you might have heard or seen back on Earth that could give us a clue as to what the government is doing?"

"Most of the stuff didn't make sense to me," Drue said. "I mean, there was a lot of alien talk after they found those ruins on Pluto, but none of the things I saw said anything about the Alpha Maraudi. And these Space Runners he mentioned . . . I kind of figured those were for use on Earth, you know? Why go to war on land when you could attack from space." He shook his head, turning back to the wall where his father had been just a few minutes before. "Why did he even let me come up here? Why would . . . ?"

He didn't finish his thought.

"Well," Iyabo said, cracking her knuckles, "we *could* just beat up this doctor and the Pit Crew. There's only eight of them and, what, like, forty of us up here who followed you out into deep space? I bet they'd fight for you now, too."

"But we can't stop the army that's coming!" Jasmine said.

"We could try," Hot Dog said, crossing her arms.

"Great." Frustration was boiling up inside Benny, and it was giving a hard edge to his voice. "We fight Dr. Bale and the Pit Crew here so that we can then fight the government? Plus a bunch of aliens? What, are we just going to lock Ricardo and everyone else up in some room like Elijah did to us? Or kick them out and make them live on the dark side?"

"Whoa, chill out, Benny," Iyabo said. "It was just a suggestion."

"Well, it wasn't a good one," he snapped.

And then everyone was quiet and looking at him again. That's when Benny realized how hot his cheeks had gotten, and that his fists were clenched at his sides.

"I'm sorry," he murmured. The people in this room—his

friends—were the Moon Platoon. His new caravan. They were trying to help. But it was all so overwhelming. "I just . . . I need a second to think."

"Yeah." Hot Dog nodded. "Sure. Clear your head."

And then, before he knew it, he was in the hallway, headed toward the elevator that would lead him up to his suite.

But he never made it there. Instead, he paused in front of the video game room, and before he could give a second's thought as to what he was about to do, he went inside. The giant space was completely covered in gray rubber tiles, and the air smelled faintly of electrical discharge and sweat. Benny walked into the center of the room and stood there for a little while.

Finally, he spoke.

"Pinky?"

"What can I do for you, Benny?" she asked, appearing beside him. Her voice was soft, comforting.

"Can you make this place like the Drylands?" he asked.

She looked at him for a few moments. "Of course."

In a flash, he was standing in an ocean of sand and dust, rolling dunes stretching out for miles and miles around him, interrupted only by the odd clumping of cacti or trees that had stopped producing leaves years before. The sky above him was cloudless, the sun blazing through a sheen of smog.

"And my RV?" he asked. "You've got pictures of it in my application footage right?"

"Behind you," she said.

He turned to find it a few yards away, unsure of whether it had been there the whole time or had just appeared.

"Thanks," he said. "You can go now."

"I'll be here if you need me," she said, already fading away.

Benny thought about trying the RV door and seeing if Pinky had pieced together the inside of his home based off the clips on his HoloTek, but he knew that even if she had, it would never feel right—like how the replicas of his family had seemed unsettlingly off when he'd been trying out the hologram-producing bracelet Elijah gave him. And besides, there was another place he wanted to go. He climbed to the top of the RV, the impossibly small hyperdrive technology sewn into his Taj space suit allowing him to feel like he was actually scaling the vehicle, just as it had let him fly over a surging river when fighting robots before his entire world had been uprooted.

He sat cross-legged when he reached the top. In the distance, he could almost make out a body of water, or maybe it was just a computer-manufactured mirage. This was the place he'd sat a million times, where he'd recorded the end of his EW-SCAB application. It was the place he went to be alone at night, especially in those long, bleak days right after his father had died. A quiet spot where he didn't have to face anyone else. Where he could allow himself to just feel, think, and be. Or, on the worst of days, to try to block everything else out completely and be comforted by silence, falling out of tune with the rest of the world.

Benny knew it was impossible, but he could almost feel the hot sting of the sand-filled breeze against his face—could almost smell a hint of motor oil drifting up from the RV. And he couldn't help but think that he'd like to sit there forever.

14.

Eventually, Benny wasn't alone in the computerized
Drylands. Hot Dog climbed over one of the dunes to his left
and stood at the top of it, using one hand to shield her eyes
from the fake sun blazing in the sky.

"Hi," she said.

"Hey," he responded.

Neither of them said anything else for a few seconds.

"Am I interrupting?" she asked.

"No," Benny said, realizing he had no idea how long
he'd been sitting on top of the holographic RV. He climbed
down and met her in front of it.

"Is this . . ." she started. "Home?"

"Yeah." He spread his arms wide. "Miles and miles of
nothing. The real thing is way hotter, though."

"Yeah, I bet. I thought Texas summers were bad, but
it's probably nothing compared to what you live in." She

150

turned around a few times, taking in the scenery. "It's kind of peaceful, though."

"Sure, when you're not worrying about water or food or bandits or anything like that. You should see the sunsets. They're insane."

As soon as he finished his sentence, the room shifted, the sun falling until the horizon burned orange, streaking the vibrant blue sky overhead and causing the smog in the distance to sparkle with iridescent light. Benny let out a long sigh, and they both stood there awhile in silence.

"It's beautiful." Hot Dog smiled a little. "But I actually came because I have something for you. It's an apology. For yesterday. I shouldn't have been talking about you with Pinky."

Benny laughed quietly. "To be honest, with everything else, I'd kind of forgotten about that."

"I meant it when I said I'm scared," she went on. "And, I don't know, talking with Pinky just makes me feel better. The same way Jasmine being so level-headed does. Or how you can seem perfectly cool standing in front of a bunch of aliens."

"Yeah, just as long as they're not EW-SCABers, I guess," he said. "What about Drue?"

"Drue being Drue is weirdly kind of nice because it means that not everything is being turned upside down. Some things stay the same." She shrugged. "Anyway, I'm sorry. It won't happen again."

Benny shook his head. "Don't worry about it."

"Well, it's a little late for that."

She smiled in a way that told Benny she'd been up to something.

"What did you do?" he asked.

"You remember what Trevone said to Drue's dad? That it would take a programmer smarter than anyone in the meeting room to get around the way he was blocking Pinky? Well, Jasmine and I were talking about it, and she realized that the second part of that was what was important. The best programmer at the Taj *wasn't* in that room."

Benny stared at her blankly for a second and then took in a sharp breath. "Ramona."

"Right. It took her, like, five seconds to figure out a way around Trevone's firewalls. Jasmine's sure he made them easy on purpose and that he was trying to tell us, figuring we were watching, but I'm not totally sold on the idea. Anyway, we can use the satellites now."

"Okay," Benny said, starting to pace back and forth. This wasn't a solution to any of their problems, but at least it was something. "So let's get together in the common room and we can start figuring out who to call. There have to be people on Earth who don't want to blow up another civilization. What if—"

"Nope," Hot Dog said, shaking her head. "Forget about

all that. You have something else to do first."

She reached into her space suit pocket and pulled out a small silver ball. Then she tossed it into the air where it hovered above Benny's head, a lens looking down on his face.

"A GoCam?" he asked. He hadn't seen one since he'd filmed himself out doing dune buggy tricks in the Drylands for his application video—although, that model was practically an ancient artifact compared to the tiny, sleek orb floating in front of him now.

"Call your family," Hot Dog said, looking serious all of a sudden. "Pinky's already set up a connection based on your EW-SCAB emergency contacts. Just tell her when you want it to go through." She shrugged.

Benny stared at her as all the blood in his body seemed to rush to his head.

"My family," he said.

"I don't have a lot of reason to call mine, Jasmine doesn't have one, and Drue is still sulking about his dad not asking about him earlier. At least one of us should be in touch with Earth and reminded of what we're trying to save." Hot Dog smiled wider. "I'm glad you have them to call."

He stood there, not moving. Finally, she rolled her eyes.

"*Go*," she said.

And Benny just grinned and started to run. He only got a few yards before he stopped, turning around in small circles as he scanned the horizon.

"Uh, Pinky?" he asked. "The door?"

A doorframe illuminated at the base of a big dune. He ran to it, the GoCam floating behind him, but stopped before going through.

"Hot Dog," he said, turning back around.

"Yeah, Benny?"

"Thanks."

She smiled as Pinky appeared beside her.

"Would you like me to program something else for you?" the AI asked. "Maybe some flight simulations?"

"No," Hot Dog said. "I think I'd like to see a little more of the Drylands while I'm here."

Back in his room, Benny hurried over to his bed, jumping on top of it and tucking his knees up under his body. The camera followed, hovering a few feet above his head as he stared at a blank wall across from him.

"Pinky," he said. "I'm ready."

The wall lit up with a wobbly blue line and a few columns of text and numbers that didn't make any sense to him. It felt like a long time passed, and with every second he got more and more worried. What if his grandmother wasn't in the RV? What if she didn't have her HoloTek on her?

What if something had happened to her and his brothers?

And then, suddenly, the screen flashed and there was his home. It was twilight in the Drylands and the inside of the RV was bathed in golden light seeping through the faded red-and-turquoise curtains that were tacked up over the windows. His grandmother sat on the threadbare gray couch, her long silver-and-black hair piled on her shoulders. She must have set her HoloTek on the coffee table that was missing one corner thanks to a mishap Benny had had years ago when he'd tripped over one of his brother's toys while carrying a heavy pipe wrench. His brothers, Justin and Alejandro, flanked her. Dust motes hung in the air around them.

"Benny!" Alejandro, the youngest, shouted.

"Hey, dumb face," Justin said with a toothy grin.

His grandmother just smiled, letting out a long breath before saying quietly, "Benicio."

For a second Benny felt a stinging in his eyes, but he blinked it away as best he could.

"Hey," he said. And suddenly, it felt like the weight of everything happening on the Moon and with the aliens was being lifted off his chest.

"What are you doing calling us?" Justin asked. "Shouldn't you be racing Elijah West or something?"

Alejandro leaned half his body over the table, practically throwing himself onto it. "What have you been up to? How many Space Runners have you driven? What kind of food do you have? A few days ago I found some candy you'd been hiding and ate it."

"Alex, shut up," Justin said. He glanced at his grandmother, waiting for some kind of scolding. When she didn't say anything, he continued, looking into the HoloTek camera with wide eyes. "What are you bringing us?"

The questions kept pouring out as their grandmother sat there, beaming at him. And Benny realized that in his rush to see and talk to his family, he hadn't thought out what he might say to them—how he could possibly begin to explain everything that was happening.

"Come *on*," Alejandro said. "What it's like up there?"

Benny's mouth went completely dry. He thought about going and grabbing a glass of water. But that would have been ridiculous since his family would be conserving every last drop they had, drinking out of the big plastic barrels strapped to the roof. Water that always had a little bit of grit in it, no matter how many times it was filtered.

"The Moon is . . ." he started. "Crazy."

"Ugh, I'm so jealous," Justin said. "I'm one-trillion percent applying next year and getting in. Start talking about me so Elijah knows who I am. And don't do anything stupid and get all the Loves banned from the Taj."

Benny forced a smile, but all he could think about was how there wouldn't be an EW-SCAB next year. For all he knew, there might not even be a Taj.

"I won't," he said.

"Tell us everything," Alejandro said. "I'm dying here!"

Benny opened his mouth, ready to somehow try to explain to them what was really going on. But the words wouldn't come. He looked at the three of them, all smiles, their eyes so wide. They had no idea how close humanity had come to being destroyed—how close it still was to being wiped out by an alien race from a solar system an unfathomable distance from their tiny RV. Life was going on as usual. They didn't have to worry, like he did, that it might be blinked out before any of them could stop it.

That's when he realized he didn't want them to know the truth. He wanted them to keep living, happy, waiting for his return and the promise of a new, better life once he got back. Why should he make them live in fear of something they had no control of?

And so he talked about everything else.

"I've driven a few Space Runners," he said, trying to add some excitement to his voice, putting on a brave face for his brothers. "I got reverse-bungie shot into the sky. I drove a muscle car over the surface of the Moon—Dad would have loved that. I've eaten so much pizza and fresh fruit and stuff I didn't even know existed." He paused, but his brothers were egging him on with their eyes, begging him to keep going. So he did. "There's a whole room here that basically puts you in a video game. I destroyed a giant robot! There's water whenever you want it and showers. I've taken *so many* showers. I've never been so clean before in my life. Oh, and watch this."

He tapped on his metal bracelet Elijah had given him and suddenly there was another Benny sitting beside him—a hologram created by a mist of nanotech image projectors.

Both of his brothers yelped with glee.

"I am playing with that so much when you get home," Justin said. "I'm pretty over that dumb holospi—"

He stopped, but Benny could guess what he was about to say.

"You guys stole my holographic spider!" he said, leaning forward. "I had big plans for that thing up here."

"Yeah, well . . ." Justin was avoiding eye contact. "You've got much cooler stuff now, right? Oh! Anyway, one of the search parties found some crazy old hood ornament and brought it back for you. You have to see it. It's so cool."

"I'll go get it!" Alejandro said, sliding out of view.

"You don't know where it is!" And then Justin was gone, too. Benny could hear the door of the RV slam behind them.

"Your brothers are the same as ever," his grandmother said. "They miss you, though. Without you here to tell them stories, they fall asleep at night imagining what you must be doing."

Benny smiled. His grandmother did, too. But this only made him feel guilty, knowing that she wouldn't be smiling if she knew everything he did. Never in his life had he lied to his family, not about things that mattered. And yet, here he was, sitting on a too-plush bed in a resort on the Moon doing just that.

He was acting like Elijah again, and he wondered how that man had gone so long knowing the things he did and not warning anyone. At the same time, he finally understood in some small way why he hadn't told the people of Earth that there was a threat out there in the stars waiting to annihilate them.

His expression must have changed, because his grandmother's face crumpled with worry.

"What is it?" she asked. "Why do you look so sad?"

"It's nothing," he said, trying to smile again. "I'm just a little homesick, I guess."

"Benicio Love." Her voice was firm. "In twelve years, have you ever been able to fool me?"

"What about when I was ten and I told you I was going to go help Dad work on a generator when I really went out to practice tricks in my dune buggy?"

She smirked. "You really think I didn't know what you were doing?"

He looked at her for a few seconds and then shook his

head. "There's a lot of . . . pressure up here. It's hard to explain, but I feel like I have a lot of people counting on me."

She jutted her bottom lip out and narrowed her eyes, a look he'd seen a million times, one that meant she was in deep thought. She considered him and the sleek room he sat in so far away. Finally, she nodded a little.

"You're strong, Benny. You had to grow up fast. Alejandro and Justin wouldn't be who they are today if it weren't for you taking care of them. I mean that as a compliment, by the way. All the kids in the caravan always looked up to you, even those who were older. Even when you were pulling pranks on them." She winked. "It's probably best you didn't take that holographic spider to the Moon with you."

"This is different," Benny said, shaking his head. "There's so much going on up here. And at the caravan I always knew what to do because I had you. Or Dad."

"You have others around you now, don't you?" she asked.

"Yeah. I do."

She smiled warmly. "That look on your face. You remind me so much of your father when he was young. You don't have all his features, but you have his expressions. Do you know what I used to say to him when he was your age? 'Loves lead with the heart.'" She laughed a little. "I wonder sometimes if he took that a little too seriously."

"Dad always thought that was so corny."

"Maybe. But I heard him say it to you boys more than once."

Benny smiled a little and nodded, staring down at his hands. "Yeah. I guess that's true." He bit his lip. She was right. He couldn't lie to her. And with his brothers gone, at least he wouldn't be scaring them with what he was about to say.

Besides—wouldn't his father have wanted him to face things head on and be honest?

"Okay," he said slowly. "There is something else."

That's when he noticed a shadow fall across the carpet. He turned to look out the window to his left and gasped.

There was something strange on the side of the Grand Dome, a dark mass of some kind. No, something was *growing* over the force field shell, already starting to obscure his view of Earth, the brown crescent of the Drylands.

"Benny?" his grandmother asked. "Is everything okay?"

He turned back to the screen to see her face crinkled in concern, the wrinkled brown skin around her eyes folding in on itself. The screen flickered twice.

No. Something was very wrong. But he swallowed hard. "Yeah," he said. "Everything's great. I think we have a connection issue. I should go. But . . . I love you guys." He smiled wide, trying to offset the hammering in his chest that he was afraid she might actually be able to hear. "So much."

She smiled, too. "We lo—"

And then the screen went black. That's when he heard the first scream from the courtyard outside his window.

15.

Alarms blared as Benny bolted into the hallway, which was already overflowing with the handful of Mustangs who had been in their rooms. Shouts of confusion filled the air as the kids struggled to figure out what was going on.

"Warning." Pinky's voice rang out around them. "An unidentified substance has latched onto the exterior of the Grand Dome. While the integrity of the shield has not been compromised, please make sure you are wearing a space suit in the event of unexpected shifts in the artificial environment."

Benny found Jasmine standing with a few other kids who had crowded around a window in the hall, all staring out into the courtyard. The dark mass continued to grow over the dome, almost blotting out Earth completely.

"Jazz," Benny said.

She turned to him, her eyes wide. "It looks like . . ."

He nodded. She didn't need to finish her thought—*whatever* was happening out there was being caused by the Alpha Maraudi. Dr. Bale had told them the aliens had the ability to control rock, and he'd seen some of that himself when he was on their ship. This *had* to be them.

He patted his space suit pocket, making sure the gold glove was inside. Just in case.

"There must be more ships out there," Jasmine said.

"What?!" Alexi, one of the Mustangs, asked. His dark, bushy eyebrows rose high on his forehead. "There are more ETs attacking? What's going on? I thought we stopped the asteroids and stuff yesterday!"

Then everyone was looking at Benny and Jasmine, shouting questions. It wasn't until Pinky appeared beside them that the group began to quiet down.

"Everyone, we're gathering in the Firebirds' common room on the first floor," she said, speaking in a tone that gave no room for hesitation. "Go. Now. I need to talk with Benny and Jasmine for a moment. Iyabo." She nodded to the girl who stood in the rear of the group. "Will you lead the way?"

Iyabo looked back and forth between Benny and the AI for a second before she nodded. "Yeah. Of course. Come on, guys."

Reluctantly, the others followed her. Pinky turned back

to Benny and Jasmine. "It looked like you needed some help."

"Thanks," Benny said. "What's going on out there?"

"You know as much as I do," Pinky said. "This would appear to be a Maraudi attack, but my sensors didn't pick up any approaching ships. Not surprising, really, but we have no way of knowing how many of them are out there. Not even *visually* now. In my estimation, the entire dome will be covered within the next twenty-seven seconds. In addition, we've lost touch with our satellites. Something in that mass is interfering with our communications."

"They're cutting us off," Benny said.

"What about the dome?" Jasmine asked. "Will it hold up?"

"It's not in danger of rupturing at the moment, but I have no way of gauging how much force this 'rock' might be able to wield. If it were to contract . . ." Pinky shook her head. "I'm not sure."

Benny swallowed hard. He'd learned since being on the Moon that a fracture in the Grand Dome wouldn't send them shooting into space like he'd once imagined, but it *would* suck all the oxygen out of the courtyard.

"Okay, worst-case scenario," Benny said. "The dome breaks. What happens?"

"The Taj has backup environmental systems, right?" Jasmine asked. "In case of an emergency?"

"Yes, but . . ." Pinky's shoulders slumped. "The emergency system acts like the force field in a Space Runner, so there's some shielding—sort of like your helmets. But it's nowhere near as strong as the dome. Structurally, the Taj's windows are a superhard polymer and most of the outside is titanium-based, but the resort wasn't built to withstand a direct attack of any sort."

"We'd be sitting ducks," Jasmine said.

The AI nodded. "Now I wish Elijah *had* gone ahead with a plan to shoot the Taj into space. At least then we'd have an exit strategy."

Benny shook his head. If the dome went, their best line of defense was gone. That meant the safest place for everyone on the Moon to be was . . .

"We should get everyone underground," Benny said.

Jasmine considered this for a moment before nodding. "That's a good idea, and those tunnels to the dark side mean we wouldn't be trapped, but . . ." She frowned. "Are we really just going to abandon the Taj and everything up here?"

"No," Benny said, taking another look out the window at the blacked-out dome. "I'm definitely not."

"I'll see if I can get the McGuyvers to help with evacuations," Pinky said.

"We should do this now," Jasmine said. "While the lobby elevator is still working. If power goes out for some reason, there's only one other way down there from the Taj."

Benny thought of the seemingly endless winding staircase he and the others had descended when they first discovered the underground city—and imagined the chaos of trying to get dozens of scared EW-SCABers down it safely.

"Yeah," he said. "Where's everyone else? Hot Dog and Drue? Dr. Bale?"

"Dr. Bale and his team are in the garage. Hot Dog is chasing after Ricardo and Trevone in the lobby. They're having some sort of argument, but . . ." Pinky's hologram flickered. She looked puzzled for a moment, and then her mouth dropped open. "A new program has been introduced to my operating system. He's taking complete control of the Taj servers. I—"

She spat a few more garbled words before her hologram disappeared completely.

"Oh my gosh." Jasmine gasped. "They've taken Pinky off-line."

"Not good!" Benny shouted.

And then he was running for the stairs.

"Come on," he said. "We gotta get down to the garage and see what's going on."

"No," Jasmine said. Benny turned back and saw that she hadn't moved.

Benny took a deep breath and nodded. "If you want to

go underground, too, I understand."

Jasmine looked up at him with one eyebrow raised. "What? No. That's not it." She glanced at the spot where Pinky had been standing a moment before. "Have some faith in me. I'm going to find Ramona."

Of course. If anyone might be able to get Pinky working again, it was her.

"Be careful," he said, because it seemed like a good thing to say. And then he darted for the stairwell door, half tripping down the stairs once he was through. On the first floor, his footsteps echoed through the lobby, with its sleek, color-changing walls and the four-story windows that had once looked out onto the Sea of Tranquility but now offered a view only of the covered dome, making the entire room seem much darker. He could hear shouts coming from his fellow EW-SCABers down the hallway that led to the Firebirds' common room, but he never paused, dashing past framed pictures of Space Runner blueprints, Taj concept art, and a giant portrait of Elijah West. The fastest way to the garage was to cross the courtyard, and he burst through the resort's front door and onto the shiny steps leading down to the dark-graveled ground.

That's when he finally paused. He couldn't help himself. He'd seen the mass accumulating on the Grand Dome from the windows, sure, but now he was there in the center of it, looking at a thick crust forming all around him. But the rock itself wasn't completely dark. It pulsed with a dull greenish light in places, seemingly at random, like chain lightning almost completely obscured by clouds.

It took his breath away, and for a second it seemed like whatever had solidified over the dome had covered his chest, too, squeezing it tight.

He gritted his teeth and managed to tear his eyes away from the sky as he sprinted across the courtyard. He was halfway to the garage when the McGuyvers raced out, on their way to the Taj. Bo moved swiftly, bounding toward the front doors on his thick, tree-trunk legs. He glanced at Benny as he passed, but didn't say anything. Ash followed behind, no match for her brother's speed.

"We're evacuating," she said. Her breath was already short.

"I know. I talked to Pinky about it," Benny said.

She paused. "You're not coming with us?"

"Not while my friends are still up here," he said. "Not until we know what's going on."

She hesitated, but then nodded. "Good luck. And let me know as soon as you have an idea what's happening." She glanced back at the garage. "I don't trust that man one bit." And then she was sprinting across the gravel again, Bo already somewhere within the Taj.

Inside the garage, Benny spotted Drue near the back of the building watching Dr. Bale and his team as they set up devices he didn't recognize. Beside the McGuyvers' office, Hot Dog was yelling at Ricardo and Trevone. It looked like she'd blocked them, holding both hands up and standing in their path.

"He *murdered* Pinky! She was standing right beside me and then she just disappeared. He's a killer!"

Ricardo didn't say a word, but Trevone stepped up to his side. "She's not dead. She was never even really alive to begin with. He just . . ."

"Turned off her personality." Hot Dog pointed a finger at Trevone's chest. "Real cool. And *you* helped him do it."

"I didn't . . ." Trevone started, his eyes turning to Benny as he approached the group. "I put up a few firewalls before, sure, but this is different. Bale's plugged his own programming into our servers. It's a complete system override. I'm not sure how to bring her back. At least not the way she was."

"But someone else up here might be able to, right?" Benny asked.

Trevone looked at him for a few beats before nodding. "She could." He turned to Ricardo. "Are we really letting him take control of the Taj?"

"We have bigger problems," Ricardo said, pushing past them and heading toward the back of the garage where Dr. Bale and his assistants were unloading one of their trailers. "What's going on?"

"The Alpha Maraudi are making a move," Dr. Bale said as he opened a big metal trunk and started rummaging around inside. "Sooner than I'd expected. They must have had ships waiting in the wings somewhere. Those blasted stealth crafts." He started tossing things onto the cement floor. "Where are the *scanners*?" he shouted at his assistants.

"Have you ever seen anything like this before?" Benny asked.

"No. But you've been to their base on the dark side. It's made up of rock just like this. Ah!" He held up what looked like a HoloTek attached to a satellite dish no bigger than Benny's palm.

"What is *that*?" Trevone asked.

"A custom radar set to detect the unknown elements that make up the composition of the Maraudi ships."

"How?" Trevone asked, taking a few steps forward.

"So we could have seen this coming," Hot Dog said. "Maybe setting that scanner up should have been your first move, instead of clearing a path for your reinforcements."

"It hasn't been thoroughly tested," Dr. Bale replied, an edge of annoyance in his voice. "And its range leaves much to be desired."

Hot Dog threw her arms out to her sides. "Uh, this blob on the dome leaves much to be desired, too. Turn it on and see who's out there!"

Dr. Bale gave her a hard look before tapping on the HoloTek a few times and then turning the screen around to them. All Benny could make out was the shell around the Grand Dome.

"Like I said," Dr. Bale continued. "The range is short. I did the best I could with the equipment I had to work with out on the dark side, but I didn't have anything close to a state-of-the-art laboratory. It's not going to pick up anything outside of the rock."

Hot Dog dropped her arms. "Oh."

Dr. Bale handed the scanner to Todd. Meanwhile, Mae continued to unload the trailers, pulling out items that Benny vaguely recognized as having been from Dr. Bale's armory, along with several of the alien samples. Drue watched every crate and piece of tech they unpacked.

"So what do we do to get this stuff off?" Ricardo asked.

"Nothing," Dr. Bale said. "We're going to hold out until the reinforcements arrive. Once my drones have cleared the way, armed Space Runners will come flying in from Earth. The Grand Dome will hold. I helped in its engineering process. It's a flawless design."

"We can't just wait for help to come." Ricardo took a few steps forward. "My friends are out there. The rest of the Pit Crew. We've lost contact with them."

That's when Benny realized that Sahar and the Miyamura twins had never come back from patrol. They must have been outside the dome, and that meant . . .

"Oh, crap," he muttered.

"They were making the rounds on the dark side," Ricardo continued. "I thought it would be good to have eyes looking out for any of those stealth ships. They're great drivers. I thought . . ."

"Pinky," Dr. Bale said, and the AI appeared beside him.

"At your service, Dr. Bale," she said. She stared at him blankly, her voice monotonous, detached. Benny hadn't realized how much he'd grown used to Pinky—had thought of her as a real person—until he heard her flat speech. Beside him, Hot Dog's chin quivered: Benny could tell she felt the same way.

"I assume that both the auxiliary tunnel and the main entrance have been covered by the alien rock," Dr. Bale said.

"That's correct," Pinky responded.

"Then we'll use the mining lasers," Ricardo said. "Or *your* weapons. We can break down the rock on the outside and get them."

"And what if that's what they want us to do?" Dr. Bale asked. "To go outside we'd have to lower the force fields at the end of the tunnels. What if there's an entire army out there waiting for us? Are you willing to take that chance?"

Ricardo didn't hesitate. "I am."

Benny looked up at him. He knew Ricardo was serious

about finding Elijah and making sure he was safe, but he hadn't realized how close Ricardo was to the rest of the Pit Crew. But of course it made sense. If his friends had been trapped outside right now, Benny was sure he would've gone after them—and he hadn't known them near as long as the Pit Crew had been living, working, and flying together up at the Taj.

Dr. Bale tilted his head back slightly as he looked Ricardo in the eye. "Listen to me. Whether you like it or not, this is war we're talking about. War has casualties. Sacrifices."

"They aren't *casualties*," Ricardo said. "They're the Pit Crew. We can save them."

"The longer we wait," Trevone added, "the more likely it would be that the aliens will have gathered troops on the ground. If we move quickly—"

"No," Dr. Bale said, and then he immediately went back to rummaging through the cargo trunks, as though nothing else mattered.

Ricardo's fists were balled so tightly at his sides that they were shaking. He turned to Pinky, who was still standing beside Dr. Bale, her eyes staring into the distance.

"Pinky, I'm taking one of the laser-mounted SRs," he said. "Open the auxiliary tunnel for me once I'm inside."

"I'm afraid I can't do that, Ricardo," the AI said without even looking at him.

"The Taj is under my control now," Dr. Bale said.

"Given the extreme circumstances, it's the only thing that makes sense. And it's time for you to make a decision, Mr. Rocha. Do you have what it takes to go after Elijah? Do you have the guts to face this alien threat, to ensure humanity's survival no matter the cost?" He looked up at the boy and stroked his beard with one hand. "Or are you a coward?"

Ricardo didn't speak. He didn't even breathe as Trevone looked back and forth between him and Dr. Bale.

"A coward like Elijah?" Benny asked, breaking the silence growing between them.

Both Ricardo and Dr. Bale turned to look at him.

"Uh, maybe not a good idea, Benny?" Hot Dog whispered.

"That's what you mean, right?" he continued. "That Elijah was a coward for not trying to destroy the Alpha Maraudi."

"We could have dealt with them years ago," Dr. Bale sneered.

That's when the lights flickered and went out, leaving the garage in utter darkness.

16.

"What's going on?" Hot Dog shouted.

"It's a blackout, obviously." Dr. Bale's voice came from somewhere in front of them.

Benny stood frozen, unable to see anything. He half expected to hear Drue scream nearby, given how much he hated the dark—but Drue didn't make a peep.

"The dome," Benny said into the darkness.

"It hasn't been compromised or else my helmet would have powered on," Dr. Bale said.

"I'll get the generators for you, Doctor," Todd said.

"They're in the second trailer," Mae said. "I'll help."

There was a shuffling nearby. It sounded like someone—maybe more than one person—had banged into one of the tables the assistants had set up. Something metal bounced on the cement floor.

"Stay *still*," Dr. Bale commanded. "There's too much

sensitive equipment lying around here."

Pinky appeared beside the man, casting an eerie glow around her.

"Apologies," she said. "There was a swell of energy in the rock around the Grand Dome that caused it to constrict. I diverted all unnecessary power to the force field, which continues to hold. Backup power should be restored in—"

Crimson lights flickered on around the perimeter of the ceiling. Benny's eyes adjusted quickly. He looked over to see Hot Dog, who was bathed red. She had her hands balled into fists in front of her stomach, like she was ready to strike at someone, but seemed to relax a bit as she blinked.

"Ah, there we are," the AI said.

"Keep all our energy on that dome," Dr. Bale said. "We can wait this out."

"Of course, Doctor."

Benny realized Drue had disappeared. He looked around quickly, spotting him making a hasty exit toward the door.

"Drue!" Benny shouted.

"No way," his friend replied without even looking back. "I'm not staying in here waiting for another blackout." And then he was out the door, into the courtyard.

"Well, Ricardo," Dr. Bale said. "You never gave me an answer."

Benny could see the muscles in the senior Pit Crew member's jaw bulge out as he gritted his teeth. "I have a hundred EW-SCAB winners to check on," he finally said. "Let's go, Trevone."

He turned on his heel and headed for the side exit that led into the Taj. Trevone glanced at Benny and Hot Dog, and then followed him out.

Dr. Bale turned to his assistants. "We need to finish unloading this equipment. Once backup gets here, things will move very quickly. We'll need deep space probes and—"

"How are you so calm about this?" Benny asked, taking a few steps forward. "We have no idea what's happening outside!"

Dr. Bale turned to look at him. "I asked Ricardo about you. He said you came from the Drylands. It's a difficult place to grow up, I'd imagine. No wonder you have such fight in you." He twitched his mustache. "But you'll be a good boy and leave this work space on your own, right? Go to your rooms. Play a video game. I don't need any more distractions."

"A *good boy*?" Benny asked.

"Come on," Hot Dog said, turning away from the man. "Let's find our friends."

Benny took one last look at the weapons and gadgets the assistants were unloading, and then turned to follow her. They were almost to the door leading to the courtyard when Dr. Bale spoke again.

"From what I gather, you and your comrades down here have enjoyed free rein, ignoring all the rules." He motioned to Pinky. "Remember, I've got my eyes on you."

"What is it about the Moon that makes adults so weird?" Hot Dog whispered.

They found Jasmine, Ramona, and Drue all standing in the center of the courtyard near the fountain of a shiny chrome hand reaching out of the pool of water, its fingertips almost touching gemlike orbs floating around it. All five of them stared up at the darkness that had blocked out the sky.

Benny realized this was the first time since he'd been on the Moon that he couldn't look out and see Earth on the other side of the dome. He shivered.

"You found Ramona," Benny said. "Good."

"She was in her suite," Jasmine said. "Ignoring the alarms."

Ramona shrugged. "Figured Pinky was fritzing."

"I don't exactly feel safe out here," Hot Dog said. "We should get inside. Just in case this thing breaks."

"Uh, is there anywhere we can go without you know who being all over us?" Drue asked.

"Who, Pinky?" Benny replied.

Drue's eyes bugged out at him. "No, I mean the ghost of Elijah West who's haunting the resort now."

That's when Benny noticed that Drue's expensive-looking black space suit was bulging out around his stomach. Something was stuffed inside it.

"Uh, what—" Benny started.

"Underground," Jasmine said. She was staring at Drue's space suit, too, nodding. "That's the safest place to be, remember." She looked around at the others, opening her eyes wide and motioning toward the door. "Even though Elijah didn't get around to installing all the cameras and stuff like he has in the Taj. At least not everywhere."

That's when Benny understood—below the Taj, they'd have privacy. They could figure out their next move.

"You know the way," he said. "We'll follow you."

"This new Pinky better have the elevators on," Drue grumbled as they climbed the steps to the Taj. "I do *not* want to have to go down that stairwell again."

Fortunately, the elevators were working—though Jasmine mentioned several times during their descent that a power outage would trap them in the shaft—and in no time, they were stepping out onto a rock slab in the underground bunker. All around them, platforms floated on hyperdrive engines alongside giant white lights that bobbed in the air. Unlike the last time Benny had been down there, people were scattered among the various levels. Ricardo and Trevone looked like they were trying to calm down a dozen kids on one of the greenhouse platforms. Elsewhere, some of the EW-SCABers who'd gone underground days ago were showing those who'd just evacuated from the Taj where everything was. Benny spotted Ash and Bo McGuyver walking between rows of Space Runners and big objects draped in dust covers— the vehicles they'd stored away underground after the first attack on the Taj.

"This does not seem safe," Hot Dog said as she walked to the edge of the rock slab they stood on and stared into the black abyss below.

"Well, there are invisible force field fences along the perimeter of each platform to keep anyone from falling off," Jasmine said. "If they're still working, that is."

"Let's try not to find out," Benny said.

One of the EW-SCABers in Ricardo's group caught sight of Benny and his friends and pointed, shouting a barrage of questions at them.

"I think my space suit is about to explode," Drue said. "We don't have time to talk to these dudes."

"Jazz?" Benny asked.

"This way," she said, pointing to a staircase leading up to a tunnel carved into the wall. "I think this side is where all the nonresidential rooms are."

They followed close behind her, passing several mining carts that were lined up near the elevators. Hot Dog looked over at them and shuddered.

"Never again," she murmured.

The tunnel snaked deeper into the Moon. Neon blue lights turned on every few feet as they rushed through. They passed several rooms that looked like incomplete research labs, the equipment still covered in plastic sheeting, as well as a sort of trophy room with framed magazine covers and portraits crowding the smooth rock walls.

"Elijah," Benny said, shaking his head.

Finally, Jasmine took a turn and entered a doorway on her right. "Yes! This is what I was looking for."

As she stepped inside, white lights turned on overhead and revealed what looked to Benny like a copy of the meeting room up in the Taj—only this one was carved out of gray rock. In the center was a circular holodesk, surrounded by a dozen rolling chairs.

Benny looked around. "So, I don't see any cameras or anything . . ."

Ramona raised her arm and tapped on her old HoloTek. "Room's clean. Only power source is the desk." She grinned. "Not connected to Taj servers yet."

"Ugh," Drue said, hurrying over to the holodesk. "*Good.* This stuff is totally stabbing me."

He unzipped the top half of his space suit and several devices spilled out onto the desk—one of the leftover black drones, a hunk of asteroid, and . . .

"Holy whoa," Benny said. "Is that Dr. Bale's alien radar?"

Drue grinned as he straightened his undershirt and zipped his suit back up. "*Yeah*, it is. I figured we could use it. And, I guess I kind of got grab happy in the dark."

"I can't believe you took all this stuff."

"I can't believe you didn't just freeze up and scream when the lights went out," Hot Dog said.

"I think you meant to say thank you," Drue scoffed.

"Wait, wait," Jasmine said. "*Alien radar?* I have to see this."

She started tapping on the HoloTek while Benny explained how unhelpful it had been upstairs. Sure enough, now that they were so far beneath the Moon's surface, it wasn't picking up anything.

"Ramona," Benny said, "maybe you can boost this thing? Like you did the satellite?"

"No doubt," she said, eyeing the device. "Major updates needed." She whistled. "Hardware, too."

"Right," Jasmine said. "I have no idea what's down here as far as equipment goes."

"Okay." Benny started pacing, trying to breathe steadily. "So, things are really bad."

"And now we don't even have Pinky helping us out," Hot Dog said.

"Well, we sort of do," Jasmine said. "Remember when

we first unlocked Pinky and she got mad at Ramona for downloading her program files?"

Ramona pulled out her Taj HoloTek and expanded it on the table. "Backups are max critical. Save your work."

She accessed a few programs that looked like complete gibberish to Benny, and then suddenly Pinky's face filled the screen.

She did not look happy.

"Of all the indignities I've suffered"—the AI's voice came out of the HoloTek speakers—"being held captive in your datapad is among the most annoying."

"Cool your coding," Ramona said.

Pinky narrowed her eyes. "My location sensors tell me that we're in one of the underground meeting rooms. You could at least port me to the holodesk."

Ramona let out a throaty giggle as her fingers flew over the screen. In a few seconds, Pinky appeared as a two-foot-tall hologram above the desk.

"That's better," she said, stretching. "Now, I'm smart enough to understand I'm a backup file from this morning," She adjusted her eyes, spinning around and looking at each of the Mustangs in the room. "So what happened to the other me?"

They filled her in on the state of the Taj. The more they spoke, the redder Pinky's face got.

"That arrogant *beast*," she said when they were finally

finished. She raised a hand to her temples as she tapped a high-heeled shoe.

"Ramona, keep Pinky's files safe," Jasmine said. "We don't want whatever programming Dr. Bale is running upstairs to infect her."

"Roger," Ramona said. "Total quarantine."

"That's smart," Pinky said. "I'll patch in to your comms, though, so I can keep talking to you." She took off her glasses and rubbed her eyes. "Okay, so the Taj is under attack and we've lost control of it."

"Any suggestions?" Hot Dog asked.

The AI turned to Ramona. "I can't believe I'm saying this, but perhaps you and I could work together to get past Bale's program? Whatever it is that's let him take control? We'd have to be connected to the servers, of course."

"That doesn't help our biggest problem," Benny said. "The dome. We have no idea how many aliens are out there, or what they want. *Or* if help really is coming from Earth since we've lost contact. We really need to get outside."

"I have some ideas about that," a voice boomed from the doorway.

Benny turned to find Ricardo Rocha standing behind them. Benny straightened his back and clenched his fingers. The others tensed up around him.

"We need to talk," Ricardo said, staring at him. "You and me. Alone."

"The last time you wanted to talk to someone alone, you sold out the Taj," Hot Dog said.

Ricardo grimaced. Though the Pit Crew member didn't respond, there was something in his expression that took Benny by surprise. It was worry or fear—he couldn't tell which. And he remembered that back in the garage, Ricardo had been adamant about finding his friends. He was used to the older boy looking stone-faced as the Mustangs' group leader, acting more like a drill sergeant than a teenager living on the Moon. He seemed somehow different now, and looked at Benny not with anger but something closer to desperation.

"I'll be right back," Benny said, nodding to his friends.

Hot Dog raised her eyebrows and looked at him like he was crazy, but he went anyway, out into the hall. He followed Ricardo into the trophy room they'd passed earlier, the one crammed full of monuments and photos dedicated to Elijah's achievements. Ricardo walked over to a framed magazine cover declaring Elijah West "Man of the Millennium."

"Don't worry," Ricardo said. "Pinky can't hear us in here." He paused. "Dr. Bale's Pinky, I mean."

Benny realized he must have been listening to their conversation for a while before coming in—that's why he hadn't seemed surprised by the much shorter version of the AI hovering above the holodesk in the meeting room.

"Right," Benny said. "What did you want to talk about?"

Ricardo rubbed his hands over his face slowly before turning to Benny.

"Trevone is the reason I'm here. He's been telling me that I've been acting like a fool for the last twenty-four hours, but I brushed him off. I was just so worried about Elijah. And now . . ." Ricardo's shoulders slumped. "Your friends back there. You trust them?"

Benny furrowed his brow. "Yeah, of course I do."

"And you'd do anything for them?"

"Sure. I mean, we haven't known each other long, but we've kind of been through a lot together."

Ricardo nodded. "So you have the smallest idea of how I must feel right now. I . . ." He hesitated, his gaze falling to the stone floor. "I *sent* my friends to patrol and look for any more signs of the aliens, yes. But also to see if they could find any evidence of whatever superweapon Dr. Bale apparently has hidden on the dark side. He wouldn't tell us about it, and I wanted to gather all the information we could. Now they're stuck out there. And we're stuck in here."

Benny wanted to ask more about this superweapon— had Dr. Bale told the Pit Crew it was hidden out there somewhere for sure?—but it was obvious that wasn't what Ricardo wanted to talk about.

"It's not like you knew this was going to happen," Benny said. "They're probably fine, hiding out in a crater somewhere." Even as he said these words, though, he knew how little good they would do. If someone had said his family was "probably fine" back on Earth, he wouldn't have felt any better.

Ricardo shook his head. "Or they're trying to fight the aliens and failing. I have to get out there and find them. I'm going to take the doctor's weapons and use them to break through this rock barrier. Trevone is already looking into regaining control of Pinky, at least enough to get us through the auxiliary port." He looked at Benny. "You've done big things up here. That's why I'm talking to you now."

"I've had a lot of help."

"Sure. But the others view you as a leader. I know how overwhelming that can be, especially if you didn't ask for it. Before I came to the Taj, I was nothing. I was street trash in Brazil."

"I heard you were some kind of soccer star or something," Benny said.

Ricardo laughed once. "I had some skills, yeah, but being the best out of a bunch of nobodies in Rio—half of us playing on empty stomachs—isn't exactly much to be proud of." He shook his head. "I was like you. The best of the caravan. But still *in* a caravan. There's only so much you can do from a position like that." He paused. "That came out wrong. No offense."

"No," Benny said. "I know what you mean. How do you

change the world from a camp out in the desert?"

"Exactly. But up here . . ." Ricardo motioned around them. He focused on the picture of Elijah. "Up here you can do anything. Or at least, that's what we all thought. Elijah once told me he invited me to stay at the Taj because he knew he needed someone to lead. The Pit Crew—even if it was just me at the time—needed a strong foundation. But look at us now."

"We can figure this out."

Ricardo looked down at him, taking a deep breath. "I need your help. You and your friends in there. I know we haven't seen eye to eye on everything, but . . ." He trailed off, shaking his head.

"I get it," Benny said. "I can only speak for me, but I'll do whatever I can. I don't know if you noticed, though, but I don't think Dr. Bale actually cares about finding Elijah. And . . . he could be right about the Alpha Maraudi wanting us to lower our shields."

"I'm willing to take that chance," Ricardo said. "I'm not just going to sit trapped down here hoping for the best. I'm going back up top and blasting my way out. I'll find Sahar and Kai and Kira."

"Trapped . . ." Benny said quietly, repeating the word in his head. It reminded him of what Jasmine had said just a little earlier, when she'd suggested they evacuate everyone. Because despite what some people thought, the tunnels leading into the Grand Dome and the garage up above weren't the only ways out to the lunar surface.

"Actually," Benny said, a smile taking over his face. "There's another way."

17.

Benny gathered his friends on the floating platform in front of the dozens of Space Runner and Moon buggy prototypes and one-of-a-kind models that had been collected underground. They'd managed to get the McGuyvers to herd most of the rest of the EW-SCABers off for a tour of the tunnels leading into the walls, giving them a little breathing room.

"So, let me get this straight," Drue said as he leaned against the electric green Chevelle they'd taken out to rescue Hot Dog. "We're going to go through the back tunnels out to the dark side of the Moon, hack the force field the McGuyvers set up there, find the missing members of the Pit Crew, and sneak back in without Dr. Bale or the Alpha Maraudi ever knowing."

"Basically, yeah," Benny said. He stared at his friends, trying to read their expressions. He thought this was a good idea—if nothing else, it meant they were actually working together with the Pit Crew—but he certainly knew it was risky.

"Cool," Drue finally said. "I'm in."

"Yeah," Hot Dog agreed. "Def."

"Once we're out there, we can use Dr. Bale's scanner to see if we can get a better idea of how many aliens are around the Moon," Jasmine suggested.

"That's a brilliant idea," Trevone said. "And I won't even ask how you guys ended up with that piece of equipment."

"I should be able to keep everyone connected via short-wave radio." Pinky's voice came through their space suit collars, Ramona's HoloTek powering her.

Benny looked for Pinky reflexively, forgetting for a second that she was a disembodied voice. "Thanks. When we get back, we'll look at getting you restored to the Taj." He nodded to Ricardo. "And we'll figure out what to do next."

"Right. *After* the Pit Crew is back safe and sound," Ricardo said. "This is going to be *dangerous*, and we need to be as stealthy as possible. For that reason, I don't think we should take more SRs out than necessary. Hot Dog and Drue are your best pilots, right?"

"You bet," Hot Dog said. "Unless we're talking about driving one of those mining carts."

Ricardo shook his head. "We'll work in pairs, then. Benny, you're with me. We'll lead the way. Ramona, you'll be Trevone's passenger. I'm counting on the two of you to get past Pinky's force field."

"Ugh," Ramona said. She was gulping an energy drink that she seemed to have produced out of nowhere as far as Benny could tell. "Flying."

Benny remembered how Ramona had spent most of their flight to the Taj curled up in the backseat with a barf bag, a green tint to her skin. He hoped she would still be able to hack and program in the air.

"Jasmine can ride with me," Hot Dog said.

"Drue, are you okay on your own?" Ricardo asked.

"Psh." Drue crossed his arms. "No sweat." He grinned. "Now, which one am I driving?"

Ricardo and Trevone looked at each other, some unspoken conversation happening between them. Finally, Ricardo nodded.

"We'll take the Star Runners," he said.

Drue and Hot Dog both took a few steps forward, their eyes bulging. "Star Runners?" they asked near simultaneously. Benny guessed they'd never heard of them either.

"Uh, Ricardo," Pinky said. "Do you really think that's a good idea?"

"If we get into a tight spot against an entire army of alien ships, there's no way we're going to be able to fight them," Ricardo said. "We'll have to rely on speed."

"Tell me *everything*," Drue said.

Trevone walked over to one of the vehicles and ripped the white dust cover off it. Underneath was a slender car that bulged out in the center with room enough to carry only a pilot and two passengers. Two wings jutted out on the back sides. The entire craft shined a stunning metallic gold.

"This is the most beautiful thing I've ever seen," Hot Dog said.

"Huh." Jasmine sighed. "He couldn't have picked a matte black for once? These are a little flashy for a covert mission."

"Flashy but *fast*," Trevone said. "The Star Runner prototypes are basically just like a Space Runner, with one key difference: they're equipped with two extra experimental hyperdrive systems in the back, giving them the ability to reach incredible speeds."

"Yes," Drue said. "Yes, yes, *yes*."

"You are *not* to engage the experimental drive unless I tell you to," Ricardo said.

"Sure. But just in case we have to, how would I go about doing that?"

"By pressing a series of buttons I'll relay to you if the time comes."

Drue frowned. "Oh."

"Sahar and the Miyamuras were supposed to scour the dark side, but they could be anywhere by now," Trevone said. "The radars in the Star Runners have a fairly limited range, so it may take some time before we're close enough to spot them or establish radio contact."

"So, search and rescue on the Moon?" Drue asked. "No problem. That's totally our thing."

"And I am *so* glad to not be the one stuck out there this time," Hot Dog added.

"Any questions?" Ricardo asked.

"Yeah, why are we just now getting to see these?" Drue asked as he waltzed over to one of the Star Runners and pulled open the pilot-side door. He shoved his head in and took a deep breath. "It's still got that new SR smell. This black leather's great and all, but does it come in any other colors?"

Ricardo ignored him, turning to Benny. "I'm driving."

"Sure," Benny said. "But if we're ever in something that doesn't fly, I'm taking the wheel."

The older boy nodded. "Deal."

The group slid into four of the Star Runners. Ramona uplinked her Pinky backup so the AI could talk to them and have limited control over the radar and guidance systems. Her voice filtered through the cabin of the Star Runner Benny sat in as Ricardo powered up the vehicle.

"I'm plotting a course through the tunnels that will lead you to the surface." A holographic map appeared on the windshield.

"Perfect," Ricardo said as his Star Runner rose into the air. "Now follow my lead."

They shot up through the huge cavern, darting past various platforms. Benny looked out the window, catching sight of EW-SCABers walking through the aisles of greenhouse levels or standing on porches made of rock jutting out of the walls, their faces all turned up to the golden vehicles ascending toward the craggy ceiling. The bottom of the cavern was nothing but an impossibly black pit, and part of him couldn't believe they'd made this trip—and survived— once already on a floating mine cart just a few days earlier.

"If you look up to your right," Hot Dog said, "you'll see where Drue carved up a big chunk of the ceiling while trying to control the laser beams."

"Hey, those lasers came in pretty handy," Drue replied. "I don't think I'm getting enough credit for inspiring that idea."

"Yeah, yeah. You're a real hyperdrive hero."

And then they were shooting through one of the tunnels carved into the walls, dim yellow lights blinking on ahead of them as they flew. Pinky outlined every turn to take, until they were approaching the end of the line—the spot that would spit them out on the dark side, near the alien base.

Only, it looked like it was blocked off.

"Pinky," Benny said, "I thought the McGuyvers just put

up a force field here, not another metal door like the one we smashed."

"According to my records, it should be an invisible barrier," the AI said. "I believe they just covered the top with Moon dust so that it blends in."

"Oh, I guess that's smart."

"Uh, guys," Jasmine said. "I'm picking stuff up on this alien radar. Some kind of structure about a hundred meters away. I think it's the alien base we found! This thing really does work."

"Trevone," Ricardo said. "What's the status on the force field?"

"Well, it's really tricky," Trevone said. Benny could hear Ramona chirping to herself in the background. "The way Dr. Bale's taken over the—"

Something shifted in front of them and the Moon dust that had been covering the tunnel opening began to drift away, blown by the faint currents generated by the Star Runners.

"Oh," Trevone said.

"Back door to the back door," Ramona chirped. "Level-one hack. I'm going into sleep mode now."

"She's good," Ricardo said quietly to Benny.

"Yeah, it's kind of ridiculous," Benny agreed. "I'm still not sure what she's saying half the time, though."

"All right, Ramona." Ricardo gripped the flight yoke as

he addressed the group again. "Close that thing up after we're through. Let's do this."

Ricardo led them out of the crater slowly, scanning the horizons, looking for any hint of an alien spacecraft. But there was nothing, just the impossible number of stars and planets blinking against the black backdrop of space.

"Looks like we're all clear for now," Ricardo said. "I want us searching in a straight line, twenty kilometers apart from one another. Match my speed, and keep your eyes peeled."

And so they separated and shot across the dark side of the Moon. To Benny, the closest Star Runner—Drue's— was hardly a blip in the distance as his eyes darted back and forth from the ground to the sky, searching for any sign of the missing Pit Crew members or the Alpha Maraudi. It might not even have been Drue, but just a trick of the light.

Meanwhile, Ricardo continuously called out on the comms.

"Sahar?" Ricardo said. "Kai? Kira? Where are you guys?"

He kept repeating their names, pausing for a few seconds afterward, but there was only the sound of his heavy breathing in the cabin.

After ten minutes or so, he banged his fist on the flight yoke.

"Pinky, are you getting anything?"

"I'm currently making do with the processing power of

a HoloTek and the Star Runner systems," the AI said. "It's not exactly what I'm used to. Even if I *were* using the Taj's servers, we haven't launched new satellites on this side of the Moon yet."

"We're stuck with radio," Jasmine said.

"Old school," Ramona's voice piped in through the comms, thin and wobbly.

"We'll find them," Benny said.

Ricardo glanced at him. "When you found that kid in the Drylands, the one on your application vid . . . how'd you do it?"

Benny thought about this for a second, hoping there was something useful he might remember. But he came up blank.

"It was just lucky, really," Benny said. "The wind had covered up any tracks, which was usually great for the caravan but didn't help when one of our own was lost." He paused. "Actually, if I'm being honest, I almost turned back right before I saw him."

"Why didn't you?"

Benny shrugged. "I knew he was out there. I had to keep looking. Well, I didn't *have* to, but I wanted to. You know?"

Ricardo nodded, and started calling out over the radio again.

A few minutes later, a new voice finally came through.

"Hello?" It was so shaky that Benny barely recognized it

as Kai Miyamura. "Is someone there?"

"Kai!" Ricardo shouted. "It's me. Where are you?"

"Suddenly there were ships," he said, his words stumbling over each other. "We weren't ready. We tried to get away, but one followed us. We took it down, but . . ."

"Is everyone okay?"

"Kira and I are fine, but Sahar . . . Something's wrong with her ship."

"Is she injured?" Trevone asked.

"I don't know," Kai said.

"What do you mean?"

"I mean I *don't know*."

"Where are you?" Benny asked.

"Who is that?" Kai replied, but he kept on talking. "We're hiding in the Mare Moscoviense. It's where she crashed."

On the windshield, a flight plan appeared. Ricardo tightened his grip on the flight yoke.

"We'll be there in no time," he said. "Everything will be okay."

"Hurry," Kai said. "Please."

There was silence on the comms after that.

"Trevone," Ricardo said, "I've never heard Kai like that. I don't think he's ever said *please* before. We're too far away from that mare right now. I need to get there fast."

A moment passed, and Trevone responded. "We'll

regroup and be right behind you."

"Hey, does that mean we're gonna—" Drue started.

But Benny never heard the rest of his question. Ricardo hit a series of buttons on the dashboard, and suddenly there was a loud metallic noise coming from behind them. Benny turned to the window in time to see the short wings that jutted from the Star Runner's side rotating, until they were aligned vertically with the car.

"Hold on," Ricardo said.

Benny had just enough time to clench the armrests of his seat before they were shooting forward at an impossible speed, the stars and planets hundreds of thousands of miles away from them suddenly nothing but blurs against the black backdrop of space as the experimental hyperdrives kicked in.

Benny thought he was screaming as his body was pinned against his seat, but the roar of the engine at his back was so loud that he couldn't really be sure.

18.

After a very long minute, Ricardo tapped a series of buttons again and the galaxy outside the Star Runner came back into focus instead of being one big smear of light. Benny swallowed hard—it felt like his stomach was in his throat—and pried his fingers off the armrests.

"Whoa," he said.

"Yeah," Ricardo agreed, a little short of breath. "You don't get used to that."

"What about the others?" Benny asked.

"They'll catch up at normal speeds. Trevone's driven a Star Runner before, but I didn't know if Hot Dog and Drue could handle it."

Benny nodded. He wasn't sure he ever wanted to be in charge of driving something that went so fast.

Ricardo pointed to a dark swath of Moon in front of them.

"There," he said. He tapped on the holographic dashboard a few times, and two dots popped up on the windshield map. "We're close enough for SR scans to work. That's them."

"Just two?" Benny murmured.

Ricardo didn't say anything, and Benny couldn't help but wonder what had happened to the other ship—to *Sahar*.

They landed next to the Miyamura twins' white Space Runners. Kira and Kai were outside, frantically walking around a big chunk of what Benny immediately recognized as alien rock. Ricardo was out of the Star Runner in a flash, and Benny hurried after him, his comm automatically linking with the rest of the Pit Crew.

"What happened?" Ricardo asked. "Where is she?"

"They came out of nowhere," Kai said, his voice high and trembling. "They were so fast."

"Monsters," Kira spat. She looked so angry, but Benny could tell she was frightened, too—her voice broke as she spoke. "There were two of them. Scouts, probably."

"We barely got away, and then . . ." Kai motioned to the alien rock.

"Get yourself together, Kai," Ricardo said. "Where is Sahar?"

"Here," Benny said, stepping up to the mass of minerals that pulsed with a dim green glow. It was just a little bigger than a Space Runner would be. "She's inside, isn't she? They grew this around her."

"They *hit* her with something," Kira said. "Not the energy bolts they were shooting at us the last time we fought them. It was different. As soon as it touched her SR, it started to spread. There was only one chasing us by then. I got it with a laser right after it attacked Sahar. I think it went down on the other side of the cliffs."

"No, no," Ricardo said, stomping over to the rock-encased Space Runner as best he could in the low gravity. "We have to get her out. Sahar? Hello?"

"Could we use your lasers to cut through it?" Benny asked.

"We don't even know which side is the front," Kai said.

"If something goes wrong and we damaged the hyper-drive, the whole thing could go," Kira said.

"Plus, if the rock explodes like the asteroids did . . ." Kai started to shake his head frantically. "No. No way. We can't do that."

"We'll get a hammer," Ricardo said, heading back to his car. "Or a chisel. There's got to be something in the emergency kits."

"Wait," Benny said. "I think I might be able to fix this."

The closer he stepped to the chunk of rock, the more buzzing he felt in his pocket—the golden glove seemed to come alive, just as it had in Dr. Bale's tent when he'd been around so many asteroid samples. Benny pulled it out of his space suit pocket.

"What is that?" Kai asked.

"Something I brought back from the alien ship," Benny said as he slid it onto his hand. "I'm, uh . . . not really sure how it works, but I think it can control this rock."

He looked to Ricardo, waiting for the lead member of the Pit Crew to give him some sort of go-ahead. But Ricardo just stared back at him.

"Or," Benny said, "we can wait and try to mine her out with a hammer or something."

"No," Ricardo said finally. "She could be hurt in there, or the environmental systems could be damaged . . ." He shook his head. "If you can get her out, then do it."

Benny nodded, and turned his attention back to Sahar's Space Runner. In all honesty, he had no idea what he was doing, but one of the Pit Crew was stuck inside that lump of glowing rock, and they needed to get to her as quickly as possible.

He took a deep breath, whispered a silent hope for the best, and placed his gloved hand on the rock. It seemed to vibrate underneath his palm.

And then suddenly the rock started to shift and move, like it was some kind of superthick fluid beneath his touch. In fact, it looked like it was *growing*, a tentacle of the sludge extending to the ground beside his feet.

Benny yelped and jumped back. As soon as he did, the rock resolidified.

"What happened?" Kai asked.

"You made it worse!" Kira shouted.

"It's alien tech," Benny said, biting his lip. "Maybe this was a bad idea."

"Try again," Ricardo said. "I don't know . . . *focus* maybe. Or imagine the rock disappearing."

He thought back to the alien ship, and how the glove had worked there. He'd had no idea what he was doing then either. In his desperation to escape, he'd just smashed his fist against a rock wall, which somehow caused it to shatter.

So he tried that. He slammed his palm down onto rock, pouring all his strength into the blow, hoping with everything inside him that it would break apart.

There was a surge of glowing energy around his hand. And then the alien rock began to crumble. He could make out the yellow paint of Sahar's Space Runner as bits and pieces fell away.

"Yes!" Ricardo shouted, bounding over to him. "Again!"

And then Benny was punching the glove against the rock covering the side of the car over and over, until the passenger door was completely freed. Through the darkly tinted windows, he could just make out the shape of a figure.

"Move," Ricardo said as he wrenched the door open.

Over Ricardo's shoulder, Benny saw Sahar, unconscious,

leaning against the pilot-side window. The dark scarf around her head pooled against the front of her force field helmet. Benny could tell by the rise and fall of her yellow space suit that she was breathing—at least she must have been getting oxygen.

Ricardo kept saying her name, more and more desperately, but she didn't respond. Finally, he took her in his arms and marched toward one of the Miyamura Space Runners.

"We need to get her in a stabilized environment so her helmet will go away," he said. "I don't even know if she can hear me."

"I'll grab the first aid kit," Kira said.

Ricardo glanced back at Benny. "Get in the Star Runner. Tell the others we found them."

Benny nodded, and made his way back to the gold vehicle as quickly as he could. Before he could even get the pilot-side door shut, though, there were voices filling his helmet, asking what was happening. He did his best to explain, all the while keeping his eyes on the white Space Runner across from him.

"They're weaponizing their control over these minerals," Jasmine said over the comms.

"It's possible they were trying to capture her," Trevone added. "They could have easily taken her onto a bigger ship if she were stranded, encapsulated in their rock."

"We need, like, a hundred more of those gloves," Drue said.

"I hate to interrupt," Pinky said, "but there's a call coming in."

"A call?" Hot Dog asked. "What?"

"From Earth."

"Oh my gosh," Jasmine said. "We're outside the dome!"

"Yeah," Benny said, unsure of why this mattered.

"That means we have satellite uplink now."

Benny grinned.

"I can create a video conference on your windshields," Pinky offered, "while engaging the autopilot to Sahar's location."

"Do it," Benny said.

The windshield flickered. On the left, a map appeared, tracing the rest of the Star Runners who were still ten minutes out from arrival. On the right side, three small squares popped up that showed the inside cabins of the crafts, his friends and Trevone all staring into their windshields. And in the center of the screen was a man seated at a sprawling wooden desk.

Senator Drue Bob Lincoln, Jr., chairman of the Congressional Committee on Lunar Affairs.

He blinked once, confusion flashing on his face.

"Uh, hi, Dad," Drue said. Benny was pretty sure all the blood had drained from his friend's face. "I mean, sir."

"Drue . . ." the man said. And then he composed himself and narrowed his eyes. "I've been trying to get in contact with Dr. Bale for the last hour and *you're* the people who pick up the call? A bunch of children? In . . . what, in Space Runners? What's going on at the Taj?"

"Well," Drue said, "it's kind of a long story."

He told his father about the rock covering the dome and that they'd gone out to rescue some of the Pit Crew members—leaving out the fact that Dr. Bale had no idea they'd left.

"Put Bale on the line," his father said when Drue was finished. "Immediately."

"That's not possible," Trevone said. "This rock is obstructing communications with the Taj."

Senator Lincoln muttered several curses. He paused for a moment, seeming to weigh everything his son had told him. Finally, he spoke again. "It looks like you're in separate vehicles?"

"That's right, sir," Drue said.

"Then someone head back to the Taj. Tell Bale that the path to the resort has been successfully cleared thanks to his drones. We're assembling troops now, and we'll be deploying within the hour. Despite these setbacks, our mission will continue as planned." He grimaced. "It's clear to me that he's incapable of managing things. I'm coming up there myself."

They all stared back at him, unsure of what to say. Finally, Drue spoke again. "I guess I'll see you soon."

His father pursed his lips. "Absolutely not," he said. "The rest of this group can relay my message. I want you to come back to Earth immediately."

"But, Dad . . . *sir*, I—"

"That's not open for discussion. The last thing I need to worry about while I'm up there is you getting into trouble." He sighed. "I trust you were paying attention during all those Space Runner lessons we bought you. God knows we paid enough for them."

"Your son is an incredible pilot," Hot Dog said, shoving her face closer to the camera in her cabin. "You should have seen him when we were attacking the asteroid field. He saved—"

"It'll make a great story for the press, I'm sure," the senator said.

Drue stared into the camera. "I want to stay up here."

"That's not going to happen. I never should have let you go up there in the first place."

"But I can help up here if you let—" Drue started.

"Your *help* is the last thing we need right now," his father said. "You're coming back to Earth. That's an order." And then he disappeared.

Silence filled Benny's cabin. It was Pinky who eventually spoke.

"The call has ended," she said quietly.

"Womp, womp," Ramona said, tapping on her HoloTek.

Benny heard Trevone mutter something to her as he looked at Drue's image on the windshield. Drue stared down at his flight yoke, jaw clenched, his perfectly parted brown hair gleaming. It looked to Benny like he was breathing heavily, his cheeks turning red.

"Drue . . ." Hot Dog said. "Are you okay?"

Drue blinked a few times, but he didn't answer. Instead, he pulled out his HoloTek and swiped through a few screens Benny couldn't see. Then he started tapping buttons on the dashboard. The dot that represented his Star Runner on Benny's radar stopped moving.

It looked like he was turning around.

"Hey," Benny said. "If you need to leave, we get it, but—"

"Leave?" Drue asked. He flashed his perfectly straight, white teeth at them, though his eyes still looked sad. "I'm not leaving. I'm going to show him. I'm going to *help*. I'll meet you back at the tunnel entrance." He paused. "Don't leave me stranded out here. Please."

"Drue," Trevone said cautiously. "What are you doing?"

"I'm going to get some info. That's what we need now that we have Sahar and the others, right?" He smirked. "I know you think you know everything, but I guess you didn't realize Pinky gave us the plans for Elijah's prototypes.

Turns out the Star Runner was included in those." He tapped on a few more buttons. "Now let's see how this baby handles at superspeed."

"Drue, no!" Benny shouted, but the boy ignored him.

And then Drue's camera shut off and his Star Runner disappeared from the radar, gone in the blink of an eye, shooting across the dark sky like a golden comet.

19.

Ricardo got out of the white car he'd taken Sahar to just as Benny closed the door to the Star Runner behind him. His mouth was dry, like it was full of desert sand, as he worried about his friend who was jetting across the Moon toward what could possibly be an entire alien army.

"Sahar's a little disoriented," Ricardo said as he approached, unaware of what was going on. "But I think she's going to be okay. We should make sure she doesn't have a concussion or anything, though. She was thrown around quite a bit in the landing."

Over the Crew member's shoulder, Benny watched Kira climb from the backseat of the SR and hold out her hand. Sahar took it and slowly got to her feet. She tried to take a step forward but wobbled a little, leaning against the door.

Then she looked at Benny. Despite what she'd been through, her eyes were still sharp and full of intensity, and they were all he could focus on. She pointed at his chest, and then beckoned to him. He walked over to her, the low gravity making it an excruciatingly long process, until finally he stood in front of her.

Sahar stared at him for a few seconds. Then she nodded.

"Thank you," she said. Her voice was raspy but firm, and Benny was so taken aback by the words that he didn't know what to say. Everything he'd read about the girl said that she *never* spoke. And so, he just stood there, looking at her dumbly, until she climbed back into the Space Runner, closing the door behind her.

Benny turned to Ricardo. "I thought . . ."

"It's not that Sahar doesn't speak," Ricardo said. "She just chooses her words carefully."

There was a glint in Benny's peripheral vision, and he turned to see two other Star Runners landing. Soon, everyone was gathered together in the crater, except for Sahar and Kira, who stayed in the car.

Ricardo scanned the sky in confusion for a moment, and then pursed his lips in frustration. "What has Drue done?"

Benny shook his head. "I don't know. He said he was going to help and then . . . he was gone."

"Based on his trajectory," Trevone said as he approached, "I'm guessing he's gone to the Taj to scope things out. But he's not responding to any communications. Possibly because he's still traveling using the experimental hyper-drives."

"I'm going to kill him," Ricardo muttered, "if he doesn't get shot down by the aliens first."

Ricardo caught the others up to speed on what had happened to Sahar. As he spoke, Trevone couldn't take his eyes off the golden glove Benny was still wearing.

"Fascinating," he said. "I have so many questions."

"Uh, yeah," Benny said. "You and me both."

"Can't we just use the glove to break the rock on the dome apart?" Hot Dog asked.

"That would take a *lot* of punching."

"If you don't have full control over it," Trevone said, "it would also put the dome's structural integrity at risk."

"Hey, guys." Jasmine stepped forward, holding out the alien radar. "I'm picking something up."

She spun the radar screen around so they could see. A few kilometers away, on the other side of a rocky outcropping, there was a triangular-shaped figure lit up in orange—one of the alien ships.

"That must be the one Kira shot down," Kai said.

"Was it purple?" Trevone asked. "A stealth ship?"

"That's right."

"Well, at least we know this radar will pick them up. That's *good*."

"Hold on," Jasmine said, drawing her finger across the screen. "There are all these weird settings . . ."

Ramona snatched the radar out of her hands and started tapping on it. "Let the master work."

As she toyed with the device, Hot Dog took a few steps away from them, looking first at her Star Runner, then in the direction Drue had headed. "You know, I bet I could catch him."

"No," Ricardo said.

"All I'm saying is that we could jet over there and back him up. I could even take the alien radar! I mean, come on. We don't know if there's one ship that shot that rock stuff onto the Grand Dome or, like, an entire alien army right outside the Taj. We could get some scans or something."

"It's too dangerous."

"I agree," Trevone said. "But if Drue *does* bring back some solid information, that will be incredibly helpful. At this point in time, intelligence is the thing we are sorely lacking. It's also our best weapon."

"And our best method of defense," Jasmine added.

"Fine," Hot Dog said, pouting. "I didn't want to drive the superfast star car anyway."

"Whoaaaaaa," Ramona said, stepping into the center of the group. She turned the alien radar around. "X-ray filter. Hard-core."

It took Benny a second to realize what he was seeing

216

on the screen. It looked like there was some sort of glowing orange skeleton walking around near the downed alien ship, only its bones were all too long and thin to be human.

But of course, it *wasn't* a human.

Jasmine gulped. "Am I looking at an extraterrestrial skeletal system?"

"Oh, that is so gross," Hot Dog said.

"Alien skellie," Ramona said with a grin. "Nice."

Trevone grabbed the radar. "These readouts are insane. It looks like Dr. Bale was somehow able to map out the mineral structure of the Alpha Maraudis' bones. But how?"

Benny thought back to the bronze-looking objects he'd seen in the shed full of alien artifacts in Dr. Bale's campsite—the ones he'd thought looked like bones. He shuddered.

"Interesting," Jasmine said, coming up beside Trevone. "It looks like they're made up of mostly metallic components."

"Uh," Hot Dog said. "So, is that thing headed our way, or . . . ?"

"It would never make it over these cliffs," Ricardo said.

"But it *could* have called for help," Benny said.

"We should get Sahar into the underground med bay," Kai said. "Why are we not in the air?"

"We can't leave Drue out here," Benny said.

There was silence for a few seconds before Ricardo spoke again.

"Let's get back to the tunnel. Everyone follow my lead."

Hot Dog glanced in the direction of the Taj. "Hopefully Drue will be back by the time we get there." She shook her head. "That idiot better not get himself captured. Or hurt."

After the bone-shaking speed they'd reached in the Star Runner, the drive back to the underground tunnel with Ricardo seemed almost sluggish, despite the fact that they were traveling hundreds of miles an hour. Along the way, Benny finally got in touch with Drue, who had apparently disengaged the experimental hyperdrives. Benny was relieved, but Drue was less than thrilled to hear from him.

"Will you *stop* calling me?" he asked. "I'm trying to focus and be stealthy! I'll let you know if I find anything."

And then the line went out.

Benny thought about calling him back and demanding that he head toward the tunnel, but he seriously doubted that Drue would listen to him. So instead, he updated Ricardo on the call they'd received while he'd been helping Sahar. The Pit Crew member kept grinding his teeth.

"If Elijah knew what was going on . . ." Ricardo growled when Benny was through. "How could I let this happen? He'd be so disappointed. After everything he's done for me, he's gone for a few days and under my command every-thing falls to pieces."

Benny could almost feel some of the same pressure that had been weighing on his mind radiating off Ricardo, the suffocating sense that there were so many people counting on you.

"You thought you were doing the right thing. I mean, so did I. And we *did* get in contact with Earth. Just not how we thought we would."

"All I wanted was to get him back," Ricardo contin-ued, "any way possible. So I let Dr. Bale into the Taj, and now . . . I think you're right. I don't think he cares about finding Elijah at all. He'd probably say anything to keep us from getting in his way."

"This isn't over," Benny said. "Once we get back and have a better idea of what's happening outside the dome, we'll make a plan. We'll figure things out."

Ricardo glanced at him. "You're, what, three or four years younger than me?"

Benny shrugged. "Yeah."

"Then how do you keep knowing what to do?"

The question didn't sound angry to Benny, more like Ricardo was bewildered.

Benny laughed. "Are you kidding? I have no idea what I'm doing. I've been freaking out the last few days." Famil-iar words started floating through his brain. "I'm just trying not to let my fear keep me from doing anything." He paused. "And, again, I'm sorry I didn't tell you about Dr. Bale."

Ricardo leaned back in his seat. "An army is coming. This is so far from what Elijah built the Taj for." He shook his head and was quiet for a moment. They were getting closer to the tunnel. Then he spoke again, without looking at Benny. "When you were out in the Drylands, did you used to stare up at the Moon and dream about being up here? I did all the time in Rio after I first heard the resort was being built."

"Every chance I got," Benny said. "I used to sit on the top of our RV a lot. Any time I could see the Moon, I thought about the Taj."

"Dr. Bale was a fancy scientist before he moved up to the Moon, you know," Ricardo said. "People like him and Drue's dad, they don't realize what something like the Taj means to those of us who grew up with nothing. To them it's a vacation hotel, a place to relax for the weekend. Or a place to house soldiers, I guess." He looked at Benny. "But to people like you and me . . . it's everything. A place where you can be anyone and do whatever you want. People from the cities probably have no idea what it's like to be on the streets in Brazil or out in the desert and to have this impossible, untouchable thing staring down at you every night. I'm well aware of how lucky I am to live up here."

Benny shook his head. "You're wrong. The Taj isn't everything. It's just a building. I mean, a really cool building, but still. It's nothing on its own. Just like my caravan back home would just be a bunch of cars without all the people."

"That sounds nice," Ricardo said. "But you know what I mean."

"I guess you're right." Benny stared out the window at the distant stars. "I wonder if the Alpha Maraudi look at Earth the same way we used to look at the Taj."

"Man," Ricardo said, sighing heavily. "I never thought of it like that."

Ricardo landed their Star Runner on the ground beside the entrance to the tunnel.

"Trevone and Ramona, stay up here to operate the force field," Ricardo said into the comms. "Benny and I will wait with you until Drue's back. Everyone else, get inside. Take Sahar straight to the med bay."

"We'll be right behind you," Benny added.

"Roger that," Hot Dog said as she followed the Miyamuras inside.

"Sahar will be okay," Trevone's voice came through the speakers. "That went well. All things considered."

Behind Trevone's car, Benny could just make out the greenish slab of rock that served as the door to the abandoned alien base. It seemed so long ago that they'd stumbled upon it, unaware of how it would change their lives—how it would completely distort everything Benny knew to be true about the Moon, not to mention the man in charge of it.

Sitting in the Space Runner beside Ricardo, it was a wonder to him that his view of the galaxy had ever been so small.

"Guys," Drue practically shouted through the comms. "Come in? Hello? Anyone?"

"We're here," Benny said. "Did you find something?"

"Uh, yeah, I did." Drue's voice was wobbling. "Pinky, can you send them what I'm seeing?"

The windshield in Benny's Space Runner flashed, and then was filled with the view from Drue's Star Runner. Hovering not far away from the covered dome of the Lunar Taj was what looked like a huge, jagged piece of greenish rock—as though someone had carved the edge of a cliff off a mountain and sent it into orbit.

"What is that?" Benny whispered.

"I dunno. I'm guessing it's, like, two hundred meters in length," Drue said. "Maybe more?"

"By my calculations, it's one hundred eighty-nine meters end to end," Pinky said. "Approximately one hundred meters high. As far as depth goes, I can't be sure from this angle."

"Okay, so I was close. There are more of the small ships like we ran into at the asteroid storm, too. They keep leaving the big rock thing and . . . I think they're parking around the Taj? It's hard to tell how many from here, but . . . Look, I don't know much about fighting or anything like that, but it seems like they're getting into formation for something."

"Oh my God," Trevone muttered. "It's another mother ship."

"Get back here!" Benny shouted, not realizing how loud his voice was until after the words were out of his mouth.

"Now," Ricardo added.

"You don't have to tell me twice," Drue said. "I'm turning around."

Ricardo looked at Benny. "How long until the Earth forces get here?" he asked.

Benny shook his head. "Hours, maybe? They might have launched already."

Ricardo turned and looked through the now-clear windshield. "We might not have that much time." His fingers tapped on the flight yoke over and over again. "I don't know what we're supposed to do. What Elijah would want."

"I don't either," Benny said. "But whatever we do, we'll figure it out together."

Ricardo looked at him for a few seconds before raising a fist into the air so quickly that Benny flinched. Then he couldn't help but laugh a little as he brought up his own fist, bumping it against Ricardo's.

20.

Inside, they regrouped on the platform where the rest of the vehicles from the garage were stored. The Miyamuras had swept Sahar off to the underground medical facility to run some scans, but Hot Dog and Jasmine were waiting for Benny and the others there once Drue had returned and they'd flown back down through the tunnels.

"Pinky sent us pictures of what you saw," Jasmine said, holding her HoloTek. It shook in her hands. "That ship is huge."

"If it's anything like that other asteroid mother ship was," Hot Dog said, "then there's no way our mining lasers can even dent it."

"Yeah," Drue said. His skin was pale, clearly still shaken from what he'd seen. "And we probably don't have enough Space Runners to throw at it since Elijah blew up so many against that last one."

"They have to be seeing that from Earth, right?" Benny said, trying to keep his cool. "So the people who are coming will expect a fight."

"You're right," Jasmine said. "There's going to be some kind of battle outside. If the army wins, they're going to send all of us home."

"Uh, I'm a little more concerned with what happens if the *aliens* win," Drue said.

"It's bad news either way." Ricardo shook his head. "And we can't count on Dr. Bale for help. He wouldn't even let me out to go find the rest of the Crew. He doesn't care about us." He nodded to Trevone. "Or Elijah."

"Just the Taj," Benny said.

"So let's take that back from him," Hot Dog said.

Everyone looked at her.

"What?" she asked. "Why not? He may have Pinky up there, but we've got all the human brains down here. We can get her back. Then we rule everything."

"The force fields *are* all still intact," Jasmine said. "We could probably keep the Maraudi and the army out. At least for a while."

"It could buy us some time," Trevone added. "Maybe enough to figure out what to do next. At least to make a game plan."

There was a rumbling sound somewhere far above them. They all looked up. Dust filtered down from the ceiling, clouding a few of the lights that floated high in the air.

"As long as the Grand Dome holds, that is," Trevone said.

Ricardo looked at Benny. He nodded to the Pit Crew leader.

"I don't want anyone to get hurt," Benny said, "alien or human. If we don't do anything and all the Alpha Maraudi get killed . . . I don't know how I could face my family knowing I didn't try to stop that. Maybe by taking back the Taj we can figure out how to contact them now that a ship is so close. We could try to come up with a way for us to help each other, or at least not destroy each other." He paused, his thoughts going back to the video of his father. "We're stronger together."

"Imagine what we could do if we understood their tech," Jasmine said. "The way they control rock. How they can apparently shape worlds, if Elijah and Dr. Bale are to be believed."

In the back of Benny's mind, a spark went off—what if they could use the aliens' knowledge to fix the ways his planet had been ravaged. To maybe even restore the Drylands.

He swallowed down the thought. It seemed too good to be true, and even if it were, they had so much to do before they ever got to that point. He cleared his throat and continued.

"If the people from Earth win and ship me back, at least this way I'd know I tried to find a way to save the Alpha Maraudi. And if they win . . . well, I definitely think it would better for us to be running the Taj and not Dr. Bale and his assistants. He might try to use that superweapon."

"Let's show this guy the Moon Platoon means business," Drue said. Then his shoulders slumped. "Aw, man. My dad is going to be so mad at me when he gets here."

Ricardo looked at each of them and smiled, grunting a little. Then he started down the steps of the platform, heading toward the elevator bank. "Let's do it."

"Ramona versus Evil Pinky," Ramona said. "Epic." She tapped on her Taj HoloTek. Pinky's face showed up.

"I want to take back controls just as much as any of you, but, Ramona, could you *not* move my programming to the background of your HoloTek?" the AI asked. "I deserve to be—"

"Mute." Ramona tapped on her screen. She shrugged at the others. "My Pinky will help."

"We'll need to get into the servers in Elijah's quarters," Trevone said. "That's where Pinky's mainframe is."

"If Dr. Bale or his assistants are monitoring the Taj's AI programming," Jasmine said, "they might notice something is up. And they have all those weapons . . ."

"What if Ramona, Jazz, and Trevone worked on the

programming while the rest of us talked to Dr. Bale?" Benny asked. "We can, I don't know, *distract* him. Maybe get some info about this superweapon of his."

"I'm glad you're lumping me into the action group," Drue said to Benny. "But, just a reminder, I could so be on the smart team."

"I can handle him alone," Ricardo said. "He still thinks I'm on his side. I think."

"No," Benny said. "We're in this together, remember? The rest of us will back you up. Once our Pinky is back in control, she can deal with him."

"Plus, if you have to fight, this way it's not three against one," Hot Dog added.

"If it comes down to a fight, you do want Hot Dog on your team," Drue said.

She grinned. "Definitely."

"Divide and conquer," Trevone said. "Just don't let him get on a HoloTek. If he sees his program's been compromised, he could shut down the system completely."

The elevator door opened. Before they got in, Ricardo turned back to them. "Okay, it's a plan," he said. "Well, sort of." Then he held his finger up in front of his mouth in a *shh* motion and jerked his head toward the elevator.

They rode to the lobby in silence. Once there, they split up, everyone nodding to one another. Out in the courtyard, Benny had to fight the urge to stop and stare at the alien rock above them. At the same time, he kept his hand in his pocket on the golden glove. Maybe it would prove to be useful again.

"Uh, guys," Hot Dog said.

She pointed in the direction of the chrome fountain. On the other side of it, Todd and Mae were setting up what looked to Benny like a big cannon pointed at the top of the dome. Ricardo took one look at them and then bolted for the garage, Benny, Hot Dog, and Drue in tow.

The inside of the building was still lit up in red, thanks to the emergency lights overhead, and Dr. Bale was at the far end of the structure, feverishly going through trunks while arguing with the new Taj version of Pinky.

"Doctor," she said, her voice lacking any emotion, "I'm not positive the dome can withstand many more of these power surges. It would be advisable to retreat to the lower—"

"I don't care about your *readings*," Dr. Bale shouted. He banged a fist against one of the tables, causing a few tools to fall to the ground, the metallic sound echoing through the garage. "I *designed* the polymer that's underneath that force field of his, and I'm telling you it can withstand these aliens."

"Doctor, the load-bearing—"

"I *know* about the load-bearing capabilities, Ms. Weyve."

He caught sight of Benny and the others approaching,

and tried to smooth down the back of his hair, which was sticking out in several directions.

"What is going on out there?" Ricardo asked, pointing toward the courtyard.

"Todd and Mae?" Dr. Bale raised an eyebrow. "I have them setting up some secondary Taj defenses. As soon as reinforcements arrive and break us out of this shell, they can take those weapons outside the dome and shoot down any lingering Alpha Maraudi ships."

"We saw what's out there," Benny said. "It's an entire fleet. There's another *mother ship*."

"How could you have possibly . . ." He turned to Pinky. "You were supposed to be keeping watch on them." He swiped a screwdriver from the table and threw it at her. The tool passed through her body, bouncing off the wall of the garage.

"Are you listening to us?" Benny asked. "There is a giant, two-hundred-meter Alpha Maraudi ship outside the dome."

"Yeah, and, like, a *lot* of tiny ships," Drue added.

Dr. Bale looked at them in confusion for a moment, and then broke into a strange, bellowing laugh. "So, they've finally realized that we're going to put up a fight. I suppose I have you and your asteroid storm to thank for that." He sucked on his teeth. "No matter. When the committee sends their ships up, they'll deal with the aliens. The particle beams I designed for them will tear the mother ship apart."

"It'll be hours before they get here," Benny said. "We talked to them. Drue's dad—Senator Lincoln is coming up here himself."

Of all the things they'd said, this was what seemed to have struck a nerve in Dr. Bale. He tugged on his beard, his mouth hanging open for a second before his lips formed a sneer.

"Doctor," Pinky said, "there's something strange happening to my—"

"Shut up," he said quietly. There was a brief moment of stillness before he slammed both his fists down on the table in front of him. "No. No, no. They think I can't handle this, but I can. All my work, and they're just going to take over—take it all away from me."

A strange grating sound, like a rusted bolt being wrenched loose, filled the garage. The floor rumbled below them. Benny turned to look through the open door leading out into the courtyard just in time to see a rolling green energy wave surge across the Grand Dome.

"Pinky—*your* Pinky was just talking about the dome," he said. "She said it might not hold up. What are we going to do if it breaks?"

"The dome won't break," Dr. Bale said, shouting each

word. "I have *faith* in my work. More faith than any of you, or that abominable AI. More faith than anyone on Earth has in me apparently." He began to walk over to his car—the Tank. "Do you think I was up here all this time doing nothing? Do you think I'm unprepared? No. I'm the savior of the entire human race. When history books are downloaded centuries from now, they will list me as the only reason there are still history books around at all. None of you get it. None of you ever have."

"Whoa," Hot Dog whispered. "Uh, maybe we should take a breath and—"

But Dr. Bale kept going. "Elijah gets all the credit for this place, for his *vision*, but what would have happened if he hadn't had me working at his side? What good is a vision if you can't put it into action?"

"Elijah created the hyperdrive technology that made Space Runners possible," Ricardo said. "That made the force fields and environments here possible."

"Maybe not the best time," Drue muttered. "And that's coming from me."

Dr. Bale spun around, pointing a finger at Ricardo.

"You worthless kids, following him around like dogs, yapping at his heels. What do you know?"

"Hey," Hot Dog said. "*We're* the ones who went against Elijah and stopped that asteroid storm."

"Ha," Dr. Bale scoffed. "I could have stopped it myself.

Would have stopped it." He was across the garage now, standing beside the Tank. "And I'll make sure they never get the chance to threaten Earth again. Whatever's out there, we can handle. My *weapons* can handle."

"Dr. Bale . . ." Benny said. "What kind of superweapon did you create?"

The man sneered for a moment. Then a smile spread across his face, showing off his teeth. "Buried in one of those craters is an electromagnetic fission bomb capable of destroying the Alpha Maraudi. Utter annihilation of their species. A weapon like the universe has never seen before. It's brilliant."

"Electro-what?" Hot Dog asked.

"You're crazy," Benny said.

"That's what they always say about men of genius," Dr. Bale said.

Ricardo took a few steps forward. "You think you're so much better than Elijah, but you're not doing this for Earth or for humanity. You're just doing this for yourself, aren't you?" He paused, taking a moment to look at Benny before turning his attention back to Dr. Bale. "You can't just destroy an alien race. It makes us no better than them. They're just looking for their Taj."

Dr. Bale clenched the fingers on both his hands. "So you are a coward after all."

"Doctor, I—" Pinky started.

233

Her voice transformed into a low-pitched drone before she blinked out of existence.

Dr. Bale turned his attention to Benny and the others. He laughed once. "Well played. But if you think it will be easy to wrest back control of the resort's AI, you've got another thing coming."

"I think you underestimate the minds at work up here," Ricardo said.

"Uh, Benny to Jazz," Benny whispered into his collar. "Now would be a good time for Pinky to take control, I think? Maybe order some SRs around?"

"We're working on it," Jasmine said.

Dr. Bale opened the passenger door of his modified Space Runner.

"Don't let him use a HoloTek!" Drue said.

Ricardo bolted at the man, but when Dr. Bale turned around, he wasn't holding a datapad: instead, it was what looked to Benny like a rifle.

"Oh, no," Benny murmured.

Ricardo put his hands up by his chest and took a few steps back.

"I know you've been running this place for a few days," Dr. Bale said. "But from where I stand, it looks like you're unarmed, and I'm the one holding a state-of-the-art plasma rifle. Now . . ." He narrowed his eyes, and it took Benny a second to realize he was looking past him, at Drue. As Dr.

Bale brought the weapon up and rested it on his shoulder, he smirked. "Did I mishear, or did someone say earlier that you're Senator Lincoln's son? I wonder if he'd be so keen to take control of this operation if he knew I had you."

Benny's eyes went wide, and he was moving before he even realized it—stepping to the side and blocking Drue. "You may have lived on the dark side of the Moon for a few years, but I grew up in the Drylands. I've seen scarier stuff than you."

"Benny," Drue said from behind him. "Don't."

"You have a lot to learn, boy," Dr. Bale said. "The Drylands are nothing. I've been living in a space suit for almost five years. Out there in the desolation."

"Yeah," Benny said. "With no one to talk to but yourself and two assistants. You've lost touch with the people you want to save."

"Don't do this, Dr. Bale," Ricardo said.

The garage was silent for a few long seconds, until the wrenching sound from outside filled the room again. Then Dr. Bale was moving, aiming his weapon, pointing it at Benny, or his friend—Benny wasn't sure who.

That's when a thunderous *boom* filled the air. Benny's ears popped, and then his helmet automatically powered on as the Grand Dome shattered outside.

As the force field around the Lunar Taj broke it sent shock waves through the resort, causing Benny and everyone else inside the garage to fall. Fortunately, the change in the atmosphere meant that the artificial gravity had been affected, and Benny found himself floating slowly to the cement floor. He was halfway to the ground when the comms in his collar kicked in and shouts filled his helmet.

"Is everyone okay?" he asked as he twisted in the air, struggling to get to his feet.

"I think so," Drue said, already up on one knee.

"The dome," Hot Dog said. "Oh, crap, are we gonna die?"

"Impossible." Dr. Bale's voice came through the speakers in Benny's collar, barely above a whisper. Benny looked over to see the man sprawled out on the floor, the weapon he'd been holding on the ground a few feet away from him.

Benny started forward, but Ricardo was faster, jogging through the low gravity, eyes focused on the plasma rifle.

"Jazz? Trevone? Pinky?" Benny yelled. "Anyone?"

"I'm here," Pinky said. "We're slowly regaining control of the Taj's systems, but I'm still powerless in the garage. It looks like the force field in the auxiliary tunnel is still holding, but the emergency environmental stabilizers won't kick in until the building is sealed."

Benny turned to the door leading out to the courtyard—it was wide open. That's when he remembered.

"Todd and Mae!" he shouted.

He looked to Ricardo, who was wrestling over the weapon with Dr. Bale, all four of their hands on it. "Go!" the Pit Crew member shouted. "I'll handle this."

Benny took a deep breath, put his trust in Ricardo, and started for the door.

When he finally made it into the courtyard, he froze. The mass covering the dome had destroyed the invisible force field and the clear glass-like polymer underneath it. The rock itself had crumbled, too. Now, a haze of debris drifted toward the ground—a miniature asteroid field studded with crystalline shards glinting in the emergency lights of the Taj. And there, past it all, was the hulking crag of a ship, looming in the distance, dozens of smaller crafts swarming around it.

Todd and Mae were bounding toward Benny. Todd kept

looking over his shoulder at the ship overhead, and Benny watched in horror as Todd ran straight into one of the stray polymer fragments, its broken edge like a knife. It sliced through the arm of his space suit. Not deeply—just enough to send little drops of blood floating out around him—but with his suit compromised, the oxygen was sucked from his helmet. Todd screamed and Mae turned around, covering the hole in his suit with one hand and pulling him through the entrance to the garage. Benny grabbed the sliding door, putting all his weight into it, until it finally gave and slammed shut.

As he made his way back to the others, the emergency environmental systems kicked in, returning Earthlike gravity and atmosphere to the room. It was jarring, and he stumbled forward, almost careening into Todd and Mae, who'd parked themselves on the ground near one of the McGuyvers' toolboxes. Farther back, Dr. Bale was on the floor. Ricardo stood over him. The weapon lay on the other side of the garage, well out of reach of any of them.

"Lock down the Taj," Ricardo shouted at Pinky through the comms. "Everything you can."

"It's only a matter of time before they get through the auxiliary tunnel," Drue said. He looked around frantically. "I mean, if they can break through the dome, they can get through that, right?"

Dr. Bale's laughter filtered through Benny's helmet. "Let them come," he said, getting up to one knee. "We can hold them off."

"Yeah," Hot Dog said. "And the dome won't break, right?"

Dr. Bale ignored her as he started for one of the trailers, motioning to his assistants. "Todd. Mae. You know what to do. We're going into full defensive mode now. Ignore these children. Shoot anything that doesn't look human."

Todd and Mae nodded, rushing to the tables. Todd's arm was wrapped in silver tape Mae must have found in one of the McGuyvers' toolboxes.

Ricardo let out a howl of anger, and then started for the door that led directly into the Taj. "Come on," he yelled. "We're done here."

The others followed him. But Benny lingered.

"It doesn't have to be this way," he said. "You can go underground. We can figure out another way."

Dr. Bale looked at him and tossed a drone into the air, where it floated. "My boy," he said, "I'm going to let you walk out of here just so you can experience for yourself how wrong you are. When they've taken you and your friends, you'll see what a fool you've been."

"*You're* the one who was just pointing a gun at us," Benny said.

"Benny!" Hot Dog shouted.

He took one last look at Dr. Bale and ran to join the others.

They darted through the hallways toward the center of the Taj, their eyes glued to the windows, looking for any sign of the Alpha Maraudi. And as they sprinted into the lobby, they saw the aliens. Small ships like the ones they'd fought in the asteroid storm landed in the courtyard, along with larger, rectangular hunks of rock that were shaped like the trailers Dr. Bale had brought into the garage.

"Trevone, what's your status?" Ricardo asked.

"We're almost done," the Pit Crew member said.

"You do know there are aliens landing outside, right?" Drue asked.

"It would be kind of hard to miss them," Jasmine said.

"Evil Pinky is a replicating virus," Ramona said. "Total malware. Needs to be deleted completely." Benny could hear her slug from a soda can. "Few more minutes."

There was a banging on the front entrance of the Taj, the sound reverberating through the four-story lobby, and Benny and the others all turned to look at the big chrome doors. Another bang. According to what Pinky had told them earlier, there would now be a thin environmental force field around the Taj, offering them a little protection and allowing the artificial atmosphere to remain intact. But how long would the emergency barrier last?

"We can't just stand around waiting for them," Ricardo

said. He grunted, shaking his head. "We're defenseless. I should have brought that plasma rifle with me. Not that I even know how to use it."

"Let's meet up with the others," Benny said. "At least that way we'll all be together."

And then they were running up the stairwell that led to Elijah's private quarters. Along the way, Ricardo checked in with the Miyamuras and Sahar, who appeared to be suffering from only a few bruises.

"No, stay down there," he said when all three of them immediately said they were on their way up to the Taj. "I need you to look after the EW-SCABers." He paused. "Have the McGuyvers prep the vehicles they've stashed down there, just in case we need to make a run for it."

Reluctantly, the rest of the Pit Crew agreed.

When they finally burst through the doors of Elijah's private quarters, Jasmine and Trevone both jumped. Ramona did not. She stayed hunched over her old HoloTek that she'd plugged into a boxy server covered in lights and embedded in a wall where a portrait of Elijah and his father had once hung. The picture was now leaning against Elijah's desk, where Jasmine and Trevone were looking at charts of the Taj.

"Where are we at?" Benny asked.

"Ramona?" Trevone asked.

"Transfer almost complete," Ramona said.

Drue stopped in the middle of the room, staring at her setup and the cords connecting her HoloTek to the server.

"I didn't think they made HoloTeks with wired connections since, like, before I was born," he said.

"Custom rig," Ramona said without looking up. "Unexpected analog assault. Genius."

In a flash, Benny was at the big window behind Elijah's desk, looking out over the courtyard. What he saw seemed impossible. He could still remember the palpable thrill that had coursed through him when he'd first driven into the Grand Dome, like his body had been completely filled with electric exclamation marks. But that courtyard—that *excitement*—was gone now. It was like the window was looking out on to another place completely.

Six small ships were parked beside the fountain in the courtyard. Two of the larger hunks of rock sat nearby, and the Alpha Maraudi were spilling out of them. Dozens of aliens. And even though Benny had seen them before— their too-long arms and legs; the bluish sheen of their skin; the quick, lithe bodies—the sight of them still took his breath away. Just as he'd noticed on the mother ship, the aliens all had different combinations and types of tentacles coming out from the backs of their heads. Blades tipped the ends of some of them, glinting in the courtyard lights, while others held devices he didn't recognize. Each of the ET soldiers he saw marching through the debris-filled courtyard wore a full mask, complementing the gemlike armor on their bodies.

"You said they needed our atmosphere," Jasmine said a little shakily as she came up beside him. "The masks must be how they can breathe out there."

"Holy squid monsters," Drue said, as he joined them. "Those things are ugly."

"They're just standing there," Hot Dog said.

"They likely have no idea what's inside the Taj," Jasmine said. "They're being careful."

Ricardo joined them at the window. He took a sharp breath through his nose as he looked out at the Maraudi gathered in the courtyard. "Elijah had shown us sketches of these creatures," he said, "but he did not do them justice."

"Bingo," Ramona said, unplugging her HoloTek. "All done."

Pinky materialized in the room, standing in front of Elijah's desk.

"That feels so much better," she said. And then she straightened her back, turning to the others. "What would you like me to do?"

Benny looked back out onto the courtyard, where the Alpha Maraudi were gathering around the cannon that Todd and Mae had set up earlier—only it had been spun around so that it was facing the front doors of the Taj.

"Oh, no," Benny murmured.

There was a golden pulse of light, and then the entire Taj shook.

"The doors are breached," Pinky shouted. "The lobby has been depressurized. I'm sealing it off. I can keep the gravity stable in there, but with a hole in the building I can't keep the atmosphere intact."

"Kill the elevators," Benny shouted. "If they don't know about the underground bunker, we don't want them finding it."

"Done," Pinky said. "I've powered down the elevator hyperdrives and parked them at the bottom of the shaft. Even if they make it down the shafts, the cars are made of titanium alloy. They'll be difficult to get through."

"The stairwell," Hot Dog said. "If they find it . . ."

Benny shook his head, trying to think of a solution. "There's no good way to block it off."

Drue's eyes lit up. "Particle beams! The drone I took! Can't we program it to, you know, shoot up the rock inside?"

"We could cause a cave-in!" Hot Dog said.

"We'd be keeping ourselves out," Ricardo said. "Trapped up here with them."

Benny nodded. "Yeah, but we'd be protecting the people below."

He looked around at everyone in the room, his friends. Slowly but surely, they all nodded.

"Do it," Hot Dog said.

Ricardo thought about this for a moment. "Okay, but we'll wait until it's necessary. Pinky, do you have access to Dr. Bale's program files? Send them to Kira. Walk her through how to control it. Figure out a way. Tell her to put the drone in place and wait for my signal."

"Done," Pinky said.

Benny looked back out the window. Smoke hung around the front of the Taj as the first of the Alpha Maraudi made their way into the resort.

"They're coming in," he said. "The Taj is being invaded."

22.

"How long will we be safe up here?" Hot Dog asked.

"I'm locking every door but . . . ." Pinky paused.

"They can blow through them with that cannon," Benny said.

Pinky nodded.

"They could bring the whole resort down," Trevone said.

Ricardo cursed Dr. Bale under his breath as he walked away from the window.

"We need to decide what we're doing right now," Jasmine said. "If we're going to try to bunker down here or head underground through the basement staircase. Every moment we waste gives them more time to infiltrate the Taj, cutting off our options."

Drue walked to the bookcase that served as a barrier between Elijah West's office and his sleeping area. "Doesn't

Elijah have an emergency Space Runner hidden up here somewhere?" He pulled on one of the shelves, causing part of the bookcase to swing open. "Maybe, like, a hyperdrive engine under his bed or something we could use to fly to the dark side and go in the back way?"

"You're wasting your time," Ricardo said. "It would be impossible to get away from all those ships right now. They'd capture us. Or worse."

"And we don't want to lead them to the tunnel," Benny said. "They'd totally trap us. And everyone underground would be in danger."

Trevone swiped the holograms above Elijah's desk until a 3D blueprint of the Taj was in front of him. "Pinky, your eyes are back, right? Can you populate this map with the locations of the aliens?" Red blips appeared on the first floor. "Okay, to get to the stairs leading underground, we'd have to make our way to the basement level. The fastest way would be down the stairwell we came up and through the lobby."

"Or," Jasmine said, stepping up beside him and pointing at the hologram. As she traced a finger across the image, a blue line showed up. "We could cut through the Mustangs' floor, go through *this* staircase, and avoid the lobby altogether."

There was a loud noise from somewhere in the Taj, and the room shook.

"They've entered the restaurant," Pinky said as the red dots moved on the map.

"We'll go Jasmine's route," Ricardo said. "Pinky, keep track of the Maraudi for us. We don't want to run into them unless it's unavoidable."

"Of course," she said.

Ramona held up the alien radar. "I'll watch the skellie-cam, too."

Benny pointed to the door. "Let's go."

They ran into the stairwell. Jasmine kept her HoloTek out, the blueprints of the Taj filling with more and more red dots. The Mustangs' floor was just a short flight of stairs down, and soon they were sprinting toward the staircase that would lead them to the basement level. Along the way, the resort kept trembling as the Alpha Maraudi filtered into more rooms and corridors on the first floor.

"They've made it to the staircase leading to Elijah's quarters," Pinky said. "You got out in the nick of time."

"Elijah would be furious," Ricardo said.

"Elijah has more important things to worry about right now," Benny said. That was assuming that the man was even still alive.

"More ships are landing in the courtyard," Pinky continued. "I think they're eyeing the garage. Bale and his assistants appear to be armed to the teeth, but I don't know what kind of fight they can put up alone."

"There are way too many aliens out there," Hot Dog said. "At least we know his superweapon isn't here."

"Technically they *could* hide in the floor," Jasmine said. "There are several storage levels under the garage."

"Yeah, great, save the mad doctor," Drue said. "I'm pretty sure that guy was going to take me hostage earlier."

"Tell him where he can hide, Pinky," Benny said as they headed into the next stairwell. "We don't want him blowing up the garage trying to stop them."

"Good point," the AI said. "I'm relaying the message now and— Wait, stop!"

They came to an abrupt halt on the stairs, almost trampling over one another. "What is it?" Ricardo asked.

"The aliens are trying to get into this stairwell. They're setting up the cannon in the lobby."

Benny looked down the steps in front of them. They still had several floors to go.

"The cannon is in position," Pinky said.

Benny looked at Ricardo. "If we're in front of that door when it shoots, we're dead."

Ricardo banged a fist against the wall, and then jumped down to the landing below them. He hit a button and opened the door that led to the Vipers' level—the third floor of the Taj. "Come on," he shouted.

Benny was the last one through. Just as the door closed behind him, he heard an explosion coming from the stairwell. His ears popped as the atmosphere shifted for a split second before stabilizing again once the hallway was sealed.

"The more rooms they take, the harder it is for us to move around," Trevone said.

"Total Taj corruption," Ramona said.

"Okay." Hot Dog raised her hands out to her sides, looking around. "There's got to be another way down, right? Don't tell me we're trapped on this floor now."

"We could break a window!" Drue said. "Float to the first floor, then break *another* window and get in."

"Those windows aren't glass and you know it," Jasmine said. "We'd need a cannon of our own to get through."

"Aren't there," Hot Dog said, "I don't know . . . ventilation shafts?"

"Wait," Trevone said, his eyes lighting up. "That gives me an idea." He started running down the hallway. "Follow me!"

Half a minute later, they rounded a corner and came to a maintenance room. "Pinky!" Trevone said, and the door slid open. He herded the rest of them inside, where the air was heavy with the scent of bleach and disinfectant.

"No offense"—Drue coughed—"but maybe one of the suites would be a better place to hide."

"We're not hiding." Ricardo grinned. "Trevone, you're a genius."

Trevone walked across the small room, past racks of cleaning supplies and extra bed linens, to a big silver hatch embedded in one wall. "This is where all the sheets get thrown so they can be cleaned. On the first floor."

"You want us to jump down two floors?" Benny asked. "We'll break our legs."

Trevone frowned. "We could make a rope out of these extra sheets."

"We don't need to," Hot Dog said. "Pinky, those files on the environmental systems I was looking at earlier." She smirked. "Why don't you just turn off the gravity?"

"Yes!" Drue shouted.

"Actually," Benny said, grinning, "we should keep it off anywhere we aren't. Let's see how the aliens do when they're trying to leap around in low g."

Pinky laughed once. "Consider it done."

There was a slight shift in the room as the artificial gravity dropped to practically nothing. Hot Dog looked around, and as she did, her blond curls drifted out from her head.

"I know we don't have time for holo-selfies, but I wish we did," she said as she walked toward the hatch Trevone was holding open.

Ricardo was the first down, followed by Benny. They floated slowly, the Taj trembling around them. A minute later, they were all standing in what Benny assumed was the laundry room—though based on the complicated-looking machines around him, it easily could have been some sort of futuristic laboratory. They didn't exactly have places like this in the Drylands.

"Jasmine," Ricardo said as Pinky turned the gravity back on in the room, "let's see that map."

"They're filtering into the other floors," she said, extending her HoloTek. "Spreading throughout the Taj in small groups now that they've found the stairwells." She paused. "Oh, no. It looks like they're in the basement level. They haven't gotten to the door leading to the underground stairs, but they'll get there eventually."

"Let's not blow up our way out yet," Benny said. "We can still make it."

"Okay," Ricardo said. "There are six of them in the lobby, right by the staircase we need. We have nothing to fight with. We'd have to sneak past them somehow."

"We need a distraction," Trevone said.

Benny held up his left hand and pointed to the silver hoop around his wrist. "Well," he said, thinking of how he'd tricked the two members of the Pit Crew standing in front of him into chasing a monster through the basement hallways so that he and his friends could access the very room they were now heading toward. "Some of us *have* done this before."

Ricardo nodded, pointing to the blueprints. "From here, we're a short sprint from the lobby. The hallway outside is still safe, at least."

"We just have to get to the server room," Jasmine said. "If we make it down the steps, we can blow the stairwell up behind us."

"Mmmm," Ramona said. "Secret server. Wonder what the hardware's like."

Jasmine shook her head. "Not the time, Ramona."

"Everyone ready?" Ricardo asked.

They nodded, and then they were running again through the short hallway. When they got to the lobby door, they stood back as Benny tapped on his wrist. A duplicate of Benny appeared in front of them.

"When the door opens, the atmosphere will go," Jasmine said, touching the side of her collar and preemptively turning on her force field helmet. The others followed her lead. "There's a *hole* in the front of the Taj now."

"Pinky," Benny said, "I'm ready."

He flattened himself against the wall as the door opened and the air changed around them. With a flick of his finger over the bracelet Elijah had given him, the holographic clone of himself darted into the resort's lobby. One of the aliens saw it, and motioned to the others, chasing the fake Benny as he darted into the restaurant.

This was their chance.

Benny motioned to the others to move, and then tapped on his wrist again to bring the cloud of nanotech hologram-producing projectors back—the aliens could look for him forever in the restaurant, but they'd never find him now.

He paused for a split second in the doorway once everyone else was through. The black marble floors flecked with gold were now covered in dust and debris. The giant chrome doors that had once welcomed them to the Taj sat against a wall, partially melted and crumpled beneath a giant portrait of Elijah in a silver suit. A part of him wondered what the grinning man in the picture would say if he saw how unrecognizable his resort was becoming, but that was the least of Benny's concerns at the moment. He followed the others as they made their way to the nearby stairwell, the doorway destroyed by Dr. Bale's cannon. He carefully stepped over the bits of blasted door and onto the landing as his friends began to hurry down as fast as they could in the low gravity.

Pinky shouted a warning. "Faster! Move! They're coming."

Benny looked back at the doorway to the lobby, but he couldn't make out any movement.

"Above you!" the AI yelled again in his collar.

And that's when he saw them. A few floors up, two masked Alpha Maraudi soldiers leaned over the railing of the winding stairwell.

They'd been spotted.

"Go!" he shouted as one of them threw itself headfirst over the side of the stairwell. The two thick tentacles on its head grabbed railing after railing, propelling it toward them with a quickness Benny could barely believe, the other alien following close behind.

23.

The first alien landed on Ricardo, knocking him into Trevone, Ramona, and Jasmine, the five of them all tumbling down the stairs together. The other hit the steps in front of Drue, Hot Dog, and Benny. Metallic red armor covered its chest, shoulders, knees, elbows, and face. The rest of its body was protected by the same sort of chain mail–like cloth Benny had seen on the alien mother ship, the silver threads in constant motion, weaving in and out of loops and knots. The soldier towered three feet over them and arched its back as the six thin black tentacles on the back of its head wound together, forming a giant mallet. With a flick of its neck, the alien rammed this new weapon into Drue's stomach, sending him flying up the stairs. Benny could hear him coughing through the comms, trying to catch his breath.

"Drue!" Hot Dog shouted.

Farther down the steps, Ricardo tackled the other Alpha Maraudi, both of them slamming into the wall. Benny spotted a flash of silver tipping the enemy's tentacles.

"Everyone go," Ricardo shouted. "I'll handle this one. Get somewhere safe."

He gritted his teeth as his fist smashed against the red rock covering the Maraudi's mouth. "Ow!" he shouted afterward, shaking his hand.

The soldier in front of Benny turned to glance at Ricardo. Hot Dog took advantage of the moment. She jumped forward and planted a foot in the alien's chain mail stomach, sending it tumbling down a few steps. She stumbled back from the force, but Benny caught her.

Two aliens separated them from their friends. There was no way they were getting past them—even if they jumped over the railing and tried to float the rest of the way down with the gravity off, those quick tentacles would surely grab them.

They only had one option. They had to get out of there—and that meant splitting up.

Trevone realized this, too.

"Get to safety," he yelled through the comms. "We'll regroup."

"Pinky," Benny said as Drue and Hot Dog followed him up the stairs, the alien close behind them. "What can you do for us?"

"Get back into the hallway you came from," she said. "I can lock the door behind you and buy you a little bit of time."

In a flash, they were back in the lobby. Six soldiers had come out of the restaurant and were now standing there, staring at Benny and his friends. Behind them, the stairwell alien launched itself through the doorway using its tentacles.

Benny, Drue, and Hot Dog ran.

"I don't guess there are any secret weapons in here that we should know about," Hot Dog said.

"Pinky, where are the SR trainers?" Benny asked as they darted for the hallway door. "Do you have control of them?"

"Give me two seconds," Pinky said.

It was actually four seconds later that three SR trainers shot through the lobby of the Taj. One pinned the stairwell alien against a wall, while the other two circled around the remaining forces. One of the Alpha Maraudi tossed something at the closest vehicle. In seconds, rock began to grow over it, and Benny saw it sputter and hit one of the lobby walls just as he crossed into the hallway and the door began to slide shut behind him and his friends.

Benny could hear heavy breathing through the comms in his helmet as they ran.

"Where are we going?" Drue asked.

"They're sealing up the garage with rock to stop me from sending out any more Space Runners. I'm not sure how many you think are expendable, but I could try to crash a few through."

"Don't waste all our possible escape vehicles," Drue said.

The Taj shook, and Benny stumbled into Drue as the Alpha Maraudi destroyed the door leading into the hallway. Aliens poured through the opening as the boys hit the floor.

Hot Dog pulled them to their feet. "This way!" she shouted as she made a sharp right into the next hallway. "I have an idea!"

Benny wasn't sure where they were headed until Hot Dog was asking Pinky to open the door to the video game room.

"We'll be trapped in there," Drue said.

"Just trust me," Hot Dog said.

He groaned, but went inside, Benny following close behind. Hot Dog lingered in the doorway.

"What are you doing?" Benny asked. "They'll see you."

"That's the point!" she said, waving at someone in the hallway.

"*Awesome*," Drue said. "We're going to die."

"Just listen to me," she said. "Earlier, Benny and I were in here and it was so realistic that Benny couldn't find the door out."

"So?"

"So they could get lost in here, too," Benny said, finally understanding.

"And this room is built to work with the antigravity systems sewn into our Taj space suits, remember? We can just float up top, wait for the coast to be clear, and sneak back out. Hidden by holograms."

"Only one problem with that," Benny said.

They both turned to Drue, who looked at each of them in confusion, then down at himself. "Oh, come on," he muttered as he stared at the gleaming, expensive black suit he'd brought from home—one that didn't have the antigravity tech from the Taj sewn into it. "You're kidding me."

"Come on, Benny," Hot Dog replied. "Gimme a hand."

She grabbed on to one of Drue's arms. Benny grabbed the other.

"Pinky, make us float," Hot Dog shouted.

And then they were shooting through the air until they were almost hitting the ceiling of the huge, rubber-covered room.

"Too bad the rest of the Taj doesn't have this tech," Benny said. "We could just fly everywhere."

"I hate this, I hate this, I hate this," Drue repeated as he dangled in the air. "If you drop me, I will never forgive you."

"Stop jerking around so much and we won't," Hot Dog

said. "Pinky, let them in. And then make it impossible for them to find the door!"

"I'm on it," the AI responded.

Suddenly, the room below them was a lush jungle, a surging river cutting through the thick foliage. Huge birds in spectacular colors flapped across the sky. There was shaking in the trees, and Benny watched something brown and furry swing on a vine across the water.

And then the aliens were filtering inside, one of them brandishing Dr. Bale's cannon. They moved carefully at first, their tentacles reaching out to touch the environment. It didn't take long for them to realize that none of the trees were real, and then they were running through the forest, passing through the light-constructed trunks with ease, looking for the three EW-SCABers.

The door shut and disappeared behind them, until Benny wasn't even sure where it was anymore.

"Okay, this is kind of great," Drue whispered, watching the Alpha Maraudi run into the wall on the other side of the room, even though it looked—thanks to the projections— like the forest went on for miles.

The aliens began to look around at one another, tentacles gesticulating wildly.

"Pinky, get us out of here," Hot Dog said.

"Finally. It feels like my arms are gonna be ripped off," Drue said, still hanging between the two of them. Then he glanced at Hot Dog. "Good idea, by the way."

She smirked. "Thanks."

They floated down slowly, hidden by a holographic cloud, until their feet were once again on the floor. The door slid open and they bolted through. Once they were in the hallway again and the door was closed, Benny breathed a sigh of relief.

"Okay," Hot Dog said. "That should keep them for a while."

"Pinky, where are the others?" Benny asked.

"Ricardo managed to knock out the alien in the stairwell, but by the time they got down to the basement . . ." She paused. "The Alpha Maraudi found the server room. Ricardo's group is hiding in the prototype storage room in the basement I showed you earlier. So far as I can tell, the aliens haven't figured out that it exists."

"And the stairs underground?" Benny asked.

"We collapsed the tunnel," the AI said. "On Ricardo's orders. I'm sorry."

He let out a long breath, and then shook his head. "It was the right move. But we need to get down there and rejoin them."

"Yeah," Hot Dog said. "I don't like being split up like this."

"Uh, or standing out in the open," Drue added, glancing around.

"There are a dozen Alpha Maraudi in the basement floor now," Pinky said, "and more streaming into the lobby as we speak."

"Too bad we only have one of those fancy bracelets," Drue said. "I doubt we can distract them all with that."

"Yeah," Benny agreed, but his mind was wandering. He glanced back at the door leading to the video game room, thinking about all the hologram pranks he'd pulled in the caravan—and those he would have pulled if he'd had the right kind of equipment. Equipment like the Taj was full of. "Pinky!" he half shouted. "How many of you could you make at once?"

"It would depend on the location within the Taj, as well as—"

"Let's say the lobby."

The AI appeared beside them, shrugging. "Dozens. The lobby is full of holographic nanoprojectors."

"What are you thinking?" Hot Dog asked.

"An army of Pinkys!" Drue said.

The AI looked at them for a second and grinned a little. Then she shifted, until she was a glowing copy of Benny.

"Or an army of you," she said. Then she shifted again and was Drue. "All of you. They wouldn't know who was real."

"That is so weird," Drue muttered.

"Is that what you had in mind?" the AI asked. "Because

the nanoprojectors from other rooms can easily be flown in to help."

Benny grinned. "That'd probably be enough to keep us hidden *and* get them to call a bunch of the aliens up to the first floor, right? We could clear out the basement that way."

Drue cracked his knuckles. "Let's do this."

Hot Dog nodded. "Pinky, tell the others we're on our way."

As they started down the hall back toward the lobby, holograms of the three of them began to appear all around.

"I hate this," Hot Dog said, eyeing one of the clones of her up ahead of them. "It's so creepy."

"I can't even tell which ones are the real yous!" Drue said.

Benny looked at the entrance to the lobby in front of them. "I think it's about to get weirder."

By the time they burst out of the hallway, the lobby was overrun with copies of themselves, darting back and forth over the marble, in and out of the restaurant entrance, and up and down the hallways and stairwells, passing through the three rock blobs that had been Space Runners just minutes before. The Alpha Maraudi tried to stop them with their tentacles, but they went right through the beings made of light. Even the screens on the walls of the lobby were being utilized—Pinky had made them look as though the room extended forever, filled with an army of

Drues, Bennys, and Hot Dogs.

"Holy whoa," Benny said.

"This is making my brain hurt," Drue said.

"It's working," Pinky said. "The aliens in the basement are headed up here. It seems like this is really freaking them out."

"It's freaking *me* out," Hot Dog said.

They sidled up against one of the lobby walls and watched as Alpha Maraudi ran into the lobby from the nearby stairwell, trying to get a handle on the situation.

"Now's your chance," Pinky said. "Go!"

They bolted for the stairs, this time making it all the way down to the basement level without being stopped. Once they were there, they sprinted through the hallways as quickly as they could. At one point, Pinky ushered them into a research lab to avoid a passing alien. But it was working. The holograms had been such a perfect distraction that Benny could hardly believe they hadn't thought of it before.

"Stay put just a bit longer," Pinky said. "The hallway is almost clear and . . . Hmmm."

"What is it?" Benny asked.

"I'm not sure. They've brought some kind of red, metallic orb into the lobby. I'm picking up a lot of energy coming off it and . . ."

There was a crackling in their comms. Benny and his friends looked at each other.

"Oh, no," Hot Dog said. "They killed Pinky."

"No," the AI's voice came again. "Well, not entirely. That was some sort of energy bomb. My servers are fine, but the holograms are not." She sighed. "How many times am I going to lose my holographic body today?"

"They fried the nanoprojectors," Benny said.

Drue let his helmet hit the wall. "I hate these guys."

The door to the research lab slid open. "The path is clear," Pinky said. "For now. Go."

They didn't hesitate. In seconds they were down the hall and around the corner, looking for the spot in the wall that would lead them to their friends. It slid open as they approached, and the three of them practically threw themselves inside. The door closed behind them.

They powered down their helmets and tried to catch their breath in the stabilized environment. Benny looked around the room. Ramona was standing at a workbench with the alien radar and what looked like several other small electronics she'd taken apart. Ricardo had taken his gloves off, and Jasmine was wrapping fabric torn from a dust cover around his knuckles.

"You're okay!" she shouted, running to hug Hot Dog.

"Good timing," Trevone said, looking up from a HoloTek he had propped up on one of the racks of old inventions. "The Earth forces are here."

24.

Benny pointed to Ricardo. *"Are you okay?"* he asked as he hurried over to Trevone's side.

"I'm fine," the leader of the Pit Crew assured him. "And I've been in contact with Kira. Everyone's holding up down below. They're just scared. Pinky told us what you've been up to. Very smart."

"Yeah, but now the hologram projectors are dead," Drue said.

Pinky appeared beside him. "Not all of them. But unfortunately we won't be able to do anything on such a large scale again."

Benny watched a fleet of green blips on Trevone's HoloTek approach the Taj. A blinking number in the top right corner kept increasing as more and more lights appeared on the screen. 42. 67. 88.

"The Taj sensors are picking up the incoming Space

Runners from Earth," Trevone said. "Meanwhile, we can only track the aliens on Dr. Bale's radar. And Ramona's taken *that* apart to try to boost its range and power using some of the spare parts from Elijah's old machines. All we've really got is the security feeds to show us the full scope of what's happening up top."

He swiped the screen, and then they were looking at the courtyard. The alien ships were still parked there, and several Alpha Maraudi seemed to be patrolling the area. A wall of glowing green rock had grown over the entrance to the garage, sealing the spare Space Runners—and Dr. Bale and his team—inside.

It was hard to believe that all this was happening just ten yards or so above their heads.

"They've gotta have more ships than the ones parked here," Benny said. "Drue saw a ton of them. They must be back inside that big floating mother ship."

A muted rumbling came from somewhere inside the resort.

"The soldiers that were trapped in the video game room have escaped," Pinky said, "by blowing a hole in the side of the wall with Dr. Bale's cannon."

"The Taj is a mess," Ricardo said quietly. "At this rate it'll be completely destroyed. Even if the Earth reinforcements do want to use it as a base, there might not be anything left of our home."

"It looks worse than it is," Trevone said. "A few key repairs and it'll be inhabitable again. Though the Grand Dome's force field will take much more time to replace. The generators that powered it are completely fried."

"Do you think the Earth army can take down the Alpha Maraudi?" Hot Dog asked.

Trevone shook his head. "I have absolutely no idea."

Jasmine raised a finger in the air. "It's not exactly comforting to say, but from what we've seen, Dr. Bale's weapons *do* work. Think about that alien ship he destroyed with one shot. And the drones. Even the cannon that the aliens are using to blow through the Taj."

"I don't even want to imagine that superweapon of his," Trevone said.

"I wish we knew where it was buried."

Hot Dog slammed her right first into her left palm. "I bet we can get him to talk."

"Speaking of which," Drue said, "you totally, like, drop-kicked an alien earlier."

"On the spaceship she head-butted one," Benny added.

"Where did that come from?"

Hot Dog shrugged. "Before I got into flight sims, I was super into fighting games, so I took some self-defense and martial arts lessons. There were a bunch of free community classes when crime started to go up in Dallas."

Drue grinned. "I like this side of you."

"You say that only because you haven't been on the receiving end of it," Jasmine said. "Yet."

Benny began to walk in little circles around the center of the room, his fingers drumming on the sides of his legs.

"Okay, so we're blocked off from the underground bunker," Benny said. "And there's about to be a big space fight above us."

"That's the basic situation, yes," Trevone said.

"If the Alpha Maraudi win, they'll take over the Taj," Ricardo said. "If they haven't demolished it by the end."

"Let's not forget the ninety-six EW-SCABers underground," Jasmine added. "Plus the McGuyvers, the rest of the Pit Crew . . ."

"And *us*," Drue said. "I don't want to end up frozen in rock or some kind of alien's pet."

"But if the Earth forces win, they'll ship us all back to Earth and try to blow up the alien home world," Hot Dog said.

"Sooo . . . what do we do?"

Benny looked at his friends, then at Ricardo. The Pit Crew member didn't say anything, but Benny could guess what was on his mind: Elijah was maybe still out there somewhere, too.

He thought about what they were all saying, and about the limited options that were open to them—as well as the outcomes they had no control over. And his mind, as always, drifted back to his family. There was a scenario he could clearly see where the human fighters took back the Taj and shipped him home to the Drylands—where within twenty-four hours, maybe, he could be reunited with his grandmother and his brothers, even if it did mean a death sentence for the Alpha Maraudi. But as enticing as the idea of being back with his family sounded, he knew part of him would never be okay with this scenario.

He wondered if all this could have been avoided if Elijah or Dr. Bale—if *someone* had tried to work with the Alpha Maraudi instead of taking up arms against them or completely giving up on humanity.

"I don't want to go back to Earth," Benny said finally. "I mean, I *do*, but I think there are bigger things to worry about here."

Suddenly, the room shook. There was a crashing sound from above, and for a moment Benny was sure the roof was going to cave in around them.

"What's going on?" Ricardo asked, jumping to his feet.

Trevone looked at the video feeds of the courtyard. "An alien ship just went down near the garage." He looked to Ricardo. "The fight has started."

"Ugh," Drue groaned, as they crowded around the feed. "Can't these cameras go any higher? I want to see what's happening."

"They're security cams. They weren't designed to watch space."

"Ramona, get that alien radar put back together," Jasmine said.

The girl clicked her tongue. "Roger, roger."

There was intermittent shaking all around them. Benny expected to see the aliens from inside the Taj run out to their ships, but according to Pinky they weren't moving at all. It was as if they weren't concerned.

And then they figured out why.

"Oy," Ramona chirped, coming up behind them. "Critical mass."

She handed the radar off to Jasmine, who gasped.

The screen showed waves of small crafts streaming from the giant alien mother ship. Their bright orange radar blips filled the sky above the Taj, like all the stars in the galaxy had congregated above the resort. There were at least as many alien ships as there were Earth forces. Possibly more.

The Taj shook around them again.

"We have to do *something*," Hot Dog said. "There's a war breaking out above us. We can't just sit around down here waiting to see who wins."

"She's right," Trevone said.

"We could try to use the battle as cover to slip out and reactivate the elevators," Drue suggested.

"That just means we'd be waiting underground,"

Jasmine said. She tapped on the alien radar and changed the setting so that it showed the walking skeletons of all the Alpha Maraudi still wandering the halls of the Taj. "Plus, we'd have to get past all these soldiers."

"So where else can we go?" Hot Dog asked.

Benny stared at the screen, trying to think of something, *anything* they could do. The skies above the Taj were now filled with the unsettling sight of countless alien skeletons flying through the air. They were lit up in orange, along with the metallic backs of their ships.

"Wait," Jasmine said. "Ramona, how much did you upgrade this scanner? Can it zoom in?"

"Affirmative," she called from behind one of the racks where she was rummaging through other devices and gadgets. "I'm a leet pro, J. Double tap."

Jasmine touched the screen a few times, until it was zoomed in on the giant alien ship. There were a dozen aliens clustered around what Benny assumed was the ship's bridge, a handful of others scattered throughout the vessel. She looked at Benny. "The asteroid mother ship was impenetrable to our lasers. But we have a secret weapon."

"That glove," Ricardo said.

Benny stared back at them, taking a moment to try to process what they were getting at. "Hold on. Are you suggesting we, what, *break into* the mother ship?"

"I am not at all against stealing that thing just for fun,"

Drue said. "But what do we do with it after?"

"We get out of here," Hot Dog said, her face starting to light up. "No matter who ends up winning this fight, they're *not* just going to let us stick around."

"Think of all the information on that ship," Trevone said, his eyes wide.

"Right," Jasmine said. "If we wanted to find some way to keep our two civilizations from destroying each other, this could be a way of doing it. There's so much we don't know about them. This could be a chance to learn."

"To try to communicate with them," Benny said, his mind spinning. "Just like we talked about earlier."

"Plus, there'd be plenty of room for the rest of the EW-SCABers on board," Jasmine added.

Ricardo's eyebrows shot up. "We could figure out if—*where* they have Elijah."

"You'd leave the Taj behind?" Benny asked him.

Ricardo took a moment before he answered. "We'd be bringing the best of the Taj with us, wouldn't we?"

Benny looked at Jasmine, his mouth hanging open. "Is this really a good idea?"

She shook her head. "Absolutely not. But I also didn't think it was a good idea to steal a car and save Hot Dog, and that turned out pretty well for us." She shrugged. "All things considered. This is definitely not something I would have suggested before coming to the Taj, but I guess things change."

"The rest of the EW-SCABers could evacuate through the back tunnel using the SRs the McGuyvers brought down there," Ricardo said. "Whoever wants to fly back to Earth can once we're in the clear."

"We'd need a way to get up to the ship and . . ." Trevone paused for a moment, calculating. "A way to get Benny to be able to touch the side of it and create an entrance." He pointed at the spot on the screen where the smaller crafts had been coming from. "This would appear to be the best place to dock. It could be a hangar of some sort."

"Uh, guys, look around you," Drue said. He motioned to the prototype Pinky had pointed out to them earlier—the one with the metal disks that shot out of the bottom, hypothetically giving Elijah the ability to safely land on a passing comet. "This thing was basically *designed* to hijack a ship."

"What do you think, Benny?" Hot Dog asked.

"You could always hand the glove off to one of us," Ricardo said. "If you're not up to it."

Benny wasn't sure about this at all, but it did seem like the only option that might not end disastrously for the Alpha Maraudi or the humans. Dr. Bale and Drue's father obviously weren't going to listen to them, but maybe they could reason with the aliens instead. Even if they couldn't, this would buy them more time.

It was a risky move, but it could work. And in Benny's gut, it felt right. Even if it sounded insane, it was at least something they could try.

"This would be incredibly dangerous," he said. "No one has to go along with this plan. I understand if you're scared. I totally am, too." He looked around at his friends. "There's no shame in staying here and hiding out."

A few moments of silence passed. Then Hot Dog spoke.

"We followed you out into deep space to shoot a bunch of asteroids and ended up in a space battle," she said. "Hijacking an alien ship probably isn't *that* much worse, right?"

"Yeah, and there's no way I'd let you guys leave me here and go play hero without me," Drue added.

Ricardo and Trevone glanced at each other. "We're in," Ricardo said.

Jasmine smiled a little and nodded. Ramona just shrugged.

"Okay," Benny said, letting out a long breath. Despite everything, he felt good having his platoon at his back. "Then let's figure out how to do this."

"This sounds very brave, but there are several variables I'm worried about," Pinky chimed in. "For example, if the aliens saw you going for their mother ship, surely some of the fighters would disengage the Earth forces and try to stop you."

"Yeah," Benny said, an electric idea buzzing in his brain. "We need *stealth*. We need the environmental mimicry systems that Dr. Bale has on his vehicles."

"That could work," Jasmine said, a smile growing on her face.

"Wait," Ricardo said. "Even if we did sneak aboard, we'd have the aliens on the ship to deal with. They won't exactly be friendly."

"We can see that it's sparsely manned on the scanner," Trevone said. "Most of the Maraudi on board must have been soldiers sent out to fight."

"But they're strong and superfast and some of them have knives in their hair. Not to mention whatever rock things they're using to take down Space Runners now. They are definitely not pushovers," Hot Dog said.

"Being a human statue is pretty low on the list of things I want to do in my life. We totally should have taken Dr. Bale's plasma blasters." Drue groaned.

"You're not helping."

"He's right, though," Ricardo said. "I mean, I don't love the idea of using Dr. Bale's weapons but . . . I don't know what else to do. We need *something*."

"Hey, trolls," Ramona called from behind one of the racks. She walked around the corner holding up a pair of silver gloves—the electromagnetic gauntlets that Elijah had used to move around Space Runners when he was still testing them out. "Aren't alien skellies made of metal?" she asked.

A moment of silence settled on the room before everyone

started talking at once. Jasmine was the only one who was quiet, as she tapped on the alien radar.

"Guys," she said as she raised her hand. But Benny and the others were still asking questions over each other.

"How do we know this'll work?"

"Do the gloves even turn on still?"

"How did I not think of this?"

"Guys!" Jasmine shouted. Benny was shocked into silence—Jasmine wasn't exactly the type to yell at them. But it worked: everyone shut up.

"There's a readout of their bone composition here," she continued. "That must be how Dr. Bale figured out how to scan for them. Part of their skeletal system is composed of unidentified elements, but the rest is mostly made up of a cobalt compound."

"They're ferromagnetic," Trevone said.

"So . . ." Hot Dog said. "Is that a yes, or . . . ?"

Jasmine just smiled. "Ramona, you're brilliant."

"Bingo, J.," Ramona said. "I keep telling you newbz that."

25.

"Okay, so, how do these things work?" Benny asked.
He stared down at his hands, the gold alien glove he'd
swiped from the first mother ship on the right, a new bulky
silver magnetic one on the left.

"They're very similar to the gravity gloves you used
in your video game exercise," Pinky said. "The magnetic
force is projected by the band on the knuckles and is activated by the button on the side of your index finger. Hold it
down to capture something in the magnetic field and move
it around. Press it briefly to create what I suppose could
be called a single burst. Hit it twice, and you'll reverse the
magnetic pull."

"Yeah, I think I'll be skipping any pulls, thanks," Hot
Dog said. "The last thing I want is a tentacle monster flying at me."

"Mine's not working," Drue said, furiously mashing the

button on the side of his glove.

"There's a power switch on the wrist," Pinky said. "But I highly suggest that you not turn it on until you're actually ready to use it. You're in a relatively small room full of metal and handling a piece of equipment you've never used before."

"I'll be careful," Drue said, tapping the wrist of the glove. "We *need* to test these out before we try to use them against an ET." He held his fist out at one of the prototype models a few feet away. "To me, my Space Runner!" he said.

Drue hit the button on the side twice, and suddenly he flew through the air, his fist ramming into the side of the car, denting the passenger door.

"OW!" he shouted.

"Drue!" Benny and Hot Dog both yelled.

He got to his feet, rubbing his shoulder. "I thought you said this would reverse the pull. It nearly took my arm off."

"Ah, I forgot to warn you that the opposite pull is quite weaker than the normal mode. You're limited to lifting things proportional to your own body weight, or else you'll be pulled toward your target."

Drue tapped the wrist of the glove, turning it off. "Maybe you shoulda mentioned that up front."

"I wonder if this is why the Alpha Maraudi tech seems to

be so mineral based," Jasmine said as she flexed her fingers inside a glove. "Encasing yourself in metal and electricity when your bones are metallic seems a little problematic."

"Possibly," Trevone said. "Just imagine what an electromagnetic bomb might do to them."

Jasmine shuddered.

"How many more of these gloves do we have?" Benny asked.

"There's a whole box of them back here," Drue said, running over to the racks. "Maybe twenty? I'm gonna toss them in the back of the Comet Catcher and take them with us."

"The what?" Hot Dog asked.

"We need to call it *something*." He set the box down beside the specialized Space Runner. "It's not just a normal SR."

"Comet Catcher." She nodded. "I like it."

Ricardo walked down the row of Space Runner models against the wall, pulling dust covers off a few of them as he went. "Most of these are relics. They run basically the same as a modern Space Runner, but have different interface systems. Pinky can't control them." He paused, glancing at Trevone. "We should be the ones to pilot the older models. We know how they run."

"Um," Jasmine said, taking a step forward and raising

her gloved hand. "I would kind of like to ride with someone. If that's okay."

"Same," Ramona said. "I get carsick."

"Of course," Benny said. "You're our strategist, Jazz. Just like with the asteroid storm. Keep your eyes on the radar and call our shots for us. Ramona, can you help her out?"

Ramona gave a thumbs-up.

"You two can ride in my car," Trevone said.

"Hot Dog, you're the best EW-SCAB pilot, so you're going to take the lead in the . . ." Ricardo paused. "In the *Comet Catcher*. The controls are fairly similar to what you're used to, with a few quirks, given the customization. Think you can manage it?"

"Ha," Hot Dog said. "No sweat."

"I'll stay in your ear just in case you need a hand," Pinky said.

"Okay," Benny said, "so I can use my holographic band to sneak out, break into the garage with my alien glove, and steal the stealth boxes from Dr. Bale's cars. We'll go invisible and save the day." He blinked, swallowing hard, thinking about how far a journey it was from the basement-level storeroom to the garage. "Easy."

"Uh, no," Hot Dog said. "You are not doing all this alone. Let's just open up the ceiling and all go out there together." She made a fist with her gloved hand. "We'll watch your back."

"That would give the aliens plenty of time to destroy the Comet Catcher," Jasmine said. "Not to mention, we'd be exposing ourselves."

"We need to do this as discreetly as possible," Ricardo said. "And we need to be *fast*."

Drue made a noise that was not quite a gasp, not quite a squeak. "Moon motorcycle," he whispered. And then he was shouting. "MOON MOTORCYCLE!"

"*Galax*icle," Pinky said.

"What*ever*. Benny! This is the best idea I've ever had. Please, *please*, let me drive you to the garage."

"A vehicle that small could maneuver through the Taj hallways fairly easily," Trevone said hesitantly.

"I should pilot it," Ricardo said, his brow furrowing. "It's a delicate piece of machinery."

"No way." Drue crossed his arms. "Benny and I got this. Besides, you need to stay down here and be ready to drive one of those dusty old models."

"It's not a terrible idea," Benny said, though he wasn't exactly sure about that. "And Drue's right. Once we're headed back with the stealth boxes, we'll want to move quickly. You should be waiting in the driver's seat."

"I'll remind you that the Galaxicle is not practical for

space travel," Pinky said. "It leaves the rider far too exposed. There's no shielding."

"It will totally make it up to that big rock ship I bet," Drue said. "No prob."

"We'll jump in Hot Dog's car when we're back," Benny corrected him.

"Fine." Drue sighed. Then he smirked. "We'll see what happens."

Ricardo looked at the two boys for a long moment before finally nodding. "Okay."

"Yes!" Drue said, slapping Benny on the back. "This is the best day of my life!"

They all turned and stared at him in silence.

"Well," he continued, "I mean, if you took everything except this ride out of the picture."

Benny glanced down at his golden glove. Jasmine was right: this could be their best chance of figuring out a solution to not only their problems but those of the Alpha Maraudi as well. And Benny wasn't going to let anyone down.

There was a loud bang somewhere above them, followed by a wrenching sound of metal on metal.

"One of the Earth SRs just slid into the east wing," Trevone said. "Minimal damage to the resort and the vehicle, but it's grounded for sure." He looked to Benny. "You should get moving."

"Okay," Ricardo said, coming up to the side of the yellow

motorcycle-shaped vehicle Drue had already mounted. "So, these buttons—"

"I got this," Drue said. "Trust me. In the time between finding out this baby existed and discovering that alien rock was growing over the Grand Dome, I was reading up on every spec and detail of this thing in Elijah's prototype files." He stroked the handlebars in front of him. "She's perfect."

Benny stood beside the slim vehicle. "You sure this'll hold two people?" he asked.

"What, you want a sidecar?" Drue asked. "Climb on. There's special gravity tech in the seat that'll keep you from flying off."

Benny slid onto the back of the seat. Drue tapped a few buttons on the small holographic display beneath the handlebars. A slight vibration shot through the Galaxicle, accompanied by a whirring noise as the two circular hyper-drive engines that were housed where tires would normally be came to life. They were rimmed in neon blue light.

"Guys," Hot Dog said. "Please be careful out there."

"Safety first," Drue said, tapping the collar of his space suit and manually deploying his force field helmet.

"If we're fast enough, we can come back, install the stealth drives, and *then* open the ceiling," Benny said. "While we're gone, maybe figure out what we're going to do once we're inside that ship?"

"The hallway outside is clear right now," Pinky said.

Drue bent down low, hovering over the handlebars. "Open the door, Pinks," he said. "Let's see what this beast can do."

"We'll be ready when you get back," Jasmine said.

The wall slid open on the other end of the room.

"Hang on, Benny," Drue said, utter glee filling his voice.

And then they were zooming forward so quickly that Benny felt certain he would tumble off the back, despite whatever tech was holding him down on the seat. The Galaxicle shot through the opening in the wall and came to a complete stop in the hallway all in the span of a second.

"Oh, man, this thing handles like a dream," Drue whispered as he rotated the bike. "You ready for this?"

Benny knocked on the back of Drue's helmet with his fist. "Get us to the garage."

Drue screamed with excitement as they raced through the hallway, the Taj around them nothing but a blur to Benny. In seconds they were in the stairwell, and as Drue pulled on the handlebars the Galaxicle reared back like he was popping a wheelie and flew up the steps. Benny couldn't help but laugh—not because any of this was funny, but because in his anxiousness he couldn't keep the sound from bubbling up inside him. Drue was doing a great job of driving them, no doubt, but it was still a terrifyingly fast ride. Benny thought about closing his eyes through the whole thing, but that seemed like it would make things even worse.

In the lobby, there were maybe five Alpha Maraudi soldiers milling about. It was hard for Benny to actually count, because Drue never touched the brakes. Instead, their bike sped out of the stairwell and toward the ceiling of the four-story room, only to dive once they were halfway across, like a bolt of yellow lightning cutting across the lobby.

Finally, when they were in the courtyard, Drue stopped.

"Holy crap," he muttered.

"Yeah," Benny agreed.

He'd watched the feeds of the courtyard from the secret storage room, but it was nothing compared to seeing what was going on in person. The dark gravel on the ground was littered with bits of broken Maraudi rock and the glittering shards that had once been a part of the Grand Dome. Farther beyond the grounds of the Taj, there were crashed vehicles—both human and alien—dotting the lunar landscape, embedded in the rocky terrain of the Moon, smoke and dust hanging around them.

Above Benny and Drue, shiny chrome Space Runners darted through space, bolts of gold shooting from weapons mounted on their hoods. The Alpha Maraudi ships were weaving around them and firing back silver energy. Benny watched as one of them shot something dark and glowing that hit a Space Runner, knocking it toward the Moon.

Rock began to grow over the car as it fell from the sky.

Looming over all this in the background was the giant rock mother ship, a good twenty miles away from the battlefield, at least. And farther back still, Earth, which felt much too far away for Benny's liking.

As his brain struggled to take in the hundreds of ships above them, he could make out no clear indication of who was winning the battle—if *anyone* was. All he knew was that the sky was filled with complete chaos.

And then he realized that below them, the handful of Alpha Maraudi in the courtyard had noticed the yellow bike floating near the entrance to the Taj.

26.

The Alpha Maraudi soldiers on the ground bounded toward them, their tentacles thrashing around their heads.

"Look out!" Benny shouted as one of the aliens with gold on its armor threw a glowing rock at them.

Drue swerved to the left, narrowly dodging the piece of alien mineral. Drawing from his experience in the fight with the holographic robots he'd had a week before, Benny punched his left fist out in front of him and smashed his finger against the button on the side of his glove. The band across his knuckles lit up. For a second, he didn't think anything was actually happening. Then he flicked his wrist to one side, and the alien went flying through the air, slamming against the side of the Taj.

"Ahhh!" he shouted, letting go of the button. "It works!"

And then debris everywhere, all around Benny and Drue—shards of the broken dome and pieces of alien rock that the Maraudi were grabbing with their tentacles and hurling at them.

Drue jerked the handlebars, the Galaxicle weaving around in a quick, irregular pattern. "Hold on," he yelled.

They raced across the courtyard at such a speed that Benny was sure they were going to crash head on into the pulsing rock that had grown over the front of the garage, but Drue swerved at the last minute and hit the brakes. They came to an abrupt stop inches away from the front of the building.

"Do your thing," Drue said as he held his silver fist out, tapping the button on his magnetic glove a few times and sending several aliens across the courtyard sprawling to the ground. "Oh, man, am I glad I played so many first-person shooters back on Earth," he whispered.

"There are three Maraudi inside," Pinky said through the comms. "I've just pinned them down with SR trainers, but you need to hurry. I don't know how long I can hold them. The cars weren't exactly meant to be used this way."

Benny raised his golden glove and slammed it down onto the alien rock so hard that he couldn't feel his palm— and immediately worried that he'd broken every bone in his hand. But he hadn't, and as the rock began to crumble Benny kept punching at it. Drue dropped the Galaxicle closer to the ground, until enough of the door was free that

Pinky could slide it open for them to get through.

"We're clear!" Benny said.

Drue turned the handlebars with one hand and sent them flying inside.

Now that Pinky wasn't diverting so much of the Taj's energy into trying to keep the Grand Dome up and running, the overhead lights were back on, the huge space of the garage lit up and gleaming, like worlds weren't at war above them. Drue hesitated for only a split second to look around, taking stock of his surroundings. Sure enough, Pinky had two Alpha Maraudi soldiers pinned to the walls—and one to the dark cement floor—using the laser-mounted Space Runners they'd flown into the asteroid storm days before. Drue shot the Galaxicle over to the end of the room where Dr. Bale's temporary base had been set up and landed. It took Benny a few seconds to get his footing once he jumped off the bike—he'd been gripping the sides of the superfast floating motorbike with his legs so hard that his muscles were cramped up.

"I'll take the Tank and the trailers," he said as he hobbled over to Dr. Bale's custom Space Runner. "You take the other two SRs. The cloaking devices are black boxes that should be stuck to the dashboards somewhere."

"Gotcha," Drue said, sprinting to the cars that Todd and Mae had driven in from the dark side.

It didn't take Benny long to get inside the Tank and swipe the stealth drive. His legs finally starting to feel normal again, he bolted to one of the trailers, then the other.

When he came out of the second, thrilled with how well this all seemed to be going, the floor of the garage was shifting. Dr. Bale and his assistants were rising on a platform out of their hiding spot beneath the cement. All three were holding weapons, pointing them around the room cautiously. A drone floated above their heads.

"What the devil is going on?" Dr. Bale asked. When his eyes landed on Benny, he frowned. "The Earth forces are supposed to be taking back the garage and liberating us. I thought that's what all this noise was."

"Doctor!" Mae shouted.

"The Maraudi!" Todd said.

Dr. Bale's eyes widened when he saw the closest of the Alpha Maraudi pinned against the wall. He took a deep breath, shifted his weight, and raised his weapon to aim at the alien.

"No!" Benny shouted. He shoved his left fist forward and tapped the button on his index finger. Dr. Bale's gun flew from his hands. Behind him, Drue must have been using his magnetic glove, too, because Todd and Mae were just as quickly disarmed.

Dr. Bale looked at Benny, his lips curled up in a sneer.

"You still don't get it, do you?" he growled. "They would kill every last one of us."

"Yeah," Benny said. "And you'd do the same thing to them. Guess you've got that in common. Come on, Drue. Let's get out of here."

Dr. Bale darted over to one of the tables where his gear had been spread out earlier—but now there was nothing there.

"My weapons," Dr. Bale said. "What have you done with them?"

"We didn't take your weapons, dude," Drue said.

Then who did? Benny wondered, but there wasn't time to worry—they needed to get back to the others, fast.

"I don't know what you think you're doing, but whatever it is, you're wrong." Dr. Bale was shouting now. "You'll find out soon enough. This universe is full of terrors you couldn't even comprehend. You're just children, and your mucking around is going to get us all killed."

"Yeah, yeah," Drue said as he hopped back onto the bike. "I kinda seem to remember us beating these alien punks before."

"This isn't over yet," Dr. Bale said. "Not by a long shot."

"Pinky," Benny said, "I don't want to hear him anymore."

"We will save humanity no matter what the—" Dr. Bale

continued, but his voice stopped piping through Benny's collar midsentence.

"There you go," Pinky said. "If only I could do the same for myself."

Benny jumped on the back of the bike floating a few inches off the ground as Drue attached one of the stealth boxes to the front of the handlebars.

"Let's get invisible," he said, pushing the button on the device. It blinked red for a split second.

The Galaxicle disappeared.

Unfortunately, they did not.

"Oh," Drue said. "Not cool."

"Well, I guess this is less obvious than a big yellow motorbike," Benny said. "It should work on the SRs, though. Let's get back down there."

Pinky slid the door open as they jetted across the garage.

"Okay, Pinky, tell the others we're—" Benny started.

There was an explosion outside as golden bolts shot from above—the Earth Space Runners were raining havoc on the courtyard. Drue twisted the handlebars and hit the brakes, bringing the Galaxicle to a halt in the doorway. As the assault continued the ground shook so violently that the Taj itself seemed to sway. The alien ships parked on the dark gravel were completely obliterated, leaving nothing but the smallest pieces of wreckage. Benny's stomach clenched—his friends were just below the heart of the attack.

"Pinky! Hot Dog! Jazz!" he shouted. "Is everyone okay?"

"We're fine, but it felt like bombs were going off above us," Ricardo said. "What happened?"

Benny watched as four silver Space Runners descended, parking beside the garage. There were emblems on the hoods that Benny didn't recognize.

"Let's go," Benny said.

But Drue didn't move. His eyes were locked on the new arrivals from Earth. Five people emerged from the Space Runners and began marching toward the garage—toward *Dr. Bale*, he assumed. Benny recognized the man leading the pack.

"Dad," Drue said.

"Oh, boy," Benny whispered.

"Dad!" Drue shouted. And then their Galaxicle sped forward, out of the garage, coming to such an abrupt stop a few feet in front of the approaching adults that Benny thought they might flip end over end.

There were immediately four weapons trained on them. Senator Lincoln stood there with his brow furrowed, hands at his sides, trying to process what was happening. Here was his son, seemingly floating in midair in the Taj's courtyard. Benny assumed it wasn't at all what he had expected to find seconds after landing on the Moon.

Finally, the man motioned to the others and the weapons were lowered.

"Pinky, connect us," Drue said, handing the extra stealth drive to Benny.

"I'm already on it," Pinky replied.

Drue slid off the bike and took a few steps toward his father. He straightened his back, standing tall. "Hi, sir."

"Drue," the man said, in barely more than a stunned whisper. Then his voice took a hard edge. "What do you think you're doing? I told you to go back to Earth." He glanced at Benny, narrowing his eyes as he gave him a once-over, and then turned his attention back to his son.

"I . . ." Drue started. "I'm sorry, but I couldn't. I tried to tell you, I'm helping up here, and—"

"Helping?" Senator Lincoln asked. He spread his arms wide. "Is *this* you helping? We're in the middle of a war zone."

"You don't understand," Benny said, getting off the bike, too, cradling the stealth drives in his arms. He stepped to Drue's side. "We're trying to find a way to save Earth *without* killing an entire species. To avoid all *this*." He jerked his head up to the battle above them.

"Of all the . . ." Senator Lincoln started, keeping his eyes focused on his son. "You have a child's understanding of how the world—the *solar system*—actually works. This is a matter of preserving the human species. We have no choice. We must do whatever it takes to survive. There's no room for error or time to think about bleeding-heart alternatives."

"Dad, please, if you'll just listen to us—" Drue said.

"That's enough." His father cut him off, pointing a finger at his son's face. "You don't have a say in this matter. You're going back to Earth whether you want to or not." He motioned to one of the other men, who started toward Drue. "Get him on a course back to DC."

Drue turned, darting for the Galaxicle.

But it wasn't there. Or, rather, it *was* there—just invisible.

"Crap!" he said. "Stupid stealth works too well!"

The person Senator Lincoln had motioned to brushed past Benny and grabbed Drue by the arm, dragging him back toward the silver Space Runners.

"Let me go!" Drue shouted, squirming in vain against the man's grip.

"This is for your own good," his father said.

"Hey!" Benny said, running forward, but the other men were faster than him and were already holding his arms back, the stealth drives falling to the ground. He looked around, trying to figure out a way to help his friend.

That's when he saw it: one of the Earth Space Runners was falling toward the courtyard, smoke streaming from its hood and leaving a thick gray line in the sky.

It was headed straight for them.

"Drue!" Benny shouted, struggling against the men holding him. "Incoming!"

All of them looked up at the silver missile of a vehicle rocketing toward them. There was no hope that they'd all get out of the way in time. Senator Lincoln cried out, raising his arms and covering his face.

Only, the Space Runner didn't hit them. Instead, it froze in the air, its hood just a few feet away from the senator's head. Through the windshield, Benny could just make out the face of the pilot, her mouth and eyes wide, trying to figure out what was going on.

Drue stood there, one arm still held by his father's flunky. The other was outstretched, his gloved fist clenched, the band across the knuckles glowing.

No one moved for a few seconds, until Drue's father finally looked up at the Space Runner, and then back at his son, baffled.

"*This* is me helping, sir," Drue said as he set the Space Runner off to one side. "Ow, ow, ow," he muttered. "This glove is totally overheating."

The man who'd been dragging Drue toward the parked Earth SRs took a few steps back, staring at the boy's glove. Benny managed to slip out of the hands of the guys who'd stopped him and hurried to his friend's side.

"What did you do?" Drue's father asked.

Drue shrugged. "I haven't *just* been racing SRs up here, Dad."

Before the Senator could respond, one of his men was shouting. Benny turned to see a dozen Alpha Maraudi soldiers swarming out of the front of the Taj. They carried black devices in their tentacles, and it took Benny a second to realize what they were: Dr. Bale's weapons.

As Benny gasped, the Alpha Maraudi opened fire.

27.

Shots of gold energy filled the courtyard as the
Alpha Maraudi fired Dr. Bale's weapons at them. Benny
darted for the stealth drives he'd dropped on the gravel
as Drue and the group from Earth took cover behind the
parked Space Runners. He managed to grab the devices off
the ground without ever slowing his stride, and in a flash
he was back with Drue, crouched behind one of the silver
vehicles.

Drue's father yelled at someone through his comm,
which was still linked to Benny's helmet. "Get me air support!"

Benny searched for the Galaxicle, but it was no use—the
stealth technology had worked *too* well. With aliens spilling
out of the resort's front entrance, Benny realized there was
only one way of getting back to his friends now, even if it
was dangerous.

"Pinky!" Benny shouted. "Change of plans. Tell the others to get in their cars and then open the ceiling. Hurry!"

A line of Earth Space Runners swooped in from above and fired on the aliens, forcing them to retreat for a moment. Benny looked toward the statue in the center of the courtyard. The big chrome hand was mangled now, but it was still able to move, along with a large section of the courtyard ground around it. As older, slightly scuffed-up black Space Runners flew out of the new hole, Benny handed half of the stealth drives to Drue, keeping two for himself.

"I'm on it," Drue said, looking over his shoulder at the Alpha Maraudi.

"Where do you think you're going?" his father asked from behind one of the nearby Space Runners.

"I'm gonna help save a couple of worlds," Drue said.

"Drue, we don't have time for this." The man slammed his fist against the side of the car he was crouched behind. "You are a Lincoln. One day, when we've molded you into a commander worthy of your name, you'll understand that your place is not as a grunt on the front lines trying to talk peace with an enemy."

"I may be a Lincoln," Drue said, flashing his perfect white teeth at his father, "but I'm also a founding member of the Moon Platoon."

He sprinted toward the Pit Crew's vehicles that were now floating by the fountain. Benny was on his heels, glancing back to try to make sure he stayed out of the sights of the aliens.

"Pinky," Drue said, his breath short as he ran. "I know this is weird, but make sure my dad's okay up here. Please."

"I'll do everything I can," the AI said through the comms.

Hot Dog's Comet Catcher was the last of the cars to fly up. Benny headed straight for it. Meanwhile, Jasmine opened the passenger door of Trevone's car. Drue tossed one of the stealth drives to her, which she juggled for a few seconds before closing the door again. And then, the car was gone. Invisible.

"Incredible," she said over the comms.

Another line of Earth's forces flew by, raining gold bolts of energy on a back section of the courtyard near them.

"We can't stay here like this," Trevone said. "We'll get caught in the crossfire."

"Head for the mother ship," Ricardo crackled over the comms. "We'll regroup there."

Hot Dog opened the pilot-side door as Benny approached.

"It is insane up here," she said as he handed her a stealth drive. "Get *in*."

He started around the car just as another wave of attacks erupted around him. Hot Dog slammed her door shut as gold beams of energy bounced off the side of the car. Benny looked back—the Alpha Maraudi were firing on them, charging from the garage and the main entrance to the Taj.

"The antigravity shields are holding for now," Hot Dog said, "but we need to go."

Benny was rounding the front bumper when something hit his back, causing him to stumble. His suit didn't seem to be leaking oxygen as he regained his footing, but a small spot between his shoulder blades was buzzing and felt suddenly hot—and the feeling was spreading over his shoulders.

By the time he realized that there was alien rock growing over him, his upper arms were already frozen in place.

"No!" Hot Dog shouted, opening her door.

"Don't come closer!" Benny yelled. "It might get you, too."

He turned his head to look at her while he still could. Her big eyes were wide as she stared at him. Farther behind her, Drue jumped into Ricardo's car before the Space Runner seemed to blink out of existence.

"Go," Benny shouted. "I'll be fine, just get out of here. I'll take another SR. There are trainers in the garage."

She blinked at him. And then the rock grew over the front of his helmet, until finally he was enveloped by darkness.

"Hello?" he called out, but there was no response from the comms. Not even from Pinky. The rock was blocking all his communications.

Benny tried to take a deep, heaving breath, but his chest couldn't inflate because of the minerals he was now encapsulated in. Oxygen continued to pour through his helmet, but that didn't help with the claustrophobia and sheer terror coursing through him as he realized he wasn't able to move a single muscle. He could hear his blood thrumming in his ears. All around him, the rock buzzed, like at any moment it might constrict. He thought of the Grand Dome, and the sight of all that superdurable polymer shattering. The only thing he had protecting him was a thin space suit.

He tried to move the alien glove, but he couldn't. His hand and wrist were just as stuck as the rest of his body.

The ground below shuddered. Around him, the battle continued.

He felt light-headed, and his heart hammered so hard he thought it might break the alien rock off him on its own. But he wasn't that lucky—he remained a statue in the middle of the Taj's courtyard, completely unaware of what was going on outside. Utterly helpless. He may as well have been stuck in a sandstorm in the Drylands, completely lost.

What he needed to do was calm down and focus. He knew this, but it was difficult to imagine actually doing it with his pulse firing like a fission engine in overdrive, thoughts flying through his mind at Star Runner speeds. Still, he tried. He closed his eyes and concentrated on his breathing, trying to get it back on track before he completely hyperventilated and passed out. He tried to center himself, imagining that he was sitting on top of the RV and looking into the horizon of the Drylands. He imagined, too, that Justin and Alejandro and his grandmother were all in the little house on wheels below him, getting dinner ready or sleeping, lost in dreams.

Somewhere up on Earth, they *were* in the RV. Benny knew this, but he reminded himself of it over and over again. He wasn't going to let this be the end of his fight to save them.

As his pulse began to slow down, he was able to think more rationally. Apart from all the buzzing around his body, his right hand was warm. There was no use trying to move, but he focused on his palm, attempting to wriggle the muscles in his hand as best he could. He still had no idea how this alien technology strapped to his hand worked, despite Dr. Bale's hypotheses, and so Benny just hoped for the best and concentrated every ounce of his energy on the glove.

It felt like it was heating up.

There was a stirring in the rock around him—something shifting—and suddenly he could wriggle his fingers and move his hand. He didn't have much range of motion but, straining, he managed to touch his chest—just barely. The alien substance seemed to melt off him, freeing more and more of his muscles. He could take deep breaths again.

He brought his hand to his head, and suddenly light was pouring through his helmet. He blinked, his eyes readjusting, and then looked down to find that the bottom half of his body was still encapsulated in the alien minerals, as though he were an ice cube that had partially melted only to be refrozen.

"Come in," he shouted as he slammed his hand down against the rock, causing it to crumble. "Anybody there?"

"Benny!" Hot Dog shouted. "Thank goodness. I was just about to come try to ram you or something to break you out of that thing. Are you okay?"

There was another barrage of golden bolts from the sky. The Alpha Maraudi were still surging out of the Taj. Across the courtyard, two of the Earth Space Runners had been covered in the alien rock. He could see several of the men still hunkered down there, trying to fight back.

"Sort of," he said, dashing for the cover of the Space Runners.

"Everyone else is on their way to the dark side," she said. "But I'm still here. Don't die. I'm coming for you."

Benny's eyes landed on a rock figure a few feet away from him—one of the men from Earth had been encapsulated. He darted over to it, slamming his palm against the statue's chest and causing the rock to crumble.

As the mineral fell away, he realized it was Drue's father.

The man was wide-eyed, his chest heaving, but he didn't shake or stumble.

"What in the name of . . . ?" he started as he and Benny took cover behind one of the SRs.

"The aliens can cover you in rock," Benny said. "You gotta watch out for that."

"I'm coming down," Hot Dog said over the comms. "I'll stop and turn off the invisibility and you can jump in."

Another wave of bolts fired from above.

"No, it's too risky," Benny said. "You might get hit by one of the Earth SRs if they can't see you."

"Okay, so I'll come in without any stealth, no problem."

"The aliens might hit you with one of their rocks!"

"Psh," she said. "Benny, I don't call myself an ace pilot for nothing."

Benny looked down at the silver glove on his left hand. A piston fired in his brain.

"Okay," Benny said. "But don't stop. Just blaze through the courtyard."

"What?" she asked. "But how . . ."

He clenched his fist. "Just trust me, Hot Dog."

"Okay. I'm going to make a pass by the fountain, then. Yeah?"

"Yeah," Benny said.

He spotted her red Comet Catcher in the distance,

shooting straight for the courtyard. He started toward the fountain, but someone grabbed his arm.

It was Senator Lincoln. "Wait," he said.

Benny looked back at him. The man was shaking the last remnants of the rock off his shoulders.

"Make sure my son is safe," he said.

Benny stared at him for a few seconds before nodding. "I will. But that means I have to go. Now."

And then he was sprinting across the courtyard as Hot Dog's custom SR dipped and weaved, avoiding shots from the Alpha Maraudi *and* friendly fire from the Earth forces.

"I see you!" she said. "Don't tell me you're going to jump on the hood or something. I don't want to kill you."

"Just don't stop!" he said.

He raised his left hand and mashed the button on the side of the magnetic glove twice as the Comet Catcher shot past him. In an instant, he flew through the courtyard, yanked so hard that he thought his fist might be ripped from his body. But it wasn't, and within seconds they were flying above the Taj, Benny magnetically attached to the trunk of the Space Runner. He climbed on top of it as best he could and took one look back to the courtyard, where Drue's dad was staring up at them. Seconds later, the man was too small to make out.

"You are insane," Hot Dog said as she turned the stealth back on so that Benny looked like he was flying on his own,

308

like some kind of cosmic superhero jetting through space. "Are you okay back there?"

"I think so," he said. Then he shivered. "Uh, maybe set us down somewhere away from the battlefield before we go all the way to the mother ship? It's *really* cold out here."

28.

They parked briefly so Benny could hop off the trunk and into the passenger seat, and then they soared invisibly through space toward the giant floating hunk of rock. Benny couldn't help but remember that the last time he was riding shotgun in a Space Runner Hot Dog was piloting, they were trying to get *away* from an alien vessel almost just like the one they were about to attempt to board.

"This is a crazy idea," Hot Dog said.

"Yeah," Benny agreed. "I know. But I don't want to back out now."

"Well, of course not. Just because it's crazy doesn't mean it's not good." She twitched her nose. "I hope."

Ahead of them, the giant alien ship, which had seemed to be floating stationary above the Moon, began to shoot forward—away from the Taj.

"What's going on?" Benny asked.

Hot Dog reached forward and tapped on the dashboard. "Come in, Moon Platoon. We're closing in on the ship, but it looks like it's flying away!"

"I hope you're close," Trevone said. "We've been monitoring the battle above the Taj. I think the alien fighters are actually losing to the Earth forces. I imagine they were unprepared for such a counteroffensive. At this rate, their entire fleet will be taken out."

"They're leaving without their fighter pilots?" Benny asked.

"It's possible they want the Earth forces to stay distracted by those smaller ships while this larger one escapes," Jasmine said.

"They're sacrificial pawns," Drue said.

"Like I said, it's *possible*. We're not sure. The radar is picking up a dozen alien life-forms inside the larger ship. Most of them are gathered in one area—probably the bridge. I'm trying to map a route inside as best I can with the various scans I'm collecting, but we might be playing it by ear once we're in there."

"Push your hyperdrives, boys," Hot Dog said, tapping on the dash. "Let's get onto that ship before it goes into light speed or something."

"I've been in touch with Sahar and the twins underground," Trevone said. "They're on standby, awaiting our status. Many of the EW-SCABers are reluctant to leave the

Moon, but one of them named Iyabo has managed to talk almost everyone into thinking it's a good idea. She is apparently really selling the fact that it would be bad to destroy an alien species. It also sounds like she has a deep-seated distrust for 'a bunch of old dudes who think they're always right.'"

"Let's not get ahead of ourselves," Ricardo chimed in. "I don't want anyone coming up here until we've secured the ship."

"What *are* we going to do with the aliens that are inside?" Drue asked.

"Commander Tull spoke English," Benny said. "We can try to reason with them."

"That didn't go so well with Dr. Bale."

"This is different," Benny said, staring down at his gloved hands. "The Alpha Maraudi are defeated. And we know about a superweapon that could destroy their entire planet. Well, we know it exists, at least. That's got to count for something, right? We have to try to get them to listen to us. To *work* with us."

"And if not?" Drue asked.

There was silence on the comms. Finally, Ricardo spoke. "Like Jasmine said. We'll have to play a few things by ear."

"I'm sending coordinates for what we believe to be the ship's hangar to you, Hot Dog," Jasmine said.

On the windshield in front of Benny, a blinking dot appeared.

"Got it," Hot Dog said. "We're going in."

As she flew the Comet Catcher toward the hulking rock vessel, Benny kept his eyes on their target spot, looking for some sort of shift in the exterior or any indication that the Alpha Maraudi had spotted them. But there was no sign of movement as they approached—Dr. Bale's stolen tech was working.

"You ready for this?" Hot Dog asked.

"No," Benny replied. He smiled. "Let's do it."

She nodded as they approached the side of the rock, Jasmine's ping mostly transparent and taking up the majority of their windshield as they closed in. With a slight rotation of the flight yoke, their car twisted, until the bottom of the custom Space Runner was parallel to the alien ship.

"Here goes nothing," Hot Dog said as she hit a few holographic buttons on the dash.

There was a slight jolt from the bottom of the craft as the two metal disks shot off, embedding themselves in the side of the mother ship.

"And now I just have to . . . ." Hot Dog murmured to herself as she tapped a hologram.

The Comet Catcher suddenly jerked through space, planting itself on the metal circles.

"Wow, okay," she said after a moment. "Those are some really strong magnets." She hit the comms. "We're attached."

"We're right behind you, but hurry," Ricardo said. "This thing is picking up speed."

"Here," Hot Dog said as she opened up the console between her and Benny and pulled out a silver wire. She handed it to him. "Just in case something happens and our car falls off, you won't be stuck on the side of an alien ship for the rest of your short life. I'll yank you back inside."

"Thanks," Benny said, wrapping the wire around his left wrist.

"Don't thank me. Pinky told us about it."

"You're welcome," the AI's voice sounded in his helmet. "Would you like me to depressurize the cabin now?"

"Do it," Benny said.

Both of their force field helmets powered on as the atmosphere inside the Space Runner changed.

"Whenever you're ready," Pinky said. "Be careful, Benny."

He took a deep breath, opened the passenger door, and then slid out into the weightlessness of space, twisting and holding on to the bottom of the car in order to try to keep his bearings. He'd been weightless in the video game chamber at the Taj and while reverse bungie jumping on the first days of his EW-SCAB trip, but never like this, traveling at high speeds in actual space. Finally, he positioned himself so that he could get his golden-gloved hand onto the ship's surface.

It occurred to him only then that he hadn't really planned on *how* to get through. He'd imagined himself slamming his fist against the outside and breaking open a hole for them, but that might mean dislodging the Comet Catcher before he had a chance to make an entrance big enough for the Space Runners. So instead he paused for a moment, thinking about how he'd manipulated the rock—accidentally—around Sahar's car, and how he'd melted it off himself just minutes before. When he'd been on the last alien mother ship, he'd watched an Alpha Maraudi control the doors with little more than a gesture—there had to be a way of getting in without *breaking* in. And so he placed his hand on the exterior of the ship and focused, visualizing the rock changing, giving way.

At first nothing happened. He groaned, pressing down harder, the soles of his boots on the Space Runner behind him for leverage. He swiped his hand across the surface, like he was trying to simply scrub the exterior of the ship away. And then, slowly, the rock began to change. It pulsed with energy and started to swirl, opening up.

He pushed off the Space Runner with his feet, hoping that adding some kind of force would make the rock open faster.

It did. In seconds there was a wide, circular hole in front of him, opening into a huge room made up of the same smooth, greenish rock as the secret alien base and the other mother ship had been filled with. Farther inside, he could see several of the purple Maraudi fighter ships. As far as he could tell, there was no movement. The place looked abandoned.

"It worked," he whispered to himself, staring down at his hand.

Then there was a sudden jerk on his left wrist—Hot Dog was reeling him back in.

Once he was back in the passenger seat, he closed the door and found Hot Dog staring at him.

"You did it," she said. "I kind of can't believe something didn't go horribly wrong."

"Yet." Benny grinned at her. "Let's get in there."

She hit the dashboard, and the Comet Catcher detached, along with the metal disks. In a flash she'd spun the car around and they were inside, parking near the new hole.

"We've landed!" Hot Dog shouted over the comms.

Benny hit the button on the stealth drive, causing the car to go visible again. "Make sure you turn off your stealth before you get out of your SR," he said. "We learned that lesson the hard way earlier."

"I'll never forget about you, Galaxicle," Drue said. "We'll see each other again one day. I promise."

As Trevone and Ricardo coordinated who would enter the ship first, Benny and Hot Dog got out, cautiously taking a look around. The hanger was huge, bigger than the garage back at the Taj, and the walls curved up to a high ceiling covered in brightly glowing stalactites.

"Jazz, there aren't any aliens around here, right?" Benny asked.

"Not according to the scanner," she said through the comms.

"You know," Hot Dog said, taking a look at the handful of alien ships parked in the corner, "a few weeks ago if someone told me I'd be seeing the inside of an alien ship, I'd probably have freaked out. But this . . ." She motioned around. "After everything we've been through in the last few days, this is kind of boring."

"I'll remind you that you said that when we're trying to get control of the ship from the Alpha Maraudi," Benny said.

"You're right. I take it back."

Within a few minutes, Trevone and Ricardo had parked their Space Runners, and the original Moon Platoon and the two oldest members of the Pit Crew were gathered near the hole in the side of the hangar. Ramona wobbled a bit on her feet, but slowly the color began to return to her pale cheeks. Benny hoped she wasn't going to be sick. Especially since her helmet was still activated.

"This place . . ." Trevone said, looking around. "I have so many questions. The first of which is why there don't appear to be any doors."

"This is what the other hangar was like," Hot Dog said. "It was completely sealed off."

"Perhaps for reasons of pressurization? Fascinating."

"We should try to close the room up before moving forward," Jasmine said. "I have no idea how the environmental systems work on the ship, obviously, but it probably isn't a good idea to leave a gaping hole in the hull if we're going to be breaking through walls."

"Benny?" Ricardo asked.

He stepped forward, placing his hand on the rock, trying to focus like he had when he'd opened the hole. As he slid his hand across the surface, the wall again began to shift, closing slowly, until it appeared to be solid.

"You're getting good at that," Drue said.

"I'm getting good at having no idea what I'm doing," Benny corrected him.

"Jasmine," Ricardo said, "get us to the bridge."

She held up Dr. Bale's radar and twisted her lips for a moment. "This way, I think," she said, leading them across the smooth floor of the hangar.

They were near the center of the room when Drue's force field helmet automatically powered down.

"What?!" he shouted, grabbing at his neck and gasping, his eyes bulging out.

"Your designer space suit is malfunctioning!" Hot Dog said, rushing to his side.

But then Drue froze and took a few deep breaths. Within seconds, the rest of their helmets had disappeared as well.

"Incredible," Trevone said, looking around. "There must be some sort of automated environmental system."

"It's not *that* impressive," Pinky said through their comms. "I could do the same thing."

They continued, until they were standing in front of a solid wall.

Everyone turned to look at Benny.

"Here goes nothing," he said, stepping up.

"Make sure your magnetic gloves are turned on," Ricardo said. "We want to be ready for anything."

Benny raised his right hand to the wall, and after a few moments a hole appeared, jagged around the edges—not at all like the clean entrance the alien had opened and closed for them on the last big ship. He looked back at the others. Ricardo nodded to him, and he stepped through.

They found themselves in a long, curving hallway composed of pale blue, semitranslucent stone, and continued onward, Jasmine directing them. As they hurried deeper into the ship, they passed by several openings in the smooth rock that led into rooms full of computer terminals and equipment Benny didn't recognize. They could have been offices or laboratories or even bedrooms—there was no telling, given the circumstances.

"Okay, we need to turn left as soon as we can," Jasmine

said, not looking up from the radar. "I think there's a large room coming up that we can cut through."

"I see a doorway ahead," Ricardo said. He was at Benny's side, leading the pack. "Let's hustle."

They picked up their pace, and charged into the room. Benny stopped a few steps inside, the others running into him.

"Whoa," he murmured.

Before them was a sprawling chamber that looked nothing like the rest of the ship they'd seen. Trails made of purple gravel cut through what looked to Benny like yellow soil. Plants—he assumed they were plants—of fiery reds and oranges surrounded them, fronds bigger than Space Runners arching over the paths. They gave way to a rainbow of other, different vegetation. Bronze trunks were topped with glowing green teardrops. A tree in the distance appeared to be shedding gossamer threads, creating a prism-like cloud around it. In the center of the room, which Benny was pretty sure could house his entire caravan, was a mushroom cap that dripped gold fluid into a quartz-lined pool around it.

"This is incredible," Benny said.

"This is *gorgeous*," Hot Dog said.

"This is likely very dangerous," Jasmine added.

"Oh come on, Jazz," Drue said, starting down one of the paths. "They're just flowers."

As he passed a green pod twice as tall as he was, several

stalks at the top unfurled, snapping the air. Drue screamed, raising his arms over his head to protect himself. But the plant didn't attack.

"Be on your guard," Ricardo said. "We'll have plenty of time to check this out later."

"Killer voice," Ramona said as she waltzed past Drue. "Impressive range."

He narrowed his eyes at her and scoffed.

When they finally made it to the other end of the alien garden, another wall waited for them.

"This is it," Jasmine said. "There are ten skeletons showing up on the other side."

Ricardo raised his silver glove in front of his chest. "We try to reason with them. But our main priority is stopping this ship and taking control."

The others nodded. Benny stepped forward, raising his right hand to the rock, and clenching his other one into a fist, ready to protect himself and the others if it came down to it.

In front of them, the final wall melted away.

29.

The walls of the bridge were the same pale blue as the hallways, but marbled with deep red splashes. Veins of light pulsed within them, as though the room itself were alive. And it was, in a way. As soon as the wall separating Benny and the others from the Alpha Maraudi disappeared, the bridge was full of movement. Three aliens rushed for them.

"Stop, we don't want to hurt—" Benny started, but the aliens were already upon them, their quickness astounding.

They weren't dressed in the full armor that the Taj invaders had been wearing, but instead in undulating chain mail, with shiny black masks covering the top halves of their faces, allowing them to open their jaws—those mouths that were too wide to be human, stretching nearly to the backs of their heads. One of them let out a sound like someone had pressed all the buttons on a keyboard synthesizer at once.

"Look out!" Ricardo shouted, jutting his fist forward as the screaming alien came within feet of Benny, a blade-tipped tentacle arched in the air above it like a scorpion's tail. The alien shot backward, sliding across the polished white floor and crashing into one of the stone computer-like terminals that lined the sides of the room. Drue raised his glove, and another flew through the giant hologram in the center of the chamber that showed the battle taking place above the Taj. The third hung in the air as Hot Dog stepped forward, her finger held down on the side of her glove. Its body was frozen, but dozens of thin tentacles whipped around its head frantically.

"Uh, Benny?" Hot Dog asked. "Maybe try that again?"

Benny stepped through the hole in the wall. The two other aliens who had come at them were picking themselves up now, looking around the room, seemingly confused as to what had just happened. The rest of the Alpha Maraudi in the bridge were dressed differently. They stood at the workstations lining the walls, their hands at chest level as their tentacles squirmed and coiled. They wore metallic robes and masks, which reflected the weaving ribbons of light that hung in the air above the terminals—the same sort of patterns, perhaps *writing*, that Benny and the others had seen in the hidden alien base. Several of them made accordion-like noises. Clipped, staccato wheezes.

It seemed to Benny like they were scared, which was a

reaction he'd never even considered.

He took a few more steps inside the room, the frenetic fight above the Taj playing out in silence in front of him. The others followed, Ricardo at his right side.

"We don't want to hurt you," Benny said, glancing at the alien Hot Dog was still holding in the air with her magnetic glove.

The only response was more of the wheezing sounds. The two aliens—guards?—who had attacked them bounced on their feet, looking back and forth between Benny's group and each other.

"Uh, guys," Jasmine said. "Did we maybe take it for granted that one of these aliens would speak English as well as you said Commander Tull did?"

"So you *are* the same humans who destroyed part of Tull's ship," a voice came from the other end of the room. It was similar to that of the alien commander Benny and Hot Dog had met, sounding as though a host of people were talking, ranging from a reverberating bass to a high, almost imperceptible whine.

On the far side of the bridge, in front of a nearly see-through section of the rock looking out onto space, was a huge egg-shaped mound of opaque purple quartz. It spun around slowly, until Benny could see the inside of it, hollow and lined in gold—a throne occupied by one of the Alpha Maraudi.

"Are you in charge of this ship?" Ricardo asked.

The alien stood, and Benny got his first good look at it. The being was tall and thin, with gemlike plates of armor on its body. Its mask was gold, and its dozens of slender tentacles were piled high above it, slithering around a glowing ball of polished red rock.

"I am," the alien said. "Vala is what you will call me."

"Vala," Benny said. "Uh, *Commander* Vala, I bet. My name is Benny Love. I'm from Earth. I mean, obviously. Like I said, we don't want to fight you. We've come to talk."

The alien guards' tentacles whipped around their heads. Vala let out a grunting noise, and they reluctantly seemed to relax.

"You may put them down," Vala said, motioning to Hot Dog's frozen Maraudi. "You have shown your power. We will talk."

Benny took a deep breath and then nodded to Hot Dog. She took her finger off the trigger button on her glove. The alien dropped to the floor and hurried away, taking its place beside the other two guards. Drue watched, then turned his wide eyes back to the commander.

"I kinda think one of those plants is making me hallucinate," he said.

"I can't believe we're talking to an alien," Jasmine whispered.

Ramona tapped on her arm HoloTek, unimpressed.

Benny glanced at the hologram, where tiny Space Runners and alien ships made of light were fighting one another.

"We knew you were destroyers," Vala said, focusing on the hologram as well. "We should have been more prepared. These ships of yours, with the golden beams of light were . . . I believe *unexpected* is the word."

"Uh, you came to destroy *us*," Drue muttered under his breath.

Ricardo looked back at him and glared. Drue didn't say anything else.

Benny stared at the commander, trying, impossibly, to place himself in Vala's shoes. The humans were putting up more of a fight than the Alpha Maraudi had expected. They were defeated, if only momentarily. But of course that was probably enough to instill fear in them. Or at least worry. This wasn't just a space battle they'd lost—their entire civilization was on the line.

So was his.

"Look," Benny said. "Those Space Runners were from Earth, yeah, but they don't represent everyone on the planet. We came to your ship because we need each other's help."

"Help?" Vala asked. A tentacle unwound from the elaborate headdress and reached down, removing the commander's gold mask and pulling it up, placing it in front of the glowing red orb. Two diamond-shaped eyes stared back at Benny, white with flickering red pupils. In the center of

Vala's head, a third eye burned a stunning blue.

Benny heard a few of the others gasp behind him.

"What 'help' do you bring the Alpha Maraudi?" Vala asked. "Perhaps I am misunderstanding the idea."

"I spoke with Commander Tull," Benny said slowly, trying to choose his words carefully. "You expected to destroy humanity and take Earth as your own as a means to save your people. I get that. But humanity isn't going to just let that happen." He pointed to the hologram. "Obviously."

"You are here to threaten us, then."

"No." Ricardo stepped forward. "We're here to work with you."

"There has to be a way to save your people *and* ours," Benny said.

"There's so much we can teach each other," Jasmine piped up from the back.

"We have learned all we need to of you and your kind," Vala said, inching closer to the hologram, staring at the alien ships being torn apart in the sky above the Taj.

"If that were true, you would've taken the Lunar Taj," Trevone said. "And we would never have been able to board your ship."

Vala turned back to them, but said nothing.

"Listen," Benny said. "I don't want either of our species to become extinct, but not all humanity thinks that way. The people you're fighting right now have a superweapon that could destroy your entire planet before you ever got the chance to evacuate. And there are people who are ready to use it against you."

"This isn't the easy invasion you might have expected," Ricardo said. "This is a war now."

"What if in trying to save your people—and in us trying to save ourselves—we end up destroying each other?" Benny asked.

The room filled with the sounds of minor chords as the Alpha Maraudi all began to speak in unison. Vala raised a slender four-fingered hand, trying to appease them. "Why should we believe you?"

Benny walked closer to the commander, until he was a few feet in front of the alien. He tossed his silver magnetic glove onto the floor of the bridge. "Look at us. We're not an army. We could have just stayed on the Moon and let them use whatever superweapon they have against you. But we didn't. We came here to warn you." He paused. "Also, we kind of want to bring other people to your ship. There are more of us, a small group on the Moon. We're caught in the crossfire."

Vala stepped closer, until the alien was only inches away from Benny, staring down at him, twice his height. "Such short life spans you have. So young. The plants you walked through existed for many cycles before you ever drew breath."

"We are just trying to survive," Benny said. "The same as you. We're each other's best chances of doing that. This is much bigger than any of us. Commander Tull told me the Alpha Maraudi were peaceful and valued reason. You may have been pushed to attack us out of desperation, but there have to be other options."

"Working together," Ricardo said, the others gathering beside him, "you'd be surprised at what we can do."

Vala looked over Benny's shoulder at his friends, and then at the silver glove on the floor. The commander grunted. "Of course, you are not saying what is also true. You have us at a disadvantage." The alien bent down and took the silver glove in its hand. "You would take the ship anyway, if we fought against you. Or you would try."

Benny didn't say anything.

Vala looked down at the glove. "So unexpected." The commander looked up at Benny. "And then again, not. Young human, it is possible we know your kind better than you know yourselves. This is why I believe you when you speak of a weapon that might destroy our home."

The commander turned to one of the robed Maraudi and barked some kind of order. The sounds of the alien language filled the air of the bridge—they seemed to be arguing with each other. Eventually, Vala's mouth opened wide and a single sound came out. It was beautiful, ring- ing through the bridge like the final chord of a symphony.

Afterward, it was quiet again.

Vala looked back to Benny. "We will grant you and your like-kind passage on our ship for now. It is possible we do have things to learn from one another. You are lucky you stand in front of one who lives up to the Maraudi's principles of reason and peace. Of knowledge." Vala turned, walking back toward the hologram. Then the commander paused, looking back over an armored shoulder. "But if you try to harm anyone or our home planet in some way—if this is some sort of trick—I will not hesitate to destroy this ship and everyone on it to protect my people."

Benny nodded slowly. "Understood."

"There are some here who are not comfortable sharing a vessel with such a destructive species."

"*We're* the danger?" Hot Dog asked quietly behind Benny.

"They can understand us?" Jasmine asked.

"We live much longer cycles than you do," the commander said. "And we champion the study of cultures other than our own. Most can understand your language, though it is difficult for us to speak. They know your world well. As such, those who do not wish to share this bridge with you will disembark in our smaller ships. As the commander of this vessel, I am allowing them to do so. Now, send for your people. But they must be quick." The commander looked at the hologram, where so few of the Maraudi ships remained in motion. One tentacle moved, bringing the gold mask back down over the alien's eyes as it reached out a hand, fingers hovering just above the Taj. "We cannot stay here long."

"Thank you," Benny said. He hurried back to his group.

"This isn't really how I imagined this going," Trevone said. Beside him Ricardo kept his eyes locked on the aliens, not relaxing at all.

Benny took a few deep breaths. "I kind of made it up as I went along."

Drue grinned. "I guess some of my charm must've rubbed off on you."

"The point is it worked, you guys!" Hot Dog said.

"I'll contact Sahar and the others immediately," Trevone said.

"Tell them to bring supplies," Jasmine said. "Food, medical equipment—who knows what they have on this ship."

"Uh, maybe some extra space suits?" Hot Dog suggested.

Ramona glanced up from her HoloTek. "I require snacks and soda."

30.

Benny and the rest of the Moon Platoon stayed on the bridge while Trevone and Ricardo went with a group of the aliens back to the hangar to await the arrival of everyone from the underground bunker. Benny noticed that both of the Pit Crew members kept their fists clenched, ready to use the magnetic gloves at a moment's notice.

Several of the Alpha Maraudi chose to leave, fleeing the mother ship for destinations unknown to Benny. In the end, there were only six aliens on board with them, including Commander Vala. Benny hardly thought to wonder where the others might be headed in the vastness of the universe—he was much more concerned with where *they* would be going next.

"My priority is to leave the immediate reach of Earth's forces," Vala said when Benny asked. "Our original mission was to collect samples from the moons of the planet you call

Jupiter, before we were diverted to your Moon after what happened to Tull. A few of our scholars are still on those satellites. We will return there for the time being, as we discover what sort of 'help' we can offer each other."

"Scholars," Jasmine said, a hint of excitement in her voice.

Vala leaned back in the egg-like throne. "We have much to discuss once we begin this journey." A few other aliens leaned in close to their commander, speaking quietly.

Benny and his friends gathered around the hologram in the center of the bridge. Silver Space Runners were beginning to land in the courtyard of the Lunar Taj, troops filtering out, charging into the resort. They were taking it back. He wondered where Dr. Bale and Drue's dad were inside. What were they planning? How much time did they have before they tried to use this superweapon of Dr. Bale's?

"You know," Drue said, "I didn't expect to feel so weird about leaving the Taj behind."

Hot Dog glanced at him for a split second before turning her gaze back to the aliens in the room. She'd hardly taken her eyes off them the entire time they'd been there. "It's not the Taj you're sad about," she said. "We're leaving Earth, too."

"And everyone on it," Benny added, turning to the translucent quartz window behind Vala's egg throne and looking at the hazy blue-and-brown ball in the distance.

Wishing so badly that he had a clearer view.

What were his grandmother and brothers doing? He realized he wasn't even sure what time or day it was anymore, or how long he'd been in space. Eventually, his family would start to worry about him, once it became clear that he wasn't returning from his EW-SCAB vacation after two weeks. His stomach churned as he thought about this, not wanting to worry them. He could feel pressure building behind his eyes—there was still so much to do, so many things that could go wrong.

But he reminded himself he was trying to do what was right, and he couldn't let fear keep him from fighting for that. He hoped for the best.

"Benzo," Ramona said, interrupting his thoughts. "Hit that wrist hardware."

He stared back at her for a moment. "You mean . . . the bracelet?"

She clicked her tongue. Benny tapped on the silver loop, causing another him to appear by his side.

An alien made a crackling sound behind him.

"It's all right," Benny said, waving his hand through his clone. "It's just a hologram."

Ramona took out her Taj HoloTek and hit a few buttons. The hologram changed, and Pinky was standing in front of them.

The AI crossed her arms. "Okay, that's the last time I get stuck in your datapad," she said to Ramona, her voice piping out of their collars. Then she turned to Benny. "You don't mind if I borrow this for a while, do you? It's not quite the tech I had at the Taj, but there are some cameras and sensors in these nanoprojectors. At least this way I can tell what's going on."

"Not at all," he said. "It's kind of nice to see you."

"Are you in contact with the Taj?" Jasmine asked.

"Not from all the way up here," she said. "We're lucky I could even get in touch with Sahar and the others via the radio." She turned around in a full circle, taking in the bridge. "This is . . . certainly a lot to process. Perhaps once we know more about their technology . . ."

The hologram in the center of the room suddenly rippled, as though it were made of water and someone had tossed a stone into it. A ribbon of green appeared above it, looping—*dancing* in the air.

"What's happening?" Benny asked.

"A communication," Vala said, standing and walking toward them. "I sent out a distress beacon the moment you broke into this room, explaining that humans had infiltrated my ship." Vala glanced at him, a flash of blue shining behind the gold mask. "We did not know what you were here for."

"So who's calling back?" Jasmine asked.

Vala's tentacles all seemed to constrict at once. "I must warn you now that you should not mistake my actions for any sort of unity between our peoples. Many of the Alpha Maraudi will not be pleased with this development." The alien turned to the hologram. "Certainly not this commander."

Vala stepped forward and said something in the Maraudi language. The hologram in the center of the room morphed in front of them, until there was another alien standing in the center of the room, a clear quartz throne in the background. Two thick tentacles were raised above its head like slick black horns. Unlike Vala, its body was thick, muscled, and bulging beneath a gemlike breastplate.

"Commander Tull," Benny said.

"Oh, crap," Hot Dog said.

Tull's wide mouth twisted. "You." There was a pause. "What a problem you have become."

And then Vala and Tull were speaking to each other in their own tongue. Benny couldn't be sure, but it sounded as though they were disagreeing, shouting over each other. Finally, Vala spoke for a long time, uninterrupted, and Tull's reaction was simply to grunt.

Tull turned to Benny. "This weapon," the commander said. "You will tell us everything you know about it."

Benny opened his mouth to speak, but realized how little they actually *did* know. Finally, he just nodded. "Like I told Commander Vala, we can work together and help each other."

Tull's lips curved into something like a smile. "Perhaps. It would be in your interest to keep us happy. As I recall from my observations of your world, *this* one is quite popular. I am certain you'll want to keep him safe."

Tull motioned to something offscreen, and in a flash there was another hologram, someone pushed into view. A man now stood in front of them wearing a deep maroon space suit. A gold mask had been placed over his eyes, but Benny could make out the three stripes shaved into the man's short, auburn beard. And of course, he recognized the gold-studded driving gloves on his hands, which were bound in front of him.

"It's . . ." Hot Dog started.

"Elijah!" Pinky shouted.

Drue gasped. Jasmine raised a hand to her mouth. Even Ramona looked up from her HoloTek.

"Somebody get Ricardo," Benny said, his heart ramming against his rib cage.

One of Tull's tentacles reached over and pulled the mask from Elijah West's face. Elijah blinked for a moment as his pupils adjusted to the light, and then he was staring back at

Benny and the others. He narrowed his eyes as he looked at them, trying to make sense of what he was seeing.

"Benny," he finally said, raising an eyebrow. "What in the name of the Milky Way galaxy have you done with my resort?"

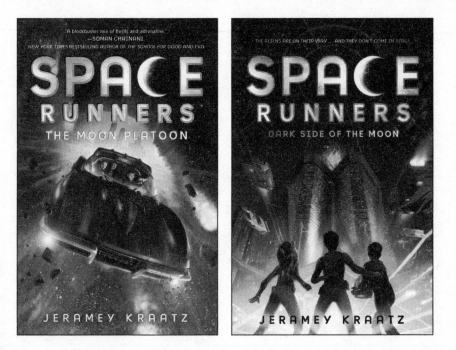